Northward

By

Chuck Radda

Acknowledgments

Thanks first to my wife Deanie who, by the final draft, had read *Northward* more than I had, but continued to plug away with suggestions and reminders that I, yet again, had spelled another "the" without the "t." Thanks to my son Chris who was my first "outside" reader this time: his input back in the summer was invaluable—all of it efficiently compressed on to a small piece of paper. I appreciated the economy. Thanks to Tom Ward, my friend of many, many decades who caused me to rethink and improve (I hope) the opening, to my brother Jim Radda and his wife Cindy Satagaj for their important feedback late and early, and to my daughter Jen Radda who keeps reminding me that a pocketbook is now a purse—because I keep "misremembering."

Thanks to my publishing partners (and skilled editors) David Fortier and Dawn Leger, who continue to provide the support and encouragement we all need sometime— that reminder that in order to write, one has to...write.

Finally, thanks to my readers. After the release of my first published novel, *Dark Time,* in 2014, many of them told me that they liked the detective better than they liked the main character. In truth, so did I.

Now that detective, Francis McNally, is back—a little older, a little different, but a lot the same. I hope that all these years removed from his last appearance, you still like him.

For Deanie

Northward is a work of fiction.

Despite the fact that there is indeed a Nunavut in northern Canada, and there is a hamlet called Baker Lake as well as a metropolis called New York City, and there do exist many other locales mentioned in this work, they are used in a purely fictitious manner.

In addition, the names, characters, businesses, events, and incidents are the products of the author's imagination. Any resemblance to actual persons, living or dead, or actual events is purely coincidental.

The Storyteller

—*There were trees covering the shoreline of Tehek. They were low, stunted by the steady northeast wind that blew down unencumbered and unrelenting from the Pole, over Baffin Bay, and into Nunavut.*

—Unencumbered?

—*Nothing could stop the wind.*

—But trees? Real trees?

—*Not like the ones you see in pictures. Scrub pine no higher than your waist, but they were trees nonetheless.*

—But there are no trees now. Only grass and sedge and flowers in July.

The child leans forward, arms supporting her head. She knows, everyone knows, but she wants to hear more about the trees...about the old times. The old man shifts uncomfortably in his seat. The arthritis has almost overwhelmed him—on some days the medicine doesn't help—but he recognizes the eagerness and the curiosity.

—*You're right, little one, but this was in the before times when animals hid in the undergrowth near Tehek while hunters and their children starved.*

—Was it Sedna? Did she trick the hunters into not seeing the animals?

The children know the myths and legends, but when the old man talks about them, they seem almost real.

—*Yes, it was always Sedna. She was ugly and her shape was frightening, but the animals did not make judgments on such things. That is what humans do. For many years our people died of starvation while the sun sank lower and the caribou ruled the winter.*

—Why did Sedna hate us?

The question arises from another corner of the classroom. The grizzled storyteller opens his thermos and takes a sip of tea as the children wait for the answer. Their teacher fidgets: Miss Laird the children call her, though he remembers only because of the wood nameplate on her desk.

Her face shows concern: the old man who knows the old ways also has an old penchant for vodka and is not above adding a bit to...to anything. He sips slowly from the thermos, a small amount (not enough to make a difference, Miss Laird thinks with some relief), then screws on the cap and finds the boy who asked the question. It was a good question but he isn't sure what it was. He straightens some of the fringe that circles his coat. His mind, sometimes as sharp as ever, goes dull for a moment. But just as he is about to ask what the question was about, he remembers.

—*Sedna does not hate us. We harm the land. We steal the water. We flatten the hills. We dig for gold, oil, minerals. And now we melt the frost. Sedna has good reason to hate us, to hate all mankind.*

He hesitates: there is a fine line between scaring the children and captivating them. He amends the statement:

—*Sedna is angry sometimes, like the rest of us. But she does not hate us.*

—Tell us about the miracle. Tell us about Tehek.

—*We can no longer count on miracles.*

—Tell us, though. Please.

He reaches for his tea once again, then shifts it away. The teacher is relieved.

"Yes," the young instructor says, capturing her students' excitement, "the children love that story."

Everyone waits.

The old man's face, weathered and grey is furrowed from decades in the inhospitable north, and maybe too many years of isolation, of sleeplessness, even of alcohol. He has paid the price for his prescience, his foresight, his gift of prophecy—all attributes that others assign to him but that he has always dismissed. Yet he cannot deny the children their story, though as with anything else that grows dimmer with age, he often has trouble believing it ever happened.

—*It was just after the solstice....*

A murmur grows. It's beginning. Every child knows the solstice, the legends, and the celebrations. He waits for a beat until quiet returns.

—*But in this solstice the happiness did not come. People were sad, children were sick, the hunters returned each day with nothing. Not even the lake would give up any of its treasures. People spoke of moving. People right here. But where would they go? Where would you go?"*

—My house is here. My grandmother is next door.

—My best friend lives up the street. Who would my best friend be?

Others join in, pick out classmates: the thought of leaving is preposterous, but not without fear.

—*Someplace warm, people said. But there were no planes to take people away. Only...here. Then one day a woman whose baby was very sick went off by herself to hunt the woods around Tehek.*

—Uki.

The children know. Miss Laird smiles. The old man will tell the story and the class will end. Whatever is in his thermos will be drunk somewhere else.

—*Yes. Uki. She had a bow and arrow, but she also carried an axe, and as the sun rose above the horizon on that short day, she cut down her first tree. The trunk was narrow and she had little trouble. Then she cut a second, and a third. Her exhaustion grew—she had no food because there was no food—and she grew weak. After the fourth tree she heard a voice behind her, or maybe in front of her, or maybe within her. And she answered, though only she heard the question, "because my baby is starving and these trees are hiding the animals."*

—Did Sedna attack her?

—*No. Nothing happened, and so Uki answered again the question only she heard. "I do not want your trees, but I must take them down so that we can hunt."*

—All of them?

—*Yes, all of them, by herself if she had to. Not even a chainsaw.*

Some of the children laugh at the anachronism; others are so mesmerized by the image that the joke is lost on them.

—*But just as she prepared to swing the axe again, a voice told her to stop. "Get the hunters and bring them back tomorrow."*

The woman didn't want to trust the voice, but darkness and exhaustion would stop her before she accomplished anything worthwhile. She returned to the hamlet and gathered the hunters. "Go in the morning," she said. "The hunting will be good."

They doubted her, scoffed at her, called her a bad mother for running off and leaving her babies unattended. It was not true: the three children were warm and dry, but hungry and sick too. To quiet their laughter she dared them. "We will go now," she said. "Not tomorrow."

When the men who doubted her arrived at Tehek, the sun had fallen below the horizon. But it went no farther west, went no lower. Minutes passed, and hours, and all that time the four men and two women hunted while the sun stood still. In the end the trees had vanished, and there were hardly reeds or sedge. There were only caribou, standing idly in the dusk as if believing they could not be seen. The hunters took what was needed, but no more. Enough to meet the crisis, to save the village, the children, the babies. Explanations were imagined and given, but Uki herself received no praise or honor; after all, she had merely relayed the news. All that time the real darkness never came.

The hunters returned, the feast began at midnight and lasted until the sun reappeared. At noon Uki went back alone to give thanks. The area looked as it always had, low growth and vegetation and animals which, if they were there at all, were hidden among the trees and scrub brush.

She stood next to the trees she had cut down: they lay where she had left them in a small clearing. Nakurmiik, she yelled, repeating it loudly in every direction. Nakurmiik. Thank you.

The children are silent, then several of them clap. The old man smiles and the expression draws in his skin and makes him look even older.

—Tell us about the woman. What happened to her?

The children know the answer. There will be no clapping this time. Hearing the old man tell it will mean more to them, but the ending is not a happy one. In the children's sanitized version Uki is forced to remain there forever to live with the spirits, never to see her own children again.

The adult version is even more dismal, filled with rape and unwanted births until such time that she has atoned for the souls her axe destroyed that afternoon. Animism makes no distinction when it comes to souls—they live within cold-stunted ground cover as well as within exalted men.

—*And every once in a while Uki would visit her children in a dream, and they would know it was their mother who saved the village, who saved the world.*

He hesitates.

And these were the blessings of the Creator.

He says the words not because it is the true ending, but of late he cannot finish the tale without crying. He hopes that maybe the children will not notice. A few seconds pass before Miss Laird steps in.

"Let's thank our visitor," she says, handing him a tissue. He is crying after all.

—You are good listeners. I will come back again.

As the children push toward the door waiting to be dismissed, their teacher puts a hand on the storyteller's shoulder.

"And they would know it was their mother who saved the village, who saved the world," she says to him, "but she could never hold her children to her breast, and they could never feel a mother's love. I remember that ending from when I was in school. You don't say that anymore?"

"Too sad," he says. "Too sad for the children."

But it's more than that. Maybe it is empathy for the woman suddenly bereft of the people she loved, or the fact that his own fantasy about rescuing Uki from the angry spirits has grown more fantastical with the passage and the ravaging of his already diminished powers. He had a wife once, a woman he had made love to. Now he can no longer imagine what that was like to hold her, how he would even approach a woman anymore. The urges, faded and muddled, remain; but the imagination will no longer support even the simplest fantasy. And if an approach were to bring more rejection, then what?

The teacher finds the old man's anorak, the boots, the mittens and, for some reason, two scarves.

"The children love your stories," she says.

"Because they believe that they could have happened," he says. "Do you, Deidre Laird?" He repeats her name, grateful for having remembered it.

"I love storytelling," she says. "It's a lost art."

He squeezes her hand for a moment. The answer has surprised him in its honesty, but disappointed him too. People, even good people, have finally and thoroughly placed themselves above divine assistance, renounced the spiritual in favor of the temporal. The old vision returns—a world spinning more violently out of control until such time that no deity—Inuit, Christian, Aztec, none—can save it.

"You too are a blessing from the creator," he says, then lets go of her hand and walks out into the reassuring cold, where he feels less like a stranger. Or worse, an impostor.

CHAPTER 1

A decades-old wind-up alarm clock jolted Derek Phillips awake at 4:00 a.m.

He has two hours. Then he and a dozen other workers will board a converted fifty-year-old military plane—an eyesore nicknamed the Greyhound for no discernible reason. Neither as sleek nor graceful as its animal namesake, and not even grey, the plane had been designed to land on aircraft carriers and speed the conclusion of the Viet Nam War—a conflict begun, fought, and drearily concluded before Derek Phillips was even born. How the aircraft relocated from the Southeast Asian jungles to the forbidding ice fields of northern Canada, or how it was repurposed from a troop carrier to a shuttle, none of the workers knew for sure. Whatever the history, the plane was Derek Phillips's carpool—his dark commute to work every Monday and home again five days later.

At such latitudes the darkness always predominated, but in the winter it felt deeper and denser—almost tangible. Even indoors—even in the bathroom where he showered and shaved—the lights seemed unable to pierce it and he found himself squinting in the mirror to trim his beard neatly. Not that his appearance meant much to anyone but himself, not since Nikki had announced shortly before Christmas that she was "off sex," or as she more indecorously put it, her legs were no longer open for business. "To be in the service of the Lord," she said "means that there are sacrifices."

More than likely her service to the lord would be temporary. Everything was temporary with Nikki: her yoga, her t'ai chi, her veganism, her teetotaling—they came and went like the sun on Christmas Day—there too short a time to be noticed. But for Nikki Phillips to reference the "service of the Lord" was so silly that even her husband—the victim of her abstinence— found it amusing. And bearable. The only facet of her life that seemed constant was her unquestionable fidelity to Derek—a quality he mostly returned in kind.

He reminded her more than once that he was also in service to a lord— that the almighty Autumn Industries paid him handsomely for the work he did, but also required an isolation and loneliness that could be mitigated only by lying in a warm bed with his wife at the end of the work week. She was sympathetic but obdurate. (Later he would learn that an Internet article had posited the connection between sex and dementia—an article which they both agreed later might be true in its inverse also.)

Despite their new, more platonic relationship, Phillips wanted to leave his wife with a positive image.

"Does this look even?" he said, surveying his beard while she stood in the bathroom doorway.

"Thicker on the left," she said, "but don't mess with it now. You'll be late."

He evened it off as best he could. "There," he said. "Wanna have sex?"

"Don't be sacrilegious."

"I'm early today. I was awake before the alarm went off."

"You know the deal," she said, folding her arms. "You can have the bathroom to yourself if you need it."

"No way," he said, feigning anger. "I'll have nothing to do at work."

"Make sure that's all you do with that thing at work," she said, then left the door open and walked away. He thought of pointing out the widely known connection between abstinence and a sense of humor, but he didn't see where that would help.

At the airfield where he and the others boarded the Greyhound the windsock hung flaccid in the early morning calm. Without a breeze the air felt unnaturally warm, but a flashing thermometer reading -35 C belied any such thought. The plane had circled and landed before the workers had even left their homes. Now they boarded, found seats, strapped in, hardly acknowledged each other, didn't speak. Thirty minutes after that, their ears buzzing from the roar of the twin turboprops, they exited. It was still dark: it would be April before conditions changed appreciably.

Derek Phillips, like the others, had come to accept it with what bordered on a quiet equanimity, though for him, the task was easier; the money, better.

While many men Derek's age were struggling to provide their families with necessities, his paycheck covered those and more. For Nikki, one of the self-labeled "weekday widows," that meant she could avail herself of the occasional trinket from a local craftsman or order new outfits from online merchants whenever she wanted. And while other children made do with improvised and amateurish summer camps in July and August, his three kids rode the coaster at Calaway Park out west, or marveled at the mall in Edmonton, and once, even, ran joyously away from the Pacific waves that crashed behind them on Vancouver Island.

Money.

And because there was enough of it, Phillips reached higher. This summer it would be Disney World. He hadn't even told the family yet, but he'd made preliminary inquiries, checked flights, found itineraries. He planned to sell the idea to his family in a month or so—a new brass ring now that the thrill of Christmas had passed. It would help them endure the unremitting winter, maybe mitigate their frustration at the sun skidding ineffectually across the southern horizon, making the world neither brighter nor warmer.

Maybe ten years down the road when Regina, his oldest, was ready for college, he'd consider a move to Toronto, or maybe west to Winnipeg or Calgary, maybe even the States. He was yet to celebrate his thirty-third birthday. There was time for these decisions.

And yet, time was becoming an issue. Derek Phillips had begun to misplace it.

He kept secret the condition, the problem, the weirdness—he never knew the right word; after all, how could he explain it? And Nikki, who tended to summarily dismiss anything she could not label and categorize—Nikki who preferred words like *stupid* and *senseless* to *curious* and *odd*, would dismiss it out of hand. Or she would advise more sleep, a proper diet, less drinking, more exercise, and of course, continued abstinence. Suggestions like those, sprinkled in with the occasional aspirin, would stretch the limits of Nikki's imagination and patience.

She was not ignorant, but her childhood had established her attitude toward ailments of any kind. Her mother had died of breast cancer at forty; her father, after suffering a stroke at forty- two, hung on for only two years before passing. Those experiences made it too easy to turn every headache into a brain tumor; every tic into Parkinson's; every cough into lung cancer.

Derek understood: if he were to confide in her that he was losing time, her diagnosis of dementia or Alzheimer's would be quick and certain.

He undertook some research on his own, learned that even men in their thirties can have TIAs—transient ischemic attacks—mini-strokes. Maybe, even at thirty-two, he was suffering from some. But the symptoms didn't align. He felt perfectly healthy, strong, and able even when he was experiencing these lapses. And really that's all they were: lapses in his day-to-day routines, some of which were almost amusing. One morning at work he awoke in his quarters at Autumn, checked the time as he always did, showered, shaved, got himself dressed, glanced at some company literature on future expansion, and arrived at the commissary for breakfast, only to find the place virtually empty. One of the food workers jokingly asked him if he wanted to crack some eggs while he was waiting. Only then did he check the wall clock—five minutes had elapsed since he stepped into the shower—five minutes in which he had cleaned up, straightened out some previous day's clothing, dressed, checked the work schedule online, verified that he'd seen it, sent an email request to the supply manager, and made his way through the labyrinth of hallways to the commissary. Five minutes. It should have taken him forty-five, or more.

A familiar voice interrupted his thoughts. Lurie. He worked security overnight but the two of them had begun their employment on the same Monday a few years back.

"What do you got, Phillips, insomnia?"

"Got up to take a leak—couldn't get back to sleep. Figured I'd beat the rush."

"Well you sure as hell beat the food," Lurie said. "And the coffee. Decaf's ready but that ain't gonna help." He held his own cup in the air, a small tag hanging over the side. "At least you get some caffeine with tea."

"Rather drink piss," Phillips said. "Tea is for the ladies."

"I thought you liked the ladies."

"Back in town, maybe."

Lurie, who was older but Phillips thought not necessarily wiser, often provided counsel anyway.

"You gotta be careful, pal. You got a good thing going with Nikki. You don't want to fuck that up."

"No worries," Phillips said, withholding from Lurie any further information about Nikki's sexual sabbatical or the irony of the warning.

A few more workers shuffled in and the room slowly filled to its normal breakfast capacity.

Though Derek Phillips had no idea why he'd been so early, he blended in, ate his usual two-eggs-over with a slice of ham, and partook in a conversation where co-workers obsessed over the fact that no Canadian hockey teams would make the playoffs again. Along with the others he damned the choking Maple Leafs and the inept Oilers, pointed out the humiliation conferred on all of Canada when a California team skated on West Coast ice hoisting the Cup. Mindless conversation, but distracting too. There was no temptation to interject anything like...*the funniest things have been happening to me.* He could contemplate it alone, or obsess over it, but not share it.

Besides, the previous week had produced a string of successive mornings during which nothing untoward happened, and Derek, who had been fighting a cold and eschewed his usual intake of weekend liquor, thought maybe sobriety was in fact the answer, that alcohol residue was the culprit and not some kind of sleep disorder as Lurie had inadvertently suggested. Or maybe that one early morning he had simply misread the clock. Occam's razor, he thought: go with the simplest explanation every time.

On more than one occasion Nikki had called him obsessive. "The pot calling the kettle," he'd laughed, but he knew the accusation carried an echo of truth. As if to confirm her belief, he secretly began noting times on an almost obsessive level, checking for instance, when he began a shower and when he ended it. Sometimes he would count while he shaved—one one-thousand, two one-thousand, then match his counting against the time on his phone. And every normal day convinced Phillips that there was little need for a solution because there was, in fact, no problem. But the normal days diminished in frequency, and even they provided some unexplainable event.

At first he was able to cover up anything out of the ordinary, as he had with Lurie at breakfast. But eventually there were witnesses, and eventually he couldn't chalk it up to misreading some clock in the shadowy morning.

CHAPTER 2

It was an exploratory assignment—a little fact-finding mission maybe half a kilometer out from the main building, preliminary to any further blasting or digging. False starts were expensive in gold mining—in any mining: moving heavy equipment and personnel into an area where some supposed discovery ended up as useless dust could waste tens of thousands of dollars. Phillips wasn't the only expert, but his sense was uncanny; and Hal Whitton, who oversaw everything at the site, openly referred to him as his personal clairvoyant. Like fishermen who seem always to know where to cast their line and duck hunters where to place a blind, Phillips could track gold. It was simple logic and observation, he maintained, and Whitton used him exclusively. And though nobody's success rate was flawless, Phillips's was approaching an unprecedented level of perfection.

"Take the afternoon," Whitton had told him that Monday, hours after his arrival for the work week. "You get three hours in, finish tomorrow morning. Usual warnings—do you need to hear them?"

Phillips shook his head. Temperature. Wind. Daylight. Dust. Communication. If he were walking from one building to the next the warnings would be no different. Long duration in the cold did not necessarily require any special vigilance, just more of it. In a way breaking up the task over two days could prove beneficial, the hiatus providing an opportunity to regenerate that vigilance. Phillips knew, as did Whitton, that this was a good four-to-six-hour assignment, one that required daylight which, in January, came at a premium.

"Stop around three," Whitton said. "When the sun gets that low, everything looks like gold."

"Or nothing does. I'll be inside at 2:55," Phillips joked, "just to make double sure."

He noted without particular emotion the digital readout that flashed near the exit: -12 F/-24C. Nothing remarkable, and besides, it was the wind that presented difficulties, and there had been no warnings or advisories for the afternoon and evening. *Dress warm—no harm* his mother had said to him thirty years before. The advice still held, he thought as he stepped outside, passed through gate security, and trudged out beyond the last storage shed. When he turned left he saw the red flag someone had planted for him maybe three-hundred meters off. His goggles fogged—colder than twelve below, he thought. Maybe fifteen, but no wind to speak of. No worries.

His chest-mounted camera and voice-activated recorder preserved his observations and commentary by transferring them to a database where the scientists and the elaborate equipment were housed. This initial survey, once its analysis was complete, would be forwarded to another inspector—a more senior employee—to double check and make the final decision. Only once had Phillips given his okay and had it overturned, and even then he was certain that the supervisor had judged incorrectly. No sense dwelling on it—this was the way the mine kept going: little discoveries led to bigger excavations led to higher profits led to trinkets for his wife and, now it appeared, led to Florida vacations.

The Monday exploratory site was a little larger than Whitton had let on, but not unusually so. Phillips took a small pick-axe from his bag and made a few tentative exploratory taps, keeping his eyes focused on his work. If they drifted up toward the low-angled sun, he'd spend the afternoon squinting, something which increased the fatigue factor immeasurably and pretty much destroyed any semblance of accuracy. He snapped photos, verbalized some observations, and occasionally looked away from the area entirely—*rest and refocus*. He worked at a steady pace. Accidents happened when people rushed—when they made little deals with themselves: *If I can finish by 2:00 I'll take an extra coffee break...if I finish today, I'll sleep in.* Phillips played no such games.

"When you finish you finish," Whitton had said, and Phillips would hold him to that.

He shook away the distractions and continued. An hour or so in, everything seemed to be going well enough, and he felt hopeful that this particular area would turn out to be productive. Could be a good one he said aloud—an unofficial analysis into his voice recorder, then added silently that the mine would keep making a profit and he'd keep getting a paycheck. He moved along, left to right, top to bottom. He really did feel it today, almost as though he were giving Whitton's clairvoyance bullshit some credibility.

Maybe he really was special, he thought, then shook away the idea immediately—people who were too special stopped respecting the elements and dangers, and just like that their frozen bodies were being identified by some distraught family member. No, he would let the day take care of itself.

It was then, while he moved from place to place and changed his angle of view almost continuously, that it first occurred to him: the sun's angle hadn't changed.

He didn't expect it to rise or set, simply crawl across the horizon as it usually did in January. But it seemed not to have moved in any direction. Maybe it was the way he was facing (though he had a pretty good sense of direction) but he seemed to encounter the glare in the exact same spot all afternoon. Was he moving along some subtle curve, or were the days beginning to lengthen? Were there fine differences he was missing? When he reached the second red marker with daylight to spare, he knew something was awry. Not even on his best day could he have worked that quickly.

What had he skipped?

What had he glossed over?

And if there were mistakes, what other ones had he made that would someday cost him his life?

He retraced his steps, looking for an area that not been left untouched, but there was none.

Scarred rock and dust, even the occasional bootprint in the dusty snow, verified his work. He checked his phone: not even ninety minutes had elapsed from the moment he left the building. One way or another, impossible or not, he was finished.

He found Whitton talking with a group in the outer chamber. "What happened?" Whitton said. "What's wrong?"

"Nothing. I just finished early."

"For the day?"

"Nope. Done."

"Was it a dud?"

"It's hot, I think. Tell the diggers."

Whitton studied him, uncertain of what it meant.

"I realize that time matters," he said, "but we can't be cutting corners either. You weren't even out there two hours."

"Things went smooth, that's all. I've marked out a few of the better spots and sent the photos on to the lab guys. You can look at them too when you have a minute. Same folder as always."

Whitton seemed to be searching for the proper response.

"That was a pretty good-sized target out there. Are you sure you got it all? I mean you didn't see a good seam and assume the rest is okay."

"I didn't bring back samples, but that's why we have the video. I can go back...."

"No," Whitton said. He looked distressed. "Unless...do you want to recheck it in the morning? Not right now...I mean, rest for a while...."

Whitton was struggling for the right way to justify a two-day job taking ninety minutes.

Phillips bailed him out.

"Tomorrow morning I'm out there," he said. "I would never cut corners, but I would never assume either."

Whitton looked relieved.

"That sounds good."

Whitton was silent for another moment, then shrugged.

"I know you," he said, "and you don't fuck up. But humor me—spend another hour out there anyway, for your own good."

Phillips knew what Whitton meant. Killing a job like that would mean everyone would be expected to work faster and harder. Management would expect it, and supervisors like Whitton would then have to deal with the accidents and mistakes. Calling this a five-hour job and then verifying the fact by sending Phillips back out there would, in the long run, keep everyone safer.

"I'm still going to charge you full price," Phillips joked.

"Absolutely," Whitton said, forcing a smile. "Can you just go through this again?"

Phillips, with the sudden gift of free time, had no problem retelling the story. This time he added a few details—how the sun seemed always to be at the same angle, how he himself had to double check to make sure there had not been some fatal flaw. Retelling it did not change the outcome, but the repetition seemed to relax Whitton somewhat.

"Listen," he said, "don't be offended, but if I didn't ask..."

"Breathalyzer? Go for it. I haven't had a drink in days, I can even pee in a cup if you want."

"Not that. Is this about...a woman?"

"A woman? Out there?"

"I mean...you got someone waiting for you back here so you cut corners to have some extra time."

Phillips smiled. "Don't get me wrong, if you have a woman for me...of course my wife would be pissed off so it'd have to be our little secret."

"Okay, okay," Whitton said. "You want to bust my balls...I just...I want to keep things normal."

"And I don't want to make trouble," Phillips said. "I'll go back out."

"Good. Good. In the morning. And listen, if others ask...."

"Migraine," Phillips said. "Does that work?"

"Perfect, so kind of lay low for a few hours."

"Until I feel better. No problem."

"And listen...later...I may want to discuss something with you later. Nothing bad.

Just...some other time. Now go rest your eyes. Not good to stare into the sun all day."

"Got it," he said and walked away, then hesitated.

"What is it?" Whitton said.

"Nothing," he said. "Your eyes play tricks on you sometimes out there. The snow, sun...it's nothing."

"But your report ...."

"It's perfect," he said. "No worries on that."

"But?"

"No, nothing. It's all good. Whatever it is you want to talk about...."

"Absolutely," Whitton said. He seemed uncomfortable. They both did.

Phillips had been candid with Whitton, had given a reasonable account of the day. But the detail he had omitted troubled him. At one point during the job he had seen something glistening nearby. At first it appeared to be just another section of flatland traced by a thin layer of snow and reflecting the sharply-angled sun, but as he focused more closely he saw more than that—he saw a large expanse of wavelets and whitecaps. This was no leaching pool or hidden lake or snowblind mirage. And as he concentrated more he heard, or maybe imagined, the clattering of surf breaking on the shore as it had on Vancouver Island, as it had on Nova Scotia when he was a child. Tehek, he thought at the time, because it was the only large lake in the vicinity. Even so, it was many kilometers to the east, twenty, maybe more. Not only that, but every lake large or small from here to Moosonee was a foot thick in ice that had been accreting since September.

There could be no waves.

There could be no sound except the ice setting and cracking, and even that was months away, and again, kilometers to the east.

He didn't share it with Whitton because everyone knew that the eyes, maybe the ears, and always the mind—can play tricks in the white cold of Nunavut.

He returned to his room and showered. Then, as he and Whitton agreed, he stayed out of the way.

CHAPTER 3

Nikki Phillips listened impatiently to her husband's bizarre account of his week at Autumn, then immediately ascribed it—as she did anything aberrant in her husband's behavior—to alcohol. Check with the others, she said, adding that she'd be surprised if many of them could even tell time anymore after the weekend binges in which they customarily partook. His rebuttal— he seldom drank during the work week—had little effect.

"It's cumulative," she said, "what it does to the brain. You don't need some shrink in Churchill to tell you that. Besides, if they think you're nuts at work, you may have no job at all. Next time this happens, maybe you should keep it to yourself."

"I did keep it to myself—I'm telling you."

"You told Whitton."

"As far as he knows, I completed a job ahead of schedule. You don't get fired for that." "You don't win friends either."

"Not interested in friends. Only interested in you, honey."

Groveling. The new normal. It didn't matter. She dismissed it as bullshit...which it was. Drivel like that was not going to change any hearts or minds.

On Sunday morning with the kids still asleep, Phillips, less hungover than usual, had rolled out of bed early, then sat alone in a dimly lit kitchen with a cup of hastily brewed coffee. Outside the darkness held sway, broken only by a streetlight a few houses down. The only sound aside from his own breathing was that of the furnace, which ran practically without interruption during January. In an hour or two the children would awaken and demand the usual Sunday flapjacks. With any luck their arrival would precede their mother's and preclude any rehash of previous discussions about their new relationship.

He had come close to exploding during the last one when she admitted that it was a phase she was going through, that crises in marriages were designed to make couples stronger. It sounded enough like some bizarre lab experiment for him to suggest she see someone about her own condition. The conversation deteriorated from there. Of course now any new dialogue would funnel into his mental state, rendering the words useless at best. And so he sat, languidly turning the pages of the local weekly while not reading a word.

The children did arrive first, one at a time, with their usual Sunday demand for flapjacks. He told them to wake up mommy, but was not disappointed when she didn't show. He generally enjoyed making breakfast even with a hangover: this particular morning was a walk in the park.

The rest of their Sunday fell along established patterns: he washed the breakfast dishes, then converted what had become an almost unmanageable pile of Legos into a fairly impressive building. The project had taken a little too long though, and the children's attention began to drift. Still, he extracted a week's worth of adventures from them, got an update on Chloe's teeth (they were all in) and Robert's alphabet tree (he had spelled a word with seven letters.) The typically laconic Regina had had little to say, but he had learned not to push her. At six years old a personality was developing, and though she was neither loving nor, it seemed, forthcoming, Phillips accepted it with his usual forced equanimity.

Nikki occupied herself with...something.

In the evening with the kids in bed and Nikki thumbing through a magazine, Derek Phillips headed off to the Naujat for a beer. This was not some act of rebellion or revenge. Traditionally the Autumn workers showed up at the end of the weekend to intimate that they had fulfilled their marital responsibilities, and that all was normal in the bedroom. It wasn't as crass or brazen as all that, but it was obvious enough so that the women in the place referred to them as "The Spent."

Women workers at Autumn were few, but for the ones from Baker Lake, the Naujat was the night spot of choice. There were other taverns, but this one was cheap, noisy, and just disorderly enough so that no reasonable conduct came under any scrutiny. And if a man and woman arrived separately and left together, nobody paid any heed: but that was a rare occurrence in Baker Lake, and on Sunday night, almost non-existent.

Among his co-workers Phillips played the part of the satisfied stud, a role that usually required little more than a look of ennui—as if there was exhaustion involved in trying new approaches only to wind up with the same old sex. He had a few beers, bitched about work with some friends, checked out some of the women, and went home. Later that night, sober and with the kids asleep, he found Nikki in bed reading, covers pulled up to her neck.

"We've all lost track of time," she said. "It's not that unusual."

"I'm not late. I came home sort of early."

"I don't mean that. At work, when you lost track of time that day. We all do that."

"Oh."

Part of him wished she was angry that he had stayed out too late. It might have shown some interest, even fear that he would find somebody else. But she knew what he knew: he loved her without limitation.

"Anyway," she said, "tell me what it feels like."

"I'm not sure I can."

"Try."

"Okay," he said and tried to imagine an analogous situation.

"How much time do you spend getting ready in the morning—you know, shower, hair,

make-up, the whole routine?"

"Depends on the day."

"Today then, this past morning."

"Half hour, maybe a little longer."

"And you have a routine?"

"I vary it occasionally, but yes. You've seen me."

"And what if you started your half-hour routine at 9:00, and finished at 9:05?"

"I'd say I lost track of time."

"No you wouldn't. If you started at 9:00 and were still at it an hour later, then I'd say you lost track of time. But this is, I don't know, just...like time is waiting for me to catch up."

"Time stands still," she said, "and yet time and tide wait for no man. Looks like you have a contradiction. But I'll tell you this: if I could make toast in an instant, boil my tea water in thirty seconds, I could get all the beds made in a minute or two, I'd be fine with it. Can you teach me how this works?"

"You'd have to be naked," he said, then headed off to the bathroom before the certain but nonetheless hurtful rejection. Moments later, his facetious suggestion having been forgotten, Nikki put her book on the night table.

"You know," she said, "if you want to quit the site work and take a desk job with Autumn here in Baker, we'll get by."

"On half salary?"

"We'll get by. You'd be home more—I could get something part time. People do it."

And struggle. Derek Phillips was not about to take an administrative job right in town and give up half his income just because his mind had begun playing tricks on him. Maybe braving the elements in a remote wilderness wasn't the proper job for a young man college-educated in western Canada, but it was indeed the job for such a young man with a wife and three children and a small home in a Nunavut community where the cost of living always ran a step or two ahead of whatever pay increases the workers received. Being able to put food on the table and clothes on the kids' backs—these were sources of pride for Phillips—for all the field workers. Pushing a pencil in a warm office a short walk from home would be an admission of failure.

"Never happen," he said.

"Just a thought. I'm going to sleep."

He told her he'd be up for a while reading. But when he heard her breathing regularly, he turned off the light: lying in the same bed with a sleeping woman who wanted nothing to do with him was somehow better. *For better or worse*—that's what they had agreed to. It was a phrase intended to cover all eventualities—physical, psychological, sexual. For better or worse. If this was as bad as it got, he could handle it.

When it became worse, Nikki had little to do with it.

Derek Phillips spent the following work week checking the time obsessively, trying to gauge where he should be in a given job. He set his phone to vibrate at fifteen-minute intervals to help him keep on track. For a while the reminders worked, but then he reduced the intervals to ten minutes and held there. Five was too much of an admission that he had lost control. Even though the week passed without major incident, the maddeningly slow ten-minute intervals drove him distracted. The following Saturday in the co-op, talking with some of the locals, he broached the topic of time lapses. Nobody thought much of it—some laughed; others expressed envy in much the same manner as Nikki had; one of them with a reputation for sleeping with every unattached woman in Baker Lake—including his former wife— saw no end to the possibilities of such a "handicap." Only the co-op owner Manitok, an Inuit herself, seemed somber and withheld comment.

He waited until the store cleared, then approached her. He had known Manitok for years. Everyone did. And anyone over the age of twenty probably remembered when she was Jacqueline Nadeau and how, for no apparent reason one day, she swore to regain her Inuit heritage and adopted the new name. Only her brother Olin called her Jackie these days, and he did so only to annoy her. It was no secret that he was rankled by his sister's affinity for the past, but nobody else seemed to mind it at all.

Her store had been the symbolic center of Baker Lake for years, decades, long before Manitok assumed ownership. People called her place "the co-op" as if there were no others, as if some indefinable authenticity had attached itself. Outsiders might have called it "authentic" with shelves of found artifacts alongside works from local artisans alongside clothing that made survival possible alongside snack food and beer that, in their own way, made survival possible. In one corner, as a concession to modernity, a Keurig spit out coffee into paper cups below cellphone cases hanging from hooks—but even then right next to some hand carved mythological figures. It was as much a junk store as a co-op, but it symbolized and unified the community, and Manitok savored the part she played.

But with that role came responsibilities—like finding out what was besetting a distressed customer.

"Everything okay, Derek?" she asked.

"It's fine," he said. "You looked so serious before."

She nodded. "Your stories," she said. "I thought of my father. He always said the mind plays tricks."

"What kind of tricks?"

"He used to call it going northward."

"A euphemism?" he asked.

"For losing your mind? No. Different. Too much cold. Not enough light. A little crazy, but a little old too."

"I'm not even forty."

"Not that kind of old," she said. "Have you told Nikki?"

"Of course. She thinks that maybe it's the alcohol. You know how weekends are around here."

"Sometimes right into Sunday morning," she said. "I make good money on alcohol and the condoms that go with it. Plus I have a young married couple living downstairs from me. I've grown accustomed to the word *indefatigable*."

"Youth," he said. "Maybe it is that lifestyle, cramming everything into two days because the next five last forever. This going northward that your father used to mention—does it stop?"

"You can't go north forever: when you get to the pole, you're going south."

"I'm serious."

"I don't believe in the Hyperboreans, if that's what you mean."

"That can't be what I mean because I never heard that word. It doesn't even sound Inuit."

"Greek. They're supposedly the people who lived north of north in some land of sunshine beyond the north wind. I guess if you go beyond the north wind, you're not cold anymore."

"Because you're heading south," he said, parroting her explanation.

"They worship the sun—I can sort of figure out why. There are so many stories, so many myths. I wouldn't put too much stock in my father's beliefs. Until the day he died he did things the old way."

"Do any of his beliefs—any of your myths involve water?"

"Of course they do. They all do. Why?"

"When people go northward, do they find water?"

"They find ice," she said with a smile, "unless it's Canada Day and that's still six months off. This is Nunavut, not Aruba."

"Do they hear the waves and smell the spray and watch the whitecaps?"

"Did you?"

"I think so."

"At work?"

"In the field, yes. Would your father say I was going northward?"

"I told you—he believed in the old ways."

"You didn't answer my question."

"You should be talking to Demarais. His life revolves around that kind of...you know...."

"Bullshit? Everyone says he's a nut."

"I don't."

"Then what is it?"

She shrugged, then picked a pair of fur-lined gloves off a table and slid them over a bit. "If I don't keep this place organized..." she said, "...people won't buy what they don't find."

"So it *is* bullshit, all the myths and legends."

She exhaled. "In this vision of yours with the water, were there sea creatures? Seals, maybe walruses?"

"I didn't see any. Does that matter?"

"My father would say if there are animals present, then they are messengers."

"And you?"

"As I said, the old ways."

"I'm not stuck in the old ways," Phillips said. "And Nikki thinks...look, you know all this. Am I crazy?"

"Only if you thought I was going to forget to charge you for your coffee and donut."

He shook his head. "You're no help," he said, but relaxed his features too. "What good is it having a native around if all she wants to do is sell donuts?"

"I'll sell you anything you can afford, and some things you can't. But advice? No. You know, we live here and we think we're accustomed to just about everything, but months without sunshine when the simple act of walking to the end of the street is a test of will—it wears you down. How's Nikki?"

"Nikki is...Nikki."

"What's her latest kick?"

"Currently? Nothing."

"No special dietary restrictions? No pulling the plug on the TV?"

"Abstinence," he said.

"Well at least it's novel," she said. "Of course if that gets around and other wives follow suit, Autumn will have to pack up and leave because the men will be too frustrated to work there. I think Nikki is on to something."

"If Autumn leaves—hey that's a song, isn't it?"

"Yes it is, go on."

"Without Autumn, how would you stay in business?"

"Better. This co-op has been around for fifty years. Now someday with the town getting warmer, Baker Lake may be a new Toronto and I'll be pushed out by a Walmart or a Hudson's Bay. But until then, I'll be here with or without Autumn. Good riddance to them."

"Business will be slower."

"And I'll have more days off. We're not a factory town but some of the old-timers are afraid we might become one."

"You're not an old-timer."

"I'm past thirty and not bitching every day about leaving. That makes me an old-timer. Here," she said, pulling four small lollipops out of the showcase. "For the kids."

"I only have three kids."

"The other one's for you. Something to occupy you until Nikki comes around."

CHAPTER 4

The thought of squeezing a conversation out of Auguste Demarais—of sitting in that dreary assisted living home at all—would have depressed him even further. Besides, the old man drank more than ever, and his fantastical stories and eye-witness accounts had grown more preposterous with time. No. Instead he would savor his conversation with Manitok, maybe cast her in one of his fantasies until Nikki came around. And it would have to be a fantasy, especially since most of the men he knew were divided between considering her a stand-offish prude and declaring her a lesbian. Neither designation seemed to bother her.

Neither was accurate: Phillips could attest to that based upon on a three-week dalliance a year before when their friendship had ascended (or maybe descended) to a different plateau. Manitok had been pining about some local guy and Phillips had been consoling or commiserating—whatever his marginally older wisdom was supposed to do. One night he wound up in her apartment and they had a kissed a few times. As quickly as the relationship changed, it reverted; and the whole incident would have been forgotten had not Manitok's brother, drunk as usual, showed up, found Phillips alone with his sister, and threatened to kill him. Even now Olin insisted that his sister and Phillips had slept together and were probably still involved at some seamy level. They weren't, they never spoke of it, they treated each other as if it had never occurred and returned to what had been a simple friendship. At times Phillips fantasized about her, even imagined little sexual exploits that had never occurred, but the facts had been informally and mutually expunged from both their lives.

Manitok was nowhere near so discreet when it came to Autumn. Her disdain for the company was incalculable—never a secret—but with the public in general she had to maintain a balance between the need for its success to provide the town with dependable income sources, and her desire for Baker Lake to become less a company town and more a small hamlet—a summer haven for hunters, fishermen, and sightseers; a winter shelter against the weather. Once at the Naujat she'd gotten into an argument with a local woman—a chemist at Autumn who had let the liquor run away with her thoughts and accused Manitok of being an *antiquarian*. When that didn't produce the desired effect, she went with *spinster*. That worked better. Then it was Phillips, himself barely able to walk a straight line, who backed Manitok away from her tormentor and got one of his friends to hold the other woman. Within an hour the fight was forgotten and the two would-be combatants were laughing about some men making the usual asses of themselves. But there was no denying that the angry words that had passed between them were the same ones that had divided the town since Autumn set up shop a decade before. Manitok's ambivalence did not begin and end at the co-op door.

And yet Autumn, seventy miles to the north, could have been a thousand miles away, so little did the connection between company and town seem to register. But about two weeks into Phillips's bizarre relationship with time, on a brutally cold Sunday afternoon, Hal Whitton showed up at the front door. Phillips was trying to entertain the kids and Nikki was grocery shopping; and for a moment Phillips merely stared—the worlds of Baker Lake and Autumn had always been discrete and, among the weekly warriors who rode the Greyhound to work each Monday, were meant to stay that way. An Autumn supervisor didn't belong in Baker Lake unless he was at the administrative office, then back on the plane and out. Not at the Naujat, not at the co-op, and especially not paying a social visit to an employee.

"Can we talk for a few minutes?" Whitton asked.

Phillips, with little real choice, gave a hesitant yes and asked him in.

"So these are the little ones, huh?" Whitton said. "This is what we come home to, isn't it?"

"You have kids?"

"Yes. They're grown now. Both in college out west. They live with their mother, but I remember what it was like."

Whitton waved to them like someone who clearly did not remember what it was like, but Phillips saved him any further embarrassment by dismissing them with a promise: no more than five minutes and there'd be hot chocolate at the co-op later. With marshmallows, he added.

Whitton let the ensuing silence gather for a moment, then admitted the obvious: he didn't get to Baker very often.

"It's not that I don't want to," he said. "Autumn owes this town a lot. But there's not much cause for me to leave the mine."

"How about to visit your wife?"

"Oh we're long-since divorced," he said. "I thought I said that."

"You said the kids lived with their mother."

"And their new father. Been ten years since we broke up. Next year it'll equal the amount of time I was married. They probably don't make a greeting card for that. Anyway, reason I'm here—I've been mulling over that job you did, you know, the six-hour task you completed in ninety minutes?"

"I told you, I don't how it happened, but it's true."

"Oh I don't doubt it. I'm just wondering if, well, are you happy at Autumn?"

"I'm not bored, I make a decent salary, and my family is well taken care of. I never really thought about much else."

"I looked up your salary. It's good. How old would you want to be before you were able to double it?"

"Double it?"

"Right now, if you stay with Autumn, keep advancing, keep at it, by 2035 you might be making twice what you're making now. You'll be pushing sixty. Your kids will be up and gone. College. Married. Maybe you'll be a grandfather. Factor in inflation, you'll still be making good money, able to travel, maybe be able to tell your boss to shove it."

"It won't be you, will it?"

"The life expectancy for my position is fairly short. You can wait and tell somebody else or, and I'm just throwing this out there, you can double it tomorrow."

Phillips didn't want to sound too eager. "Does this involve a casino trip?"

"Not at all. It involves a change in jobs."

"You're firing me?"

"A change within the company."

"Something legal?"

"I told you, it's a job change, call it a restructuring of responsibility. It's an opportunity for you to make a good living, maybe retire early. I mean what you do with your money is...."

"I get the money part. What will I be doing to make this...this windfall."

"First thing you'll do is get off the plane tomorrow morning and come straight to my office so that I can lay everything out for you. But since you're curious—and you should be—Autumn is...hey, this is confidential, okay?"

"Sure."

"I mean you want to tell your wife, that's fine, but beyond that...."

"Confidential. Got it."

"Autumn is branching out. The mine here is going to be productive for a while, and out west we have oil fields. But the climate is changing, and we can either moan and groan or we can take advantage of it. About twenty miles east of the mines is what we think may be a vast underground oil stockpile. The climate now, the permafrost, is at a critical stage. At the current rate of warming and assuming normal weather for two years, we're that far away from its being feasible to drill, to build, to lay a pipeline. Others are going to realize this too. We have a lease on a small parcel of land near Tehek, but that lease will expire next year. We need to be coy about what we're doing, apply for a renewal, expand the area, and start construction. Once we do that, we can count on the legal system siding with us, but until then we may have to skirt some issues."

"Drill on land that isn't yours."

"Explore."

"Semantics, but let's say you do. Why do you need me? My talent is with minerals."

"Your talent, Mr. Phillips, is with getting things done. That's all. I'm asking you to get things done faster. Now I've got construction crews ready to go, but I need expediters, people who are going to know what to do and tell others to do it. I can hire people to scout the area and look for the prime places, or I can have you do it in one quarter of the time and do it alone. Secrecy is important here."

"Is it legal?"

"It's not illegal. Not really."

Phillips laughed. "Explain the difference."

"Nunavut is a new territory—not even twenty years old. It's kind of developing as we watch. The rules are shaky and there's room for, well, adjustments. There are lots of people—officials—who want to see it become more than an ice field, and they can skirt some of the issues, especially in areas that aren't posted."

"No disrespect, Mr. Whitton...."

"Hal."

"No disrespect, but just because a piece of land doesn't have a no trespassing sign on it, I don't think you can just take it."

"That would be for the courts to decide. Let's not get ahead of ourselves. Now, your wife. You can tell her what you're doing, but you won't be coming home for a while. You'll have to concoct a story to explain your absence to everybody else: a sick relative maybe. And Nikki will have to defend your story."

"She might not go for it if it's not legal."

"Remind her about the money, about what it would mean for the kids and her. I'm not asking her to do anything wrong or hurt anybody, just go along with your story."

Whitton took a deep breath and exhaled loudly, like someone who kept making the same valid point and never receiving any confirmation.

"You're not a native, Phillips. You weren't born here in Baker, right?"

"Right."

"So you like the town, probably. You're settled—I understand that. But towns like this one, they're dying. Look around you. Look at the standard of living. At the homes. At what people do to earn a buck."

"It's like every other small town in Canada, in the world."

"Without resources," Whitton said. "That's the difference. What's going to happen when the temperature goes up a few degrees and ice on the lake isn't quite so thick, and the permafrost level rises, and some of the wildlife that visitors come to watch and even hunt move on to the north. You'll have better access with less ice—you might have cruise ships coming out of Moosonee and sailing into Baker Lake, but then what. A few little shops selling Inuit art? Stories of the wildlife that *used* to be here? I don't see that happening."

"And oil will help?"

"A storage depot on the lake here, tankers hauling the product south."

"So you're talking about a pipeline."

"Right on down to the lake. It won't affect the town. It'll be out of sight."

"It's going to be harder to hide the storage depot."

"We can move it farther east, but the thing is those crews when they arrive here—maybe they stay for a while, spend some money. You want to make the town accessible for them. Now I know you're thinking the Exxon-Valdez and a few million dead ducks and fishes. This coastline isn't Alaska—not an obstacle course. No hidden reefs. Even the radar is better now. And double-hulled vessels are a lot less vulnerable."

"How long?"

"How long what?"

"How long would I be gone?"

"On the initial assignment, a month, maybe a little more. I know the kids are a factor, but you can call them, talk to them, feed them whatever story you want. What do you think?"

On the job Phillips made decisions every day, but this one extended beyond himself.

"When do you need to know?"

"If I find you in my waiting room tomorrow morning," Whitton said, "we pursue it. If not, we find someone else."

"Are you going to tell me this is the chance of a lifetime?"

"If I have to explain that to you, you're not the person I thought you were. Have a good day, Phillips. Don't forget the hot chocolate for the kids."

In the moments after Whitton left, the man sat in silence until his daughter Regina poked her head in.

"I don't like him," she said.

"You're very perceptive for a six-year-old," he said.

"That's what Mommy says. What does that mean?"

He laughed. "Get your brother and sister. Time for marshmallows."

CHAPTER 5

I promised myself I wouldn't complain about the cold—that I knew what awaited me in the northern Canada winter. I kept that promise until I was about ten feet removed from the single- engine Cessna that deposited me and five others on the tarmac of Baker Lake Airport. It was only then, inside the spartan but functional box that serves as a terminal, that I complained.

One of the other passengers smiled.

"First time here?" she asked. Her only luggage was a small, black leather briefcase: something about her demeanor told me she'd been here before.

"It is," I said. "It's quite bracing."

"Haven't heard that word used to describe it," she said. "But yes, bracing. There's a car here to take us into the hamlet."

"Where it's warmer?"

"Inside the buildings, I suppose. Believe me, this is nothing," she said. "Wait until the sun goes down or the wind picks up, or both. Come on or you'll die before you get out of the airport."

"And that would be embarrassing?"

"It would hurt tourism. Come on."

It was late in the day, but I knew that fact only because of a blood-red kitchen clock hanging above the exit door from the terminal. When you're that far north in the winter, it's pretty much twilight all the time and clocks become especially important. Or completely insignificant.

The woman with the briefcase led me over to a counter and told me that my luggage would soon arrive, via the pilot. No flashing lights on a large carousel—just a lady unloading a plane and hauling the stuff inside on a large-wheeled cart.

As she predicted, the pilot—she had identified herself as Captain Norris—was now doing double duty as a skycap. She and my new friend knew each other.

"Shelley," she said to the pilot, "this is..." she looked sheepish. "I guess I should have gotten your name before I volunteered."

"McNally," I said. "Francis, or Frankie, or Mac. I answer to all of them."

"Shelley Norris," she said. "Sometimes I get a chance to talk to passengers while they're boarding. Didn't get a chance this time. Thanks for flying with us."

"There's an *us*?"

"Sort of. Another pilot and I fly this route. How was the flight?"

"Boring. Tedious. Bumpy. Cramped. Cold."

"In that case would you like to fill out one our surveys?"

I liked her immediately.

"I want you...just you...to fly me out of here in a few days. And maybe there could be a smidge more heat."

"That is a problem," she said, handing me her card. "It's easier with pressurization. I'll try to get a camp stove back there. For next time."

"Or a kerosene heater. Something safe."

She laughed. "Pocket warmers may be your best bet," she said, then handed me a brown carry-on from the cart. I didn't bother telling her that I hadn't *chosen* her airline at all. The plane was there with an empty seat. Shit luck—nothing more.

When she asked how long I planned to stay, I told her a couple of days should do it. Her schedule was fluid, she said, but she would try to accommodate me. In real life I'd have tipped her, but in real life the pilot would probably be insulted if you threw him (or in this case *her*) a twenty when you deboarded, then thanked the person for not crashing. I followed the others to the waiting car, but then stopped, raced back, and handed Captain Norris a twenty. "Thanks for carting off the luggage," I said. She looked surprised—held it out in front of her like a venomous snake.

"You're welcome," she said. "But this is mostly for not crashing the plane, right?"

"Eighteen of it. The other two is for the carry-on."

"If I'd known there would be a tip involved, I'd have tried even harder not to crash. Thank you, Mr. McNally."

"Frankie's good," I said, then raced back to the car and squeezed between two men in the backseat of some throwback sedan, an Oldsmobile I think. The suitcase woman from the terminal rode up front with the driver who looked twelve but who seemed to show the rudiments of a slight beard. And his voice had dropped to a more mature level, providing me with some assurance he was legal...or close.

I leaned forward to give myself some breathing room.

"So you've been before?" I said to the woman.

All the time," she said, and extended a still-mittened hand. "Marianne Austin, like Texas, not Jane."

"Jane?"

"The author. You know, *Pride and Prejudice*? She spells it with an *e*."

"Saw the movie," I said, and immediately had to force myself from falling into another funk. When Linnie got sick we stopped watching all those classic movies on TV. She had always read a lot and always had a pulse on what looked to be good entertainment. Since the diagnosis, though, most of her reading has centered on lung cancer and how to beat it. It's one of those comeuppance diseases, you know like when a heavy drinker gets cirrhosis or an obese person gets heart disease. People tend to nod and say I told you so without actually saying it...and you'd like to punch their fucking heads in. (Linnie will vouch for the fact that I don't curse much, but all bets are off when some asshole agrees that a victim of an illness should die.)

Linnie never smoked, never worked in an asbestos mine, and never did any of the things that are supposed to give you that comeuppance—she just got a cold that wouldn't go away and then one day a specialist said it was lung cancer. Linnie's first question was would she make it to her next birthday in October. The specialist was apparently too special to make prognoses, but we found out from other physicians that she probably would. That was six months and one specialist ago. I remember how on Labor Day she took a bit of a downturn, and by mid-September we could see the end accelerating toward us. But then a new regimen and there she was racing to the front door and giving out Twixes on Halloween. It's been kind of a status quo since.

The mention of *Pride and Prejudice* had been one of those traps—what I call any kind of occurrence that pops up and reminds you of some unpleasantness you're trying to forget. I didn't feel like explaining all this to Ms. Austin and the other two riders, so I just made some comment about Austin, Texas, being a lot different from Baker Lake, Canada, and hoped she wasn't interested in pursuing any other avenues of conversation. She was.

"Here on business?"

"Yes," I said. "You?"

"No other reason to be here in January, unless you're into wildlife photography. Citizens have reported some bears lately—gotta be careful. They can be aggressive."

"You mean the bears, right?"

She laughed. "I should have been more specific. Yes, the bears. Some citizens can be, too. Everyone gets a little ornery shut in like this every winter"

"Which lasts what, eleven months?"

"Not quite that long—you see your first snow maybe mid-September, then by October the temperature is stuck below freezing all day—it's pretty much downhill from there until, well until March when it starts to turn a little. By mid-June all the snow is gone. I guess eleven months isn't that much of an exaggeration. Never counted."

"Summer's coming."

"I guess," she said, "but let's call it the eve of rising temperatures. There's probably a fifteen-letter Inuit word for that—I'll have to find out.

She asked if I was staying at the hotel. I told her I wasn't aware of any other options, especially since I wasn't planning to stay long—two or three days. She said it was a decent place, and I admitted that I had grown accustomed to a lot of indecent ones, especially when I was working full time.

"Lot of traveling, huh?"

"Quite a bit," I said, though the indecent places were the ones I surveilled, usually from the comfort of my car. I wasn't ready to share with Ms. Austin the fact that I was (or had been) a PI. Admissions like that tend to defeat the purpose of being a PI. In truth, after I retired and included Linnie in my travels, I became very particular about where we stayed, mostly to make up for all the times I'd left her at home. For a couple of years we went everywhere together—I had seen too many older couples wait for the opportunity to go places, then suddenly find themselves ill and stuck at home permanently. Actually, when I retired three years ago, we pretty much abandoned our house—spent most of our time asking neighbors to keep an eye on things while we were driving through Arizona or riding some tour bus in Hungary. There were places between Arizona and Hungary too. It was a hectic two years, but it ended seemingly in the blink of an eye: she got sick and didn't get better. I spared Austin the details.

"I stayed there once myself," she said, referring to the hotel "until I got settled. Now I have a place. The hotel manager had a crush on me so I got extra towels."

"My God, why would you ever leave?"

"I know. Extra towels keep people coming back. Maybe you'll get them too, though I think he favors women. Anyway, I'm pretty much a full-time part-timer here now."

"How's that?"

"Sporadically. I work for the government, cover most of Nunavut, which is like saying I cover Europe. Kind of a lot for one person—lots of travel; of course the population density is too small to measure—there are only two dozen actual locations only a few of which have an actual population."

"Like here."

"One of the bigger ones. My stop," she said to the driver, who pulled over, then got out to get her bag from the trunk.

"Enjoy your stay," she said to me, and I watched her traverse a short walkway to a low, square building with an unlit sign I couldn't read. The driver waited for her to get inside, explained to us that that's what he did for everybody, told some horrible anecdote about a man who slipped, hit his head, went unconscious, and froze to death after some cab driver had dropped him off. "Not gonna happen again," he said, though when he dropped the rest of us at the hotel, he sped away before any of us reached the door. He probably considered an attractive woman like Marianne Austin more worth protecting than a bunch of old timers checking into the only hotel in town.

He wasn't the only one who felt that way.

The clerk at the main desk—the only desk—sporting at least a few days' growth of beard and green toque asked me, before I even gave him my name—if I'd come in on the same plane as Ms. Austin. Even if I hadn't I would have said yes, since whatever crush he had developed during her hotel stay remained active, and the opportunity for extra towels loomed.

"She said this was a pretty nice place," I said to him. I wanted to see him swoon again.

Mason. That was the name on a little silver nameplate he wore as, perched on a high stool, he handed me some paperwork. It's a trivial matter, but I don't think I'd ever been at the front desk of a hotel and talked to a seated reservations person. It's one of those stand-up jobs—like a train conductor or a store clerk, but Mason (I assumed that was his first name) seemed very comfortable on that stool and I was willing to avoid future small talk just to get to my room and out of the clothes I'd been in for some thirty hours. Nobody flies direct from Westchester County to Baker Lake without seeing most of the United States and Canada along the way. I once had to fly to Detroit to get to Albuquerque—that was almost logical compared to this recent itinerary, one which included Toronto, Saskatoon, something called Churchill, and here, each aircraft increasingly small and noisy (and cold) along the way. So no, I'd save any chatter with Mason for a later date—or would have had there been soap in my room.

So back to the main desk.

"Sorry," Mason said, "got a woman who does that but sometimes she doesn't."

"Maybe it's time to rewrite the job description," I said when he gave me a small wrapped bar.

"Room okay?" he asked. I told him it was.

"You up here on business?"

I told him I was.

"With the mines?"

This was the conversation I thought I'd avoided.

"Maybe. Not really sure. I'm meeting with a client."

"You a salesman?"

"No."

"FBI?"

"You don't have an FBI in Canada."

"But you aren't from Canada," he said, and removed his sunglasses for the first time—they may have been those photosensitive lenses that darken in the light of day (not that there is much) but they seemed too dark for the dimly lit lobby. He squinted at me as if he had just spotted a shard of spinach in my teeth, then put the glasses back on.

"So?"

"No, not the FBI. Not the CIA. Not your CSIs."

It occurred to me that a previous visitor here, a man I knew quite well, had probably undergone the same inquisition, so I stole a piece of his identity.

"I sell stocks and bonds," I said.

"Both?"

"Yes. Why not?"

"No reason. You know I always wondered what the difference was. I mean I hear that someone's wealthy from stocks and bonds, but...hey, I can always Google it, right? Don't want to hold you up."

He was smiling. I think he knew I was lying, and by agreeing not to push it, he simply underscored the fact. I mumbled something about finding time later to maybe go into it with him—I figured I could Google it myself by then—but he said no, he was self-taught and this would help continue his education.

"Tell you what though," Mason said, "I can direct you to your client if you'd like."

"Got to get cleaned up a little first, but I do need to find the co-op."

"Which co-op?"

I knew there were two and I know who owned each one.

"The one Manitok runs."

"That's her Inuit name, of course," he said, playing the tour guide-cum-local color expert. "She's right down the street." He led me to the door and pointed to it. "It's slippery up here, but this is a survivable journey," he said. "Be careful, some journeys aren't."

"That sounds ominous," I said. "How about the journey to my room? Does that seem safe?"

"If you don't slip on that bar of soap."

He'd already pulled out a laptop. "Gonna look up that bond stuff," he said.

"Have fun," I said. I'd have to use my phone to do some research. Just to keep up. I suppose if I'd told him the truth in the first place—well, it's always the first lie that screws things up.

CHAPTER 6

That previous visitor here...a man I knew quite well...the stocks-and-bonds guy...Martin Wilkes.

His phone call on January 15 should not have come as a surprise. The date marked another anniversary of the "Miracle on the Hudson," which had become the focal point in his life.

Martin Wilkes—on January 16, 2009, as the world celebrated an aviation marvel—phoned and told me that his wife, a passenger on that luckless, then seemingly charmed flight, had been rescued like the other 149 passengers, only to vanish that same evening. Not even a week later (and after I had practically guaranteed her safe return) she lay dead in a medical facility deep within the Canadian Arctic, a victim of exposure and of her own self-destructive tendencies. I can spin the story with details and emphasize the suicidal tinge to her death, but failure really has no suitable euphemism. Either you do the job or you don't. Either you find the missing person or you admit the failure. If that pilot Sullenberger had *almost* made a safe landing and *almost* saved 150 lives, I doubt if his name would be enshrined in any hall of heroes, or played in the movies by Tom Hanks. The fact that I *almost* went to the Arctic in search of her, and that her husband *almost* rescued her would make for a pretty dismal movie, one that not even Tom Hanks could salvage.

For me the Miracle on the Hudson always belonged to others. Not to me. Not to Wilkes.

This January 15, the house was still redolent of Christmas. For Linnie and me the holidays had gone as well as we could have expected. We had shared a few good days when we opened some presents and even had some people over, but mainly we watched the holidays pass by without us. Since there was no fear that our artificial tree would dry out and burst into flame or that the LED candles would tip over and start some conflagration, we let things be. We had discussed the possibility that this might be our last Christmas together and that there was no point in following any established protocol. But after a while even artificial greenery seems to wilt, and on that evening I'd decided to return the place to some normality. With Linnie upstairs asleep I had disassembled the tree and moved a table back to its non- holiday location. I had just retrieved the tree storage carton when the phone rang—203—a Connecticut area code, and a number that seemed familiar. Then I remembered the date and I knew.

I didn't think Wilkes was calling to celebrate, any more than Germany celebrates D-Day, or the invisible inhabitants of the moon quote "one small step..." to commemorate the day some alien monster jumped all over them.

But I knew it was Wilkes, renewing an alliance that had begun as pure happenstance.

Nine years before, one of his regular clients had given him my name. Older guy named Blackmoor—gotta be eighty and probably still kicking ass, or chasing it. I'd done some work for him once and I guess he liked me and thought that Wilkes would too. Blackmoor didn't consider whether or not I'd like Wilkes, and that task took some time. Some of it was me, of course. I'd just passed fifty in 2009 and I was set in my ways, expecting people to act the way...well, the way I expected them to act. But the rest of the problem was Wilkes himself—I just thought he was dishonest, maybe not with his investors or his company, but certainly with himself. When Keira went missing—that was his wife—he vowed to do whatever it took and spend whatever it cost to get her back. I'm dead certain he believed his dedication was genuine. But those feelings existed more on a theoretical level than an emotional one, and he always seemed more inconvenienced than worried, at least until he finally went all in. When it was over he was shocked and despondent over Keira's death, but I think he was insulted too, and that seemed like an odd reaction.

Comparisons are odious, so let me just come out and be odious: Linnie and I have plenty of secrets—little bits of trivia we don't bother sharing. But we still know everything significant about each other. Wilkes, though, seemed to know almost nothing about the woman he was married to—had been married to for some twenty years—other than the superficial knowledge that they were husband and wife, that she took care of the kids while he worked, that she tended to groceries and cleaning and maintaining a home while he filled in with anything else. It was match right out of early television with the parameters clearly delineated.

I assume they celebrated anniversaries and birthdays, had regular sex, maybe even said *I love you* on occasion; but when she ran off that day, he could not fathom any possible reason for it. It was only when he came to grips with his own lack of understanding, even though it was too late, that he became more likable...which made my failure to bring Keira home more of a burden. It still is.

I'd blown cases before; in fact, inasmuch as virtually every case ends with someone getting some really bad news, I guess I blew them all. But death was a hell of a lot more final than proving to a Yonkers attorney that, yes, his wife was sleeping with her golf instructor; or informing a banker over in Eastchester that he was right—his treasurer with a weakness for slow horses was availing himself of the odd-thousand dollars on occasion—and losing it at the track. Very few people were ever truly happy when I completed an assignment—except me. I earned a good living by being proficient at what I did. But the Wilkes case—I have trouble finding any upside to that.

To his credit, Wilkes never held it against me—even admitted more than once that no PI could have done much to exorcize the demons with which Keira Wilkes lived. Maybe that's true. But I'd exacerbated the situation by being stubborn. I had protocols, procedures that had proved their efficacy over a lifetime. Sometimes they involved a good deal of caution—a knowledge of just when a certain stage of an investigation should be reached, or delayed, or rejected out of hand. And so, nine years ago, when Martin Wilkes insisted on heading north on what appeared nothing more than a random and amorphous search, I advised against it, refused to sanction it, and absolutely rejected his suggestion that I accompany him. And of course like the proverbial blind horse stumbling upon some creek, Wilkes did find her...and almost as quickly lost her for good. Another two days, I told myself afterwards, and I'd have been there. Whether that would have made a difference is debatable, even unlikely, but guilt doesn't always operate on a level playing field or within the more logical recesses of one's mind. I wasn't responsible for the death of Keira Wilkes, but the days when I truly believe that are rare, and this was not one of them.

I felt almost relieved to hear his voice.

"I just remembered the date," I said. "I thought you might call."

"But you answered anyway."

"I'm getting older now," I said. "I can't afford to make any more enemies. I don't want to have one of those wakes with no mourners."

"All your clients will be there."

"I said *mourners*. Bad news and a bill—that doesn't create friendships."

"Everybody sends a bill, Mac. That's how the economy operates. Thank God for that or I'd be out in the street. How's retirement?"

"How'd you know?"

"You told me a few years back you were ready. You're not the type to think of things without doing them. So?"

I told Wilkes what I was up to—how I'd migrated from full time investigations to part-time instruction at various police stations. He acted enthusiastic, but I know Wilkes—when he works, he works. A part-time job would have him crawling up walls...or standing out on Whitehall Street with pamphlets and a tin cup.

"Your wife must be happy," he said. "Linnie, isn't it?"

"Yes, she's adjusting."

"Tell her I was asking for her. Reason I called—I'm down in Greenwich for a meeting that just ended—I was wondering if you wanted to have a drink somewhere. Just catch up. I'm like ten minutes from you."

"If you're that close, stop by."

"I don't want to impose. It's kinda late."

"For dinner maybe. I'm still five hours away from sleep."

"You don't mind?"

"Of course not. One thing—Linnie's under the weather—she'll be sleeping."

"Well then we can do this another time. Goddam flu has half the company out."

"Nothing like that. She had a little surgery about a month back. You know how recovery can be."

"Not really. A month? Did she fall?"

"Lung cancer."

The gasp was audible.

"Jesus! That's...my God, Mac..."

"Bad, I know. But people do survive it these days."

"How long? No, no, that's not what I...when did this happen?"

"Late fall."

"Neither one of you smokes. What the fuck?"

"That was more or less our reaction. You don't have to be a smoker, I guess."

"Is she having treatments?"

"Chemo, before and after the surgery. We'll see. People can survive for a good while even if the operation doesn't clear everything."

"I read about that immune therapy."

"Immunotherapy. Yeah, lots of good things happening. I'll tell you about it when you get here."

"God, no. I'm not going to bother you. Another time."

"A year, Wilkes? Linnie and I are going to be fighting this for a year if we can, maybe longer. You mean I can't have anyone visiting for a year? You know the address. Come on over. But let me warn you—the house is a little bit...um...Christmasy. Don't get me wrong—I'm not preserving the atmosphere. We just, you know, let things go."

"You can't worry about shitty little housekeeping things when your wife is sick. I really don't want to impose."

This was the new Wilkes—the post 2009 model—still reliving and maybe atoning for the life he'd squandered with Keira. His priorities had been reordered too late: now he was the spokesman for involved and honest marriages, putting others first. Turning him away would have spoiled all he believed in, so I assured him I could pour a drink or make coffee on my own and verified the directions. In the fifteen or so minutes I would have before his arrival, I stashed a few red candles in the cabinet and replaced the fake spruce over the mantel with some floral wall hanging Linnie had bought a few years back. Lots of purples and yellows that transformed the house into Easter, having skipped every occasion in between.

Linnie was dozing but I told her Wilkes was going to drop by. She was not pleased.

"The place is a mess."

"I cleaned," I said.

"I know how you clean, Mac."

It was the kind of statement that, before she got sick, would have preceded her jumping out of bed and retrieving the vacuum from the hall closet. Not this time.

"Use clean glasses, okay?"

"Isn't *dry* good enough?"

A half smile. There were times during the day when she was up and about and as normal as she'd ever been, but she wound down quickly in late afternoon and disappeared after dinner which, at times, she hardly touched. I'd like to think it was a mere condemnation of my cooking skills, but it was the cancer and the treatment and probably the occasional bout of depression thrown in for good measure.

"I got this," I said. "We'll be quiet."

"As if I could stay awake. Say hello for me."

I kissed her and went back downstairs, then waited until Wilkes's headlights lit up the front windows. I looked around the room one more time. Everything looked fine until I opened the front door to let him in and cringed at a half-dead wreath with a faded bow.

"Oops," I said. "More work to do."

"It'll get done," he said, shaking my hand. "I'm overdressed."

He was. I don't think I've worn a topcoat in decades, but his made me feel I was missing out—black wool and perfectly tailored with a yellow paisley tie that was perfectly Windsor-knotted showing through at the neck.

"Compared to me," I said. At least I wasn't in my bathrobe...yet.

"I still play the role," he said, then shook his head in disgust. "Suits. A room filled with them. God they're insufferable."

"*Your* friends," I said. "Can't wear jeans on Wall Street, can you? Not if you want to drive a car like that."

I pointed to the driveway where a gleaming black vehicle shone in the streetlight, brighter still with a thin layer of snow surrounding it. I couldn't tell the make or model, but dark shiny cars under artificial light always look impressive.

"Bought it used," he said. "My boss thought I should drive a Mercedes so I drive a Mercedes. Can't keep the goddamn thing in repair, but that's part of the cachet...there's no better morning greeting than *Fuckin' car's in the shop again.* That's how you say 'I drive a Mercedes' without sounding arrogant. Tell me how Linnie is holding up."

"Speaking of being in the shop...."

"I didn't mean...."

"Wilkes, we still laugh. You can too. Everything is day-to-day whether you're sick or not. We don't let it consume us."

"Must be hard not to."

"Linnie has never been a brooder. Her *woe is me* maximum is about ten seconds. How are your kids?"

"They're fine," he said. "Brett's in high school where everyone's as surly as he's always been. Now he's beginning to see what that looks like and he's becoming more bearable. James is just...James. Rolling along from day to day. He talks about his mother more than Brett does, but he's okay."

"And business?"

"Market's through the roof. You know what happens next. Hole in the roof followed by rain."

"So I should sell both shares of PanAm stock?"

"They may have nostalgic value: I'd hold on to them. Back in '09 the tailspin was bottoming out.

That's all changed."

"Must be the president."

"I can't say it's not, but I didn't vote for him. That's between you and me—I have to maintain my Republican values if I want to work for T&B."

"And you were seeing someone a while back, right? Elizabeth something?"

Of course I knew her name—Elizabeth Hadley—a woman I had vetted without Wilkes's knowledge because...well at this point the whole process was so ingrained that I couldn't help myself. And after all he had done to reexamine his life and make changes, I just didn't want him to be disappointed. He had mentioned the woman once and I immediately conducted a small-scale investigation. I called her the grey lady—a nickname that had little to do with hair or skin color or murky background but everything to do with the color palette of her clothes—an inexhaustible parade of grey which ranged from battleship to gunmetal to slate with infinite shades between. But her history was black and white: a research analyst in Wilkes's own building, married once, a clean divorce, no hints of anything untoward. And she was physically striking—close to six feet, perfectly proportioned, carried herself without a scintilla of self-consciousness, even wearing heels when the mood suited her—grey ones. It may have been unseemly to investigate a friend's potential fiancée—to tail her for a few hours one afternoon—but in my sometimes fevered mind, I felt that providing a safe relationship would somehow atone for the previous failure, at least where Wilkes was concerned. Some days I even come close to believing that.

I was disappointed when he said they had called it off.

"Not officially," he said. "I guess we left the door ajar."

"Did you give it a chance?"

"Probably not," he said. "I'm not really ready to give chances, you know?"

"Well, it's been...."

"Going on ten years, I know. I think when I'm ready it won't seem like so much of a risk. Maybe she's the one."

"She may not wait," you know. "Lots of men out there to compete with."

"I know, but I don't have to worry about the short ones. She's pretty tall."

"You have certainly figured out the odds, Wilkes."

We talked about nothing for a few minutes—the general sorry state of the world from the point of view of two men whose view was no less myopic than anyone else's that comes from a digest of unnewsworthy TV reports and Internet rumor. I'm not sure how long we sat there trying to make small talk— I don't think it was either of our fortes—before we lapsed back to our wives. For each of us nothing else mattered.

I offered him coffee, he declined. We made one last stab at talking about nothing—I think it was the Knicks or something to do with sports—before Wilkes stood.

"I should be going—got a long drive."

"No such thing in a Mercedes. I didn't even offer you a drink. You used to drink gin. Boodles. You introduced me to it."

"Still do. Some other time maybe."

"Coffee then?"

"I should be going. Homework to check. And I don't want to be a bother."

"I press a button, I drop in a pod, I place a cup underneath. Coffee. Kids won't do their work until you get home anyway."

"They're pretty conscientious, especially since Brett has come to realize that getting into college is his ticket out of my grasp."

But finally Wilkes relented.

"The caffeine will keep me awake on the Merritt," he said.

"Good. Then you can tell me why you're really here."

"I told you. I was in the area...."

"I'm retired, Wilkes, not comatose. Now formulate whatever the hell you came here to ask me. I don't need charts and graphs like in work. Just shoot."

"It's nothing. Not with your wife sick and all."

"If you leave and don't tell me, don't you think I'll find out in an hour anyway? Did you forget how good I am?"

He nodded and sat back down. I let the Keurig do its work, settled up on the cream and sugar requests, and came back in with two cups.

"Like I said, quick. Now what's up?"

"I know you're retired, Mac—knew it before I called—but I was hoping I could get you do one more job. I just didn't know about Linnie then—that she was sick and all. You work through all this first and then maybe some other time...."

"In my line of work, there's seldom room for *some other time*. The coffee will keep you awake long enough to drive home *and* tell me about this...job...assignment...favor. Which is it?"

"All three, I guess. And one more thing."

I could see the hesitancy, and it was more than just Linnie's being sick. I made it easier for him.

"You might as well say it, Wilkes. It's at the North Pole again, right?"

"There's no actual pole there."

"Really? What do the polar bears lean against? Or aren't they real either?"

We'd been groveling for conversation before; now we were loosening up, and without liquor.

"I believe those bears are real. The anoraks and boots too. All real."

"Nunavut."

He nodded. "As I said, Mac, this is not something you have to do."

But it was. I couldn't bring his wife's case to a satisfactory conclusion, but at least I could try to keep another one from ending the same way.

CHAPTER 7

Wilkes laid the half-empty coffee mug on the end table.

"A few days ago," he said, "I got a call from Baker Lake. Remember Manitok?"

"I remember the name. Of course I'd actually know her if I'd been there."

"I really didn't come here to have this conversation again, Mac. You weren't going to rescue Keira, nobody was, not even if you ionically transported yourself there and got there *before* she did. I'm sure you realize that."

"Ionically what?"

"Don't dwell on fine details. You made what we at T&B call a nonviable promise—you didn't have all the facts. You didn't know her. Hell, I didn't even know her. Can we move on?"

I started another rebuttal but he held up both hands.

"Listen, Mac, I don't want to be a pain in the ass here, but a good host should make his company feel at home. Dredging up old and uncomfortable topics isn't the way to do it."

"I gave you coffee."

"And it's delicious. I just don't want the agita that goes with it. Now the missing guy's name is Derek Phillips. He's not Inuit but he works up at the mines. Got a wife, three kids."

"That gives him four reasons to disappear, or else no reasons."

"What do you mean?"

"Guys who run off usually find that family life is not what it was cracked up to be and look for a way out. Guys who don't run off have the same motivation—gotta stay for the family. In other words his family situation doesn't necessarily help me. Is this his first marriage?"

It must have been right about there when I realized that in my attempt to be glib and knowledgeable, I had pretty much described Wilkes's own situation with his wife running off and abandoning the family.

"Sorry," I said. "Just running my mouth."

"Saying aloud what I think about every day doesn't bother me. And I don't know if this is his first marriage. I just know the outline here."

"If he has a girlfriend or two, there could be debts involved."

"Don't know that either."

"Derek Phillips. If I Google him?"

"Nothing there. The Internet doesn't know he's missing."

"It will, soon enough."

"I wish I had more information for you, Mac, but Manitok was a little vague about particulars."

"Think she's the other woman? I mean shouldn't the guy's wife be the one looking for a PI?"

Wilkes shrugged, but he looked dubious. Then again, he'd been at Tolliver & Byrne so long, he had to be thinking like an investor, not an investigator—though even there I'll bet we had more in common than he thought.

"Tell you what," I said. "With my situation...."

"Can you recommend someone good?"

"Really?"

"I didn't know about your wife so I can't in good conscience ask you to go. I figured there must be a list that only PIs would have—you know, who the good ones are."

I hated the idea of delegating *my* job to someone else, but Wilkes was in luck. I'd been to a conference in Toronto in 2012 and picked up some names—top investigators from several provinces—I was sure I hadn't thrown it away. Pretty sure.

"Of course," he said, "Nunavut isn't really a province."

"And they weren't represented. But I have a list somewhere," I said. "Some pretty good men and women work in the Toronto area. It's not a list you'll find online, but it covers the U.S. and Canada, even some of Europe. These are people who are going to cost quite a bit of course."

"I don't think money is an issue," Wilkes said. He was less enthusiastic at the prospect of someone else doing this, but he knew I wasn't going to leave Linnie alone.

"It's going to take some time to turn up those names," I said. "I no longer have a filing system to speak of, but I have a drawer full of Post-it notes."

"Aren't you supposed to post Post-it notes?"

"You've found the flaw in the system. Let me give you a call tomorrow or shoot you an email. I have your address."

"Fair enough. I'll tell Manitok she'll get a list of potential investigators and she can maybe choose one."

"Is she married now? Manitok?"

Wilkes laughed. "When I hired you to look for Keira, do you remember the first thing you asked me for?"

"Of course—a list of old boyfriends."

"And I was upset at the time because I was sure you were headed off in the wrong direction entirely."

"I probably was."

"Not entirely—it was a childhood friend that set her off. Now I have the same question—what difference does it make if she's married?"

"Just adds to her availability."

"I get that part, but she's not the type to get involved with a married man."

"There's a type? That's like the *law-abiding citizen*: everybody is one until he isn't."

He exhaled loudly. "I guess because I know her, I dismissed that possibility out of hand. Can't do that, huh?"

"No, though your observations count for something too. She could be just the spokesman for the group—they figure she knew you, you knew a PI, bingo. The thing is, if she's sleeping with this Phillips guy, then we have a lead, even a motive. You say he's been missing a week or so."

"A little more."

"And no one has heard from him either. No ransom note? No phone calls? Nothing like that?"

"I don't think so. I didn't ask a lot of questions—I figure you'd know—or maybe some other PI would know what to ask."

"How did she sound?"

"I don't know what you mean"

"You give a lot of financial advice, right? When the market goes down—even for a week or so—like after the Brexit vote a few years back..."

"So you follow stuff like that."

"I don't have a retirement plan," I told him. "My investments pan out or we don't eat. In your case, when the market drops, don't you deal with a lot of panicky phone calls?"

"I get my share."

"So you understand urgency as opposed to, oh maybe, simple concern or curiosity. How did Manitok sound?"

"Calm, I guess. Certainly not panicky. But that's her."

"But if she's calling from a thousand miles away...."

"Two thousand."

"Even better—if she's doing that she's desperate: there are plenty of good PI services in Canada. But if she doesn't sound desperate, then there's a reason, and I think the reason is...despite what you believe about her...."

I waited for him to finish the sentence, but he just smiled.

"Not gonna say it," he said. "I trust my judgment about her."

"That counts for something," I said. It's true. When you're drawing a picture of a client or a suspect, you take whatever input you can from people you trust.

We finished our coffee, he declined a second cup, I assured him once more that I'd find the list. It was getting late.

"At least I'll be awake for the ride home," he said, then stood, put on his coat, and walked toward the door. Just as I reached for the knob to open it for him, he stopped me. "Oh, one more thing," he said.

"What are you, Columbo?"

"What?"

"TV detective. Used to walk away from the suspect just far enough for the guy to feel relieved, then turn around and say 'oh yeah, one more thing' and then drop a bomb. Do you have a bomb?"

"I have a...a firecracker."

"Manitok is sitting in your car waiting to come in?"

"Of course not."

"She's sitting in *my* car?"

"Not that either."

"Then the only other possibility that would make you this suddenly nervous is that you gave Manitok my phone number and you want to get out before she calls. What time will that be happening?"

"I told her not to call until she had spoken to me again. I wanted to talk to you first, see if you were willing. Now I understand it's really not feasible."

"So she won't be calling?"

"She agreed to wait."

"Wilkes, I just can't get you to think like a PI. It's 9:15. They're an hour earlier in Nunavut, right? I think I remember that. I figure she'll wait until 9:00 her time, then she'll call. Whether you tell her I can't do it or she doesn't hear from you at all, she's calling. If she's going a couple thousand miles for a PI, she's not going to sit back and just hope for the best, not with a missing person involved"

"If she does call," Wilkes says, "then I apologize. She agreed to wait."

"Desperation doesn't allow for delays, but beyond that, she probably wants to make her own case. Here's my suggestion—we sit around a little longer, have another coffee, maybe watch the Knicks for a while, wait until 10:00 just for the hell of it. What do you say?"

He agreed, the on-again off-again topcoat landed on the chair, and—since he didn't like basketball much—we found some news channel for background noise and drifted from topic to topic for a while—his kids, work, the house which he would have loved to sell but didn't want to uproot the boys. I'd always considered him a humorless person, but then I had only known him at an awful time in his life. Now, in this awful time in mine, he was more personable, even shared some funny stories from work which I'm sure were confidential. No names, he said, and wisely too. I do have a knack for finding information.

At 9:48 the phone rang. Wilkes shook his head.

"And sometimes people find me," I said.

He looked apologetic: I wasn't that sure he was that sorry.

CHAPTER 8

I won't lie and say that Manitok made such a compelling case that I couldn't wait to get started. In fact I turned her down at first—even told her the truth about Linnie's condition. When she heard that, she said something like *of course you can't leave*, but she was waiting for me to say oh yes I could. So I did, in a way. I told her we'd talk about it, Linnie and I. Manitok claimed to be okay with that, but I knew by her tone she thought I was putting her off only to delay the obvious. She wasn't quite so okay with my asking her if she and Derek Phillips were sleeping together.

"That, Mr. McNally, is none of your business."

"That, Ms. Manitok, is exactly my business. When you hire me, everything is my business. Now you don't have to tell me everything, but it's still my business."

That may have chilled the friendly conversation a bit, so I assured her I wasn't about to post her answer on some social media site, but that if she wanted me to find this guy, I had to have all the information I could, and that restricting me to nothing more than general knowledge would render my chances of success only slightly better than hers and not worth the investment. And it was an investment: she and a dozen or so others had put together enough to cover my transportation and accommodation expenses, and leave me a couple thou to play with. I think they thought it was very generous, it wasn't: if Manitok hadn't been a personal referral from someone I felt an obligation to, I'd have dismissed the offer out of hand. Instead I agreed to call in the morning after I'd had time to reassess. Wilkes, hearing only my half of the conversation, smiled when I hung up.

"Well that takes me back," he said. "My first conversation with you was pretty much like that. Do you ever want to know anything other than who your client has slept with?"

"It's a good starting point," he said. "People will admit to all kinds of stupid or horrible things, but they lie about sex. Everyone does it. I just want to know the extent."

"Then what?"

"I can still work with them, or for them. It just establishes a baseline."

"Inquiring into a stranger's sex life never is a good icebreaker. You pissed her off, right?"

"Same as I pissed you off. I don't think she took it well, but she's a big girl. Besides, once a client calls, she's no longer a stranger. Come on, Wilkes, you know how I work. I'm not going to dance around an issue that could be vital. And I'm not preaching here, but what if this really is a crime? What if Phillips really is in trouble? Then the niceties of life disappear regardless. I'll call her in the morning."

"And tell her no."

"That's the plan."

"At least you were polite to her, even if it was just a favor to me."

"So what's wrong with that?"

"Nothing. Everything. I'll let you get some sleep. Give Linnie my best."

"You've never even met my wife, have you?"

"One of these days."

This time he got to the door and past it. After I'd straightened out the place, I was a little more honest with myself about taking the job. Yes, I owed Wilkes a favor, but there was another reason I wanted to do it. PI work is dying.

That's not an easy admission to make, but I can't keep poking fun at all the new investigators who do all their work sitting on their asses in front of a laptop or hanging out in a coffee shop with a smartphone and looking at video from some surveillance camera. I can't keep doing that because it works for them and it makes me feel like a dinosaur. There remain some things you need to see firsthand, observe, register—a man having a late dinner with some unidentified woman in a hotel restaurant might not turn up on the Internet, although in these days of Instagram and Facebook and ongoing surveillance—not to mention imagined exposés masquerading as investigations, maybe it would.

When I first started out, I felt smarter than everybody else because I worked my ass off. And I didn't have to operate within any system. A police detective might catch a...let's say a robbery and investigate. Maybe a week goes by and the guy's homing in on a suspect or two, then just like that he's pulled off that case because some superior says that another one needs looking at "right away." Then someone else picks it up and maybe wants to go at it differently and so...it's back to square one. But me? I handled one case at a time, two if one was ongoing and didn't require constant surveillance or monitoring. I had control.

Another thing: cops work shifts—even the best of them have to clock out once in a while. I never did. If I wanted to put in an eight-hour day from 4:00 a.m. to noon, then that was my day. And if it extended another hour or ten, I didn't have to dicker with some supervisor about overtime. I'm not belittling what the cops do: unlike many of them I've never been shot at or called upon to some scene with an active shooter. If I have been shot at, the gunman missed so badly and from such a great and silencing distance that I didn't know about it. And cops' wives notoriously pay a high price: If Linnie did, she never let on.

None of that really made me smarter—that was just hard work—but nowadays I can be just as smart with a two-minute Internet search. And if I'm a hacker or even if I know one (and truthfully, I don't know anyone who doesn't know one), then everything is available to me. I stayed away from the "dark web" and its catalogue of sexual deviates, but that doesn't mean I never asked people to go there for me—or that it didn't pay off. That politician sending pictures of his dick to some girl—you really think that's an isolated incident? People these days are so infatuated with their electronic devices that they don't realize that everything they do is out there—forever. I don't have to find pictures of the guy sleeping with his best friend's wife—all I have to do is find the ten-thousand emails they've exchanged, or the phone records from their cell providers, or the cell phone photo of their little excursion through Central Park when he snapped an innocent picture of the foliage around the reservoir and it went to the cloud, placing him undeniably there when he was supposed to be in work. And I can do all this while I'm watching reruns of Columbo or Kojak, those throwback PIs who wore out shoe leather and listened to the hi-fi instead of the wi-fi.

In 2009 when Martin Wilkes came to me in desperation searching for a missing wife, I dazzled him with all kinds of seemingly private information about his personal and business life, data I accumulated in a few hours.

Nowadays it would take me a few minutes, and I wouldn't need the phone next to my ear calling in favors from other PIs.

So yes, I wanted the case, but I was not planning to take it. Running off on Linnie would be analogous to this Derek Phillips guy running out on his wife and three kids. When I finally dragged myself upstairs that night—coffee never keeps me awake—I thought about Wilkes some more. Life could not have been easy for him these past eight years, not only because he'd lost his wife, but because he felt responsible for it. There's no workaround for guilt, and my knowing that made denying his request—and Manitok's—that much easier.

I went upstairs and shaved. Most men do that in the morning, but I always seemed to be rushing and wound up missing spots. At night it was almost meditative, like reading before bed. When I finally got to the bedroom I smelled...coffee. I was marveling at how the aroma had spread throughout the house when the light flickered on and I saw the cup on Linnie's end table.

"Figured we were gonna talk," she said. "You want another cup too?"

"What are you doing awake?"

"Well," she said, "that's a difficult question to answer. For a while I was awake because I was curious about the voices downstairs, then I was awake because I wanted to know what Wilkes wanted, then I was awake because I was too furious to sleep because you made me out to be some fucking invalid. Which I'm not."

"Of course you are. That's why I love you."

"This is not funny."

"The cancer isn't, but this conversation sure is."

"Don't be an asshole, Mac. You made it seem as though I was dying up here, that if you left the house I wouldn't survive your absence. It's a wonder you have time to take a leak anymore with all that pressure. Or go out and get the mail. All sorts of bad shit could happen then."

She was waiting for me to respond, to remind her that she was desperately ill, but we had had this conversation and similar ones before.

"So you heard."

"I heard. I heard you offer to give him a list of some second-rate PIs in Toronto?"

"They're not second-rate."

"Are they as good as you?"

"These days, with everything online...."

"Are they?"

"Probably not."

"Half as good?"

"Maybe."

"So you're providing a list—one that you don't even have—of mediocre investigators who are probably retired or fucking dead. It's a good thing you aren't a paid advisor—or Manitok doesn't live close enough to punch your face in."

"I thought women scratched more than punched."

"You're lucky I'm an invalid. Look, either tell her yes or no, don't send her on a fruitless search for some deceased PI."

"Some of those detectives worked for companies—good companies. And they were young."

"Or maybe they passed the business down to their kids who kept the name and ran it into the ground. You can't do that to her. Why not just take the job? I don't require any special care these days, at least not from you—and Newland said that days like this were an aberration—that when I was tired I should rest, and when I felt good, do whatever I want."

"Newland's a quack. If she were any kind of real doctor, she wouldn't have limited herself to oncology."

"All right," Linnie said, "obviously we're not going to talk about this rationally—for some reason. But if we were, I would guess that more people recommend Dora Newland every day than recommend the Toronto Association of Deceased Investigators. But that's okay. You can pass on this chance at atonement and use me as an excuse. I don't mind."

I was about to say I didn't need atonement, but that would have been foolish. So I added a third person.

"Wilkes says I don't need to atone for anything."

"But what do you say?"

"You don't have to ask."

"Mac, listen, what kind of case is it?"

"A missing person."

She smiled. "From my mouth to God's ears. Take the job. You're not going to undo what happened to Keira Wilkes. And it's true—you don't need to atone for anything. But how many times have you mentioned that case?"

"Thirty-five. I've been a counting."

"Thirty-five a week, maybe."

"And what if I don't find this guy...this Derek Phillips? Then I'll make things worse."

"But you'll be there. You'll have gone the extra yard. Regardless of what happens you won't mope around because you stayed home, didn't go all out. I know you. You're not afraid of failure: you're afraid of not living up to your own standards. I'm not going to enable that. Take the job. And take back what you said about Newland. That was dumb."

I put up a few more mild protests, but Linnie was right. I wanted it. Real or imagined, failures can eat away at you, and chances to erase them seldom drop into one's lap.

*****

After Linnie dozed off I lay awake for a while reconfiguring my plans for the next week, then feeling some regret over my dismissive comment about Dr. Newland "settling" for oncology. Some attempts at humor are just lame. Newland is terrific. For one thing, she has no diplomas hanging on the wall behind her desk or, for that matter, anywhere else in her office. There is no indication that she's even a physician, other than the fact that she occupies an office in a Manhattan medical arts building that's walking distance from several downtown hospitals. I like her willingness not to show off the fact that she went to school, choosing instead to decorate her walls with black-and-white prints of seascapes in thin black frames. Subdued. Understated. Not medical. Kind of classy.

"Sag Harbor," she said on that first day in her office when I noticed them. "My parents had a place and they gave me a camera instead of a boat so I had to settle."

"You took those?" They looked professional.

"With film," she said. "They go back a ways."

"I go back a ways to film too," I said, though my photos of people behaving badly probably lacked the aesthetic appeal of Newland's.

"Photographer?"

"PI."

She smiled. "I better be careful."

Too late. I already knew about Sag Harbor, and I knew about the Shore Road home on Boothbay Harbor up in Maine where the Newlands currently vacation, and I knew about her husband Barry who served as a freelance security advisor for several major financial institutions, and for that matter I knew the couple's children's names too, though how Sheridan and Maddy were faring in school lay somewhere outside my...well, my purview, to use the correct term. I did know their teachers' names though.

I know this all sounds creepy in this NSA-era when everything sounds creepy and secrets on Facebook ripple randomly through Alabama, Andorra, Austria, and every other location in the alphabet; but even though I was retired when Linnie got sick and we first met Newland, I hadn't lost my touch for discovery or my ability to differentiate an investigative probe from everyday questions and answers. There's never a substitute for experience.

No diplomas on Newland's walls that day? No problem. I'd vetted Dr. Dora Newland as well as, maybe better than, most of the targets I'd dogged for embezzlement or insurance fraud or abandonment, and found not even the slightest blemish: she was the right person, even to the point of putting the onus on Linnie to decide what she felt capable of on a given day, in a given hour. Newland was not a quack—it was a dumb thing for me to say, even in jest.

I woke up in the morning feeling as though I owed the doctor an apology, but instead I kept another promise: I called Manitok while Linnie clicked through the travel websites looking for the best flight to Nunavut. There's no such thing—I learned that from Wilkes—but it gave her something to do while I convinced Manitok that I would be there as soon as I could and was looking forward to this assignment. As I said, I don't lie to Linnie, but I'm more flexible when it comes to others.

CHAPTER 9

In the mid-sixties, Amber ranked number 460 on the list of most popular girl's name in the United States, behind Josephine and Kelli with an *i*. Despite that, we have two of them as neighbors, both born in the sixties, women a few years younger than Linnie and I who help out whenever they can. They love Linnie and tolerate me: they might as well be clients.

From the day of Linnie's diagnosis, they declared themselves her caregivers—no small feat since Linnie doesn't like receiving care. She would never allow herself to become some kind of convalescent requiring continuous monitoring, though there are days when she fits that pattern. Amber days, I call them. Neither friend has ever failed us.

It was they who, after we decided I should take the assignment, convinced me not to ship Linnie off to the Glen, the Taj Mahal of convalescent homes, even after I'd called in numerous favors to get her a week there. In truth, I didn't want to do it, but I didn't want to impose on our neighbors. Of course when they caught wind of my plan, they threatened to barricade the street to keep any transporting vehicles away. I'm not sure they wouldn't have done it.

Their willingness to be Linnie's secret caregiver—disguised as recipe experimenters, TV critics, or simply drop-by neighbors, excised some of the guilt from my leaving. A fourth for pinochle would not be a problem either: the Ambers' circle of acquaintances far exceeded ours. And apparently covered all genders—something I learned my first night in Baker when I called Linnie on Mason's landline and was greeted by a deep voice informing me I'd reached the McNally residence.

"The lady of the house," I said, "if she's available."

The man laughed. "You must be Mac. I'm Jack—Amber's insignificant other."

"Which one?"

"Which *other* or which *Amber*?"

"Probably doesn't matter. You must be playing cards," I said.

"Winning too," he said. "Let me get Linnie for you."

I expected to hear a brightness in her voice, if that makes sense, but I didn't. My first notion was to tell her she needed rest more than company; but that would have been a convenient lie: she needed both, so I avoided the subject beyond asking her how she felt. I told her about the flights, mentioned the weather of course, and the darkness. No, no polar bears or reindeer yet, not even that much snow, but the people were friendly and I hoped to get started in earnest the following morning.

She listened—politely I guess you'd say. She knew I didn't want to bring her down with health questions, not when we already knew the answers. The closest we approached that topic was her asking me when I expected to be home.

"I'm settled here, one day up at the company, two at the most," I said. "Fly out the next morning, home by Friday evening. It takes forever to go short distances up here."

She seemed agreeable to that schedule, though of course her having convinced me to take the job left little room for her to complain. I reminded her to watch the Ambers—that their cheating at cards was well known. She reminded me that I was worse and that she'd be fine. That constituted our discussion of health. It was not a reassuring call, but I thanked Mason for the use of the phone, asked him to add the cost to my bill.

"With stocks," Mason said, ignoring me entirely, "you actually own part of the corporation. With bonds you're more or less lending money to that corporation and they keep paying you interest."

"Very good," I said. "I can work out a prospectus for you if we get the time." He smiled: he was even more certain than before that I was lying.

"Think Mason is my first name?" he said.

"I do." He didn't deny it.

"Mac," I said—he knew my full name from the register. "Just call me Mac."

"Mac," he repeated. "Fun jousting with you."

"Have we been jousting?"

"More like parrying I guess. Kind of enjoyable—it can get a little tedious running this place."

"How long have you done that?"

"Twenty years—been in Baker most of my life. Moved up here from Brossard, just across the river from Montreal. I was just a kid."

"Quite a move."

"I went to McGill—got into that great engineering program. Lots of your people going there these days."

"*My* people?"

"Americans. College is cheaper up here. Anyway, got my degree and could have gone into research, kind of wanted to, but I got this job offer, came up here, met Tanya—here we are.

"Meeting a girl changes things."

"No regrets—not in that area. We're still married, Tanny and me, got a couple of grown kids living near Montreal."

"And you stayed here. The hotel recruited you?"

"What? Oh, geez no. Had another better job, but since I got banged up I've been here at this desk."

"That better job...with Autumn Mines?"

"Autumn," he said. "Just Autumn. The *mines* part is understood. If you want to sound authentic...and it appears to me that you do..."

"Your injury. How'd it happen?"

"You don't strike me as an ambulance chaser, Mr. McNally. Supplementing your investment income?"

"Just wondered if they made good. Sometimes large corporations with sharp legal minds get away with stuff."

"I got a fair settlement."

"That's good then. I'd have thought an engineer would be out of the danger areas in a place like that, but I guess accidents can happen."

"They can," he said. "But it all worked out."

"Yeah, you said that. Twice actually."

I smiled because I knew I was getting under his skin a little, but I'd have bet anything he took a screwing from Autumn.

"That must be because it's doubly true."

"Must be. What does...what's your wife's name again?"

"Tanya—Tanny to everybody here."

"Tanny. Hmmh. What does she say about your...whatever...settlement, agreement?"

"She's accepted it."

"Does she work?"

"Teaches part-time at the college here. Literature. Culture. Plus she's writing a novel."

"What kind?"

"I guess it's a mystery—or it is to me. She only lets me read a little now and then. She's pretty good."

"Is she as smart as you?"

"Smarter. Do you want to joust some more or do you want to come clean?"

I shrugged. "I'm a retired PI. No big deal."

"Your secret's safe with me. But I'm not going to be one of your clients."

"I wasn't asking."

"You were vetting. You might not even realize you're doing it anymore. What you think is conversation is a little like a...like a pre-acceptance checklist."

He was right. I had probably honed my investigative skills to the point where simple conversation eluded me. I don't know if that's a bad thing, and I don't think Mason thought that either. The fact that he probably could have used a lawyer when he was injured, not a PI, made the entire conversation less significant.

"It's your job," he said. "No worries. Of course Manitok is a different story. She told me you were coming, and if she told me, well then...I don't think she fully grasped the P part of PI."

"Appears that way."

"Anyway, be careful crossing the street. Things tend to freeze a bit around here."

"Is that what happened to you? Slip on the ice?"

"Something along those lines," he said. He was not going to tell me, at least not yet. I was almost out the door again when he yelled *Lefebvre*. His last name, I assumed.

Over the years I'd met people who were underemployed, well-educated, or just innately intelligent, who'd somehow wound up waiting tables in a diner, or checking in merchandise behind some Home Depot, or operating the carousel at a county fair. There was always a good reason—some little disaster that ambushed and restrained them. What was most surprising was that in most cases, the people weren't bitter about it. They might have been embarrassed or disappointed, but I think when we're working we're somehow satisfied by the very act—the specifics become secondary. Mason Lefebvre was probably like that.

Knowing that, and even sensing a calmness and equanimity in him, I was still curious about what had happened to force him into a sedentary job and what role Autumn had played in it. But, as he said, he wasn't hiring me. And I still hadn't met the people who had actually done so.

CHAPTER 10

Mason's warning that it was "slippery up here" was not an exaggeration. Twice in the fifty yards it took me to get from the hotel to the co-op, I had to catch myself—stop and regain my footing. That balance is not what it once was. To the town's credit, the Baker Lake Department of Public Works (which, Mason joked, was a guy with a bucket of sand) had done a pretty good job of ensuring safe passage on the more treacherous steps and walkways, but it had to be a frustrating battle in a place that never sees a noonday sun or a temperature much above zero.

But I found the co-op easily enough: a 4x8-foot professionally painted sign that read CO-OP made it quite a bit easier. My actual arrival, though, was less than graceful. Though I didn't stumble and fall into the canned goods, I did assume that the door would close behind me...like in a normal place of business. It didn't, so instead of a few welcoming words for the new guy in town, I got a not too gentle reminder from a bearded man in a red vest that doors don't close themselves. I wanted to remind him that they actually do with the advent of a little piece of machinery called a door closer about a hundred years ago, but I wasn't there to make enemies—that process would undoubtedly come later and require even less effort.

"Sorry," I said, then noticed that he had broken away from a larger group gathered near another one of those pod coffeemakers. I guess in the workplace that's become the new water cooler, the focus for gossip and general chatter. I had no gossip, but I moved toward the group anyway, waited for a break in the conversation, then asked if someone named Manitok was around.

"She's here." It was a woman's voice. "She's me. Are you McNally?"

I said I was, but I said it quietly. I'm not used to being introduced to the public at large, having based my entire working career on people not knowing my name and having no clue just what the hell I was doing in their company lounge, hotel lobby, apartment hallway, parking garage, deli across the street, or once in the car behind them on a Ferris wheel. Manitok might just as well have thrown a lanyard around my neck reading *Francis McNally, Private*

Investigator. Don't tell anyone! In fact she did the next best thing, though she did lower her voice a bit when adding, "This is the guy I hired."

I was tempted to restate Mason's observation and ask what part of the term *private investigator* she didn't understand, but as Linnie is wont to say, pretty girls get away with all kinds of shit. (Since she's always been one, I trust her judgment.) And Manitok was a pretty girl. I said before that Linnie and I never had children, but Manitok was about the same age as some of my nieces and every bit as cute: short dark hair—arrow-straight with bangs—and a slightly bronzed, perfectly even complexion, the kind that differentiates young people from...well, me for instance. Childless uncles tend to spoil nieces and nephews, and I was aware that such a tendency could create problems when one of those nieces and nephews actually hires you.

Manitok was not, of course, a New York metropolitan name; but if she was some holdout against modern tradition, her appearance didn't show it: jeans and a red fleece vest over a standard-issue black sweater. Even a little lipstick, I thought, though for all my observational skills, women's make-up eludes me.

I should say that if I owned the red fleece concession in Baker Lake—maybe in all of Nunavut—I wouldn't be worried about the stock market, rogue states, sea level rise, or anything else. To be honest, some vests were more reddish orange and others were more of a burgundy. But good old-fashioned fire-engine red was the *color du jour*...of every *jour* I imagine.

Manitok introduced the other members of the little klatch: Hannah who runs a small art workshop and gallery; Victor, some kind of official in town who has something to do with buying and selling land; and Willis, a fisherman in the summer and expedition guide in the winter—and monitor of doors left unclosed. He gave me his card, white on white with an embossed polar bear on the front and his name on the back—not the polar bear's name: Willis Traynor—Guide.

His skin was lighter than the others', including Manitok's, and with the blue eyes and sandy hair, I figured Traynor for a transplant, maybe like Mason back at the hotel. He didn't say enough for me to pick up an accent, but if he'd said he lived around the corner from me in Westchester, I wouldn't have been surprised.

And there was another young woman. Carol. She looked, well, damaged. You can tell when people have faced some bad shit and not been able to get past it. There's something palpable in the misery or the regret or whatever manifests itself in victims' eyes. And I thought, either she's getting counseling or in need of it. True, none of these people's personal lives was any of my business...yet...but she stood out: if she were in fact one of the contributors to my stipend, I immediately felt I owed her more than I owed the others.

None of them looked at all miffed when Manitok led me away to talk privately, so I told them I was happy to have met them. Linnie says that's *phatic*—a phrase that continues a conversation but doesn't mean anything. Since she told me that, it's really hard for me to tell someone who wishes me a nice day to have one himself. Phatic—like *glad to have met you*—but the weird thing is, in this case at least, I think *they* truly were glad to have met *me*. I didn't know what they expected, but I had a pretty good idea that Manitok had bolstered my reputation by twice, if not more.

"Those are friends?" I asked. "Yes."

"Close friends?"

She looked quizzical.

"Close enough," she said. "Why?"

"Tell me about Carol."

"But isn't that your job? To investigate people?"

"I'm here to find your missing citizen and I plan to do that. Carol—she's one of Derek's, right?"

"Derek's what?"

"This is going to go better if you don't question my questions."

"I don't care if it goes better," she said. "But I just want it to go somewhere. Asking personal questions about friends of mine—friends who have nothing to do with anything—doesn't move us along."

This was one pseudo-niece I was not in danger of spoiling.

"Understood," I said. "Carol is off-limits. So let me withdraw my impertinent question and make an observation: there's something between her and Phillips and it's something that could maybe help me. Now if I were a cop, I could maybe go through the legal system and find a way to pry some information out of her. And if I were working back home and wasn't restricted by time, I could set up surveillance and guzzle coffee for a few days while I found what I needed to know. Sorry to sound mercenary, but you didn't gather enough money to allow for that and I don't have enough warm clothes or a car—which I don't plan to rent. So moving us along—as you put it—isn't helped by impeding the investigation."

"Are you finished?"

"No. But if you're okay with a slower and gentler pace where I ask polite questions for a day or two and then go home, so am I."

I wasn't trying to browbeat or intimidate her. Just as well—her expression never changed.

"So," she said. "I guess you're used to getting your own way, aren't you?"

"I'm accustomed to doors closing behind me, but beyond that, I'm really pretty flexible. Now which one of those people is his wife and why isn't she joining you and me?"

"You didn't answer my question."

"Actually I did. This little territorial dance where we stake out our area and defend it—I've done it before and so have you apparently. I never saw much good come from it, but tell me if I'm wrong and I'll dance some more. Otherwise...the wife? Which one?"

"She's not here."

"I didn't think so."

"These days she has enough problems trying to get by."

"But wouldn't a lot of those problems be solved if someone found her husband? We do want to find him, don't we? Everyone seems a little ill at ease."

"I wasn't ill at ease on the phone until you asked me if I was sleeping with the man I wanted you to find."

Oh yeah, that. I explained to Manitok that it was a logical question, one which even though it may have seemed more titillating than investigative, was designed to test the waters. I confessed that Wilkes never cared much for that approach either, but it's never meant to be insensitive, just inquisitive, and a touch disorienting. When she ignored my explanation, I knew I hadn't convinced her. The process of making enemies—a process I had honed during my career—seemed even easier in Baker Lake.

"Carol is Derek's sister-in-law," she said.

"That's not a deal breaker as far as sleeping arrangements. I've been around long enough to know...."

"She's his wife's sister," she said, her voice many decibels higher than when we'd started. "They wouldn't do that to each other."

Hannah, the artiste, must have heard the change in tone and yelled over to ask if everything was all right.

"Getting' there," I yelled back, then lowered my voice for a more reassuring "just getting to know each other." I didn't want a third party arbiter. Hannah, to her credit, didn't come storming over. It wouldn't have helped, though it might have prompted me to book a flight home sooner than I'd planned.

"Your friends," I said. "They're protective."

"We watch out for each other."

"Who was watching out for Derek Phillips? Wasn't he part of your group?"

"He hung around on occasion."

"Every day?"

"He worked at Autumn so he couldn't have been...."

"Every day when he wasn't working? Did you see him every day he was...well I was going to say home, but maybe this was his home."

"He has a home. I told you, a wife and three kids."

"Actually Wilkes told me that. You haven't told me much of anything."

"Well, I don't think he was fucking anybody else and I know he wasn't fucking me."

"Never? Or lately?"

"Never."

She was tough, unflappable, immovable—choose your favorite adjective. Let me add that she was also lying. Once I realized that, I could, as Manitok said, move us along.

"As merchant and customer then, did you see him a lot?"

She glared at me. I guess if you're not used to disdain and revulsion, this would be a traumatic moment, but I've seen worse expressions over the years, more hateful and angrier, sometimes from people who could mop the floor with me. I will admit that the proliferation of guns has made situations like this a bit more tenuous, but I usually have a good sense of whether someone is a murderer, and exiting the United States always lessens the possibility that someone is armed. Manitok was not, but the secretiveness annoyed me. Then that attempt to shock me with a few f-bombs struck me as silly and childish. I would have said that to her, but I didn't want to be the one to speak next, so I let her stew while I took out my phone and checked the time.

"I saw him most days," she muttered, finally. "Toward the end we talked a lot."

"Toward the end of what?"

"Will you let me finish?"

"I heard your voice drop—you were finished. Toward the end of what?"

"Before he disappeared. He was...he was having some difficulties."

"Marital?"

"It wasn't that simple. He felt he could talk to me."

"Look, I don't want to piss you off any further, I really don't. But you seem too smart not to realize that if he's telling you problems he's not sharing with his wife, then...go ahead, fill in the blanks."

"It doesn't have anything to do with this."

"Okay," I said, and let out an extended exhale that comprised a whole gamut of emotions. She picked up on at least one.

"You're angry."

"Yes I am. Let me explain why. I'm a licensed professional in the State of New York. I follow a code of ethics, part of which says that my clients tell me when there is confidential information that I can divulge. I can't pry secrets out of you, then walk down the street telling them to strangers, not even to a cop...unless—and this is a big unless—I have to in order to prevent serious or imminent harm to others. Serious or imminent harm."

She started to say something, but I stopped her.

"Let me finish. We have a missing person in a hostile environment. To me that hints at serious and imminent harm. So yes if you confide in me, but by requiring my silence you endanger someone else—including yourself or me—then my silence is off the table. Are we clear?"

She more or less spat out her agreement.

"Good. I'm not trying to uncover any dark secrets. If there's a drawerful of titillating pictures, sell them to the *Enquirer*, but if there was something in his conversations that you didn't pick up on, maybe I might."

"I don't think he said these things to his wife, to Nikki. But she and I come from different places."

"I don't think you mean geography, right?"

"I don't," she said, told me to wait a minute, then without my asking rousted her acquaintances from the co-op—I'm not sure what she said to them, but they seemed okay with leaving.

"If you kill me," I said, "those others will still be witnesses."

That almost drew a smile. Almost.

"Let's get something to eat," she said, then provided me with a couple of dining choices, most of which I'd read about, and one, the Sixty-Seven, that I hadn't. I was in fact pretty hungry. Before I could ask her who was going to run the co-op while she was gone, she hung a sign on the door—*Back in 30 min*.

"We can talk there," she said. "You really need more information and I don't feel like standing here for an hour, filling you in.

"The sign says thirty minutes."

"Then thirty will do."

It's always a good admission for clients to make—the awareness that they've been holding back, that I know it, and that I can't do anything until they stop. That's when I usually hear *let me be honest you with Mr. McNally* and that's when I get the first ten percent of the story. Then later, half of the rest of it, and so on. Do the math—all those halves—in the end there's always that little fraction....

CHAPTER 11

The Sixty-Seven reminded me of the kinds of luncheonettes we used to have in the United States, and one in particular: Jim's or Bob's or Bill's—a common name—and people would drop in for a quick sandwich and a Coke, then be on their way. My father took me there for ice cream a few times; it wasn't so much a planned trip as it was convenient, occupying the corner right across the street from an Esso station where an actual attendant pumped gas.

Establishments like that comprise a niche now satisfied, maybe even satiated, by the pervasive fast-food industry and the even-more pervasive automobile. But entering the somewhat noisy Sixty-Seven, finding a square wood table (with no tablecloth) and some straight-back cushionless chairs, reminded me of that place to which, as a child, I had always planned to go alone someday. It closed before I ever got my driver's license.

I shared my little reminiscence with Manitok who added that we could also get ice cream at the Sixty-Seven, adding "and it doesn't even melt on the way home."

Polar humor, but the change in venue had apparently helped us exude some civility, maybe reduce the sniping. The waitress greeted Manitok by name, then looked askance at me until Manitok apparently gave some silent signal that I was okay. Only then did I get a menu.

"I'm here a lot," she said.

"Apparently with a lot of creepy men," I said. "I don't think the waitress thought I was anything other than a serial rapist."

"Sharon is online too much, can't separate the bullshit from the news, but she's all right."

"She's probably on the phone with the Mounties right now," I said. "Tell me, what kind of name is Manitok?"

"If you spell it with double-i in the middle, it means rugged. With a single i, just an Inuit name."

"But not your real name."

"Jacqueline Nadeau. My brother calls me Jackie to piss me off, but most people get by with Manitok."

"Rugged."

"Not really. Not a hunter. Don't fish or hike. Not much of an outdoors type. The waitress that gave you the evil eye? Just so you know, people have become protective."

"Of you?"

"Of me, of themselves, of the community. Protective and suspicious. Autumn made us that way."

"Did they make you pains in the ass, like you were back in the store?"

"I was following your lead, Mac."

She smiled slightly—it may have been more of a smirk—but things were a little less icy. Indoors.

"How did Autumn turn you into a...a hesitant responder?"

She removed her toque, at which point I realized I was still wearing mine and tossed it on the bench.

"It's a strained relationship we have with the company," she said. "Without them we have less and revert to fifty years ago, trying to scrape by on seasonal tourism; with them we have to keep our guard up so that they don't screw us over."

"How would they do that? Fire people? Bring in workers from the outside?"

"No, although they could. It's more than that."

"Like?"

"I'll give you an example. Three years ago just before Christmas, they called a meeting for the entire hamlet and had it in our town hall auditorium. Food and drink, music, decorations. It was more of a party and we were invited to celebrate the new Baker Lake, the one where another two-hundred jobs would be added and the town would grow dramatically and there'd be a new school and all kinds of other improvements."

"In return for your soul. This is not exactly a new story."

"Maybe less soul than spirit. We had to allow them to build a new mine less than ten miles out of town, and less than ten miles from the lake, our lake."

"That you named the town after. And that was a problem?"

She nodded, then held up while the waitress brought us some water and asked if we were ready to order. I hadn't even looked at the menu. I told Manitok to pick something that didn't contain blubber or bear meat. She shook her head in mock disgust, made sure I wasn't a vegetarian, then ordered two BLTs and two draft beers. When I asked what kind of drafts they had, she lsughed. I took that to mean choices were not available.

"The new mine was a problem," she said, picking up the thread. "We'd learned to turn a blind eye to environmental hazards seventy miles away. It wasn't right, but we'd learned. But a few miles upstream? That was different."

"So the town said no."

"Some did, some didn't. Finally it came to a vote with reps from Autumn buying up ad space in our weekly and even online, then hosting little get-togethers to plead their case; and jerks like me going door to door telling people to vote no. It was tense. Every little gathering was people conspiring for or against."

"But you won."

"And made some enemies, people who won't shop at my place. But a polluting mine that close to the lake, practically on top of streams that feed in—it would have been a disaster."

"Environmentally or spiritually? You mentioned spirit before. Not soul, spirit."

"We have areas that we treat with...with special respect, reverence. Sites of old villages where ancestors lived, paths they took, even migration trails that animals used...still use. We don't build shrines and make pilgrimages, but we know they're there and we don't want them defiled. The hostility to me has faded, but for the people living in poverty, they see me as the villain. I kept them from getting ahead."

"Are you worried, I mean about your safety?"

"For a while I was. Someone smashed a window on the door of the co-op and I heard some name-calling, but it's basically calmed down. As the culprit who doomed Baker Lake to stagnation, I make a pretty good symbol, like the little inukshuk in the store window..."

"The what?"

"It's a human-shaped figure made from piling stones on one another. Ancients used them to direct animals on migration routes. The caribou would see the shape in the distance, assume it was a human, and go a different way."

"Where the real humans were waiting to slaughter them."

"It wasn't for sport, Mr. McNally."

"I was just making a joke. And call me Mac, or anything but Mr. McNally."

I glanced around to see if anyone was evil-eying us (or more particularly Manitok) but we seemed to be completely unnoticed.

"So your reign as town pariah is over? I mean here we are being waited on courteously by someone who knows you well enough. Should I worry about the bacon being poisoned?"

"Eat too much bacon and you won't have to worry."

"I believe it was you who ordered the BLTs. And you implied it was not short for blubber."

"You'll be fine—no poison, just a nice dose of nitrates. And no one eats blubber. Have you read anything since *Nanook of the North*? These days local places will even deliver if I ask. Some days I just can't get out of the store."

"Come on," I said. "You can't ever be that busy."

"Saturdays after paychecks and the boys are home from Autumn, then Monday when they head back and the wives have to stock up for the week. There are times."

"Nikki Phillips one of those wives?"

"They called themselves the Autumn Widows."

"That's pretty grim. Or maybe even clairvoyant. Why do they do that?"

"They're alone all week, have to make do with the kids and the house, all that. It was kind of like a support group."

"Was?"

"They don't meet anymore. It's a little too real. It's been tough for Nikki: three kids, no help."

"I keep hearing that and I believe you. But if my wife were missing, I'd be grasping at every straw in hopes someone would find her. I'm kind of that last straw, right? And yet, she wasn't at the co-op and when I got there, and nobody even called her to let her know help had arrived."

"Maybe your relationship is different from Nikki's, but I'm not sleeping with her husband."

"You already said that. Is anyone else?"

"You're the PI."

"See? Again, that's not helpful. You're like the guy who turns up at the doctor's office, isn't feeling quite right, but says nothing to the doctor in hopes that, being the professional that he is, he'll be able to discern the illness by having the nurse weigh him. Sometimes even the professionals would like a clue, maybe a list of Derek Phillips's lovers. Is there a list?"

She shook her head.

Of course Manitok was right about the differences between Phillips's marriage and mine. I could have explained all of that to Manitok—maybe even filled her in on why I was hesitant to take this job—but an extensive discussion of Linnie's illness would have further muddied the waters, and I needed to get to the bottom of this "different relationship." I was becoming more certain that Manitok, if she was holding back, wasn't holding back much—that maybe she knew about as much as Phillips's wife did.

When the sandwiches and beer arrived, I took a break from my so-far ineffectual questioning. I hadn't realized how hungry I was until I tried remembering the last time I ate—a breakfast sandwich that had been constructed several breakfasts before in a little café in Churchill. And the beer was good, though a little too bitter for me. Manitok said that Baker Lake now possessed a brewery and that this was some of the product from the latest batch.

"A brewery. You're not living in the dark ages after all. Of course in America we have one in every abandoned factory building, but you'll catch up. What did you and Derek talk about in the co-op?"

"Nice segue, Mac."

"Gotta work on those. Did you talk about his marriage?"

"That you should really hear from Nikki."

"And I'd like to, but she's not here."

"I'll tell you what I do know. Basically Derek thought he was losing his grip."

"On his wife? Was she the one with somebody else?"

"Of course not."

"Losing his grip? Are we still talking about his sex life?"

I actually got a laugh out of her, one which unfortunately sprayed a small mouthful of that bitter ale on the table. I signaled for the waitress and she brought some more napkins.

"You're gross," Manitok said.

"I'm not the one who spit up. And anyway, it was funny."

That much she didn't deny as we dutifully restored the table to its former condition.

"Losing his grip," I said. "How? The cold? The dark?"

"He was experiencing odd sensations, and don't say that again."

"You mean don't ask if we're still talking about his sex life, right?"

"You can't help yourself, can you?"

"Okay," I said. "No jokes. What kind of odd sensations?"

"For one, he was feeling time stagnate."

"You mean stand still?"

"He said stagnate. He couldn't explain it. But I know he told Nikki. The problem with her is she isn't good at accepting things like that."

"Accepting isn't an option when you're married. If it were...."

And then despite my misgivings, I was sitting there talking about Linnie's cancer, the prognosis, the regimen, her desire for me to finish this job.

"Maybe you should go home after all."

"Can't do that: I told you, when Linnie says go, I go."

She didn't believe me, so I wasted the next ten minutes of our allotted thirty rehashing Wilkes's attempt to save his wife in 2009, my guilt over having failed to help him, Linnie's awareness of my regrets, and most of all her basic independence and strength. I was hoping Manitok would buy at least half of it—that would be enough—though it was all true. She listened. She looked wary. In the end she agreed that maybe my assessment of my wife's feelings had been correct, but she also thought I should have contradicted her.

When she continued to hammer away at my shirking responsibilities, I finally stopped her.

"I'm here now. Can we finish one thing at a time?"

"Yes."

"Derek was losing time? Gaining time? Stagnating time?"

"All of the above," she said. There was still reluctance. "He couldn't explain, but it was as if time didn't exist."

"That's a pretty hard concept to grasp. Give me an example."

"Examples don't make sense, but, well for instance, in work he might be given a job that should take maybe an hour. In ten minutes he'd be done."

"And the job was done right?"

"And he could remember having completed every step."

"How often did this happen?"

"A lot, but not consistently. Days might go by when everything seemed normal; then it would happen again, out of nowhere. It was maddening."

"*Maddening* as in he finally couldn't take it anymore and killed himself, or maddening in the fact that he confided in his wife and she thought he was nuts, so he started up with someone else?"

"Keep harping on to that and you'll be the one wasting time."

"I'll never ask again."

And I wouldn't, but not out of politeness. I already knew the answer. Manitok had more than a humanitarian interest, but it was more than a sexual one too, so I figured it was time to talk to the person with whom he was actually supposed to be having the sexual one.

"Where do I find his wife, what's her name?"

I knew her name, but I wanted to hear how the word came out of Manitok—the tone, the inflection. I wondered if she would sneer at it, or maybe spit it out like a bad pistachio nut. She did neither—which told me less than I wanted to know. But everything tells you something.

"It's a little late for a visit," she said, "what with the kids and all. Let me call her—maybe she'll see you."

"Does she know about you?"

"You said you'd never ask again."

"It's a problem I have. I'm working on it. Does she know?"

"She knows I own a co-op."

I waited.

"Okay, Mr. McNally, I think she has her suspicions about her husband. But not about me."

"My job doesn't involve lectures or penance. Or embarrassment. But if some relationship between you and Derek is responsible...."

"It isn't," she said. She tapped a few numbers on her phone.

"Nikki," she said. "Manitok. There's an investigator here who has some questions about Derek. Would you be willing to talk to him?"

She looked at me, shrugged. Either Nikki had said no or was formulating a response.

—"No, he's from the States."

—"A couple of days I guess."

—"He tries to be."

—"Fifteen. I'll tell him. You all right?"

Whatever the response was ended the conversation.

"Fifteen minutes," she said. "It's a five-minute walk."

"What do I try to be?"

"What?"

"On the phone just now. You said 'he tries to be.' Tries to be what?"

"Pleasant," she said.

"And my success rate?"

"Finish your beer before it goes flat."

CHAPTER 12

Nikki Phillips's eyes showed the strain of what her life had evolved into—a continuing cycle of single-mother responsibilities and demands that had sapped her of both optimism and hope. Despair is a gradual acquisition—one that takes hold only when we're sure beyond doubt that a situation can never improve—that what we face on our most miserable day is as good as it's ever going to get, but still not as bad. Two weeks isn't really enough time to fall into a chasm that deep, but it often serves as an indicator; and that in itself is cause for people to keep asking what's wrong or commenting that we look tired. Encouragement and support generally make us feel worse.

I've seen it in my family and seen it in my job, even felt that, with Linnie's diagnosis, it could easily afflict us. I'd like to say we don't let that happen, but it's more she than we. In addition, we're together in our little bubble: Nikki Phillips is alone. Now I know that if her husband's philandering is common knowledge, it would not be unusual for her to seek comfort somewhere else, but I just had the feeling that wasn't happening when I finally arrived at her front door.

Our introduction was what I would have to call uneasy—a situation I could have expected. She may have been put out by a late visitor, but I was there on her behalf, trying to find her husband. I didn't expect a ticker-tape parade or a home festooned with streamers, but I thought she might see me as a way out. She didn't.

Even now, though, I can't be critical. As I said, her face showed that strain, but it also showed a gash under her left eye—something I automatically would have blamed on a husband if there had been one present. Maybe she had found someone, a partner who brought a violent streak with him. Before I could even register the thought, she rebuffed it.

"My daughter," she said. "Regina sometimes acts out."

"Oh."

"You sound disappointed. You thought it was Derek?"

"I thought it was...an adult."

She knew what I meant, but shook her head.

"Nope, just my little shit of a daughter."

"And she likes to play with a kitchen knife?"

"With whatever is handy. This time it was a paintbrush. We were arguing—Derek is better with her than I am, but with him gone, she makes it hard."

We sat on either side of a roughened wood coffee table in a tastefully decorated but dim and predictably gloomy living room. Nikki Phillips didn't possess the youthful beauty of Manitok, though I had the feeling there wasn't much difference in their ages. Manitok, of course, was not regularly assailed by a child with a pointy weapon: sometimes that makes a difference. Still, not only am I not a very good judge of those matters, but my eyes, half-frozen shut and tearing profusely from the cold when I arrived, did not allow for much clarity. Even five minutes later, and even after she had brought me a dampened facecloth, the room still looked just a bit blurry.

"You come from a warmer climate, Mr. McNally," she said.

"It would be difficult not to."

She nodded. "We're not even above the Arctic Circle," she said. "It's the everlasting shame of Baker Lake—living in the cold and dark and we can't even call it the Arctic."

I told her to feel free to stretch the truth. Her gallows humor in the face of adversity and uncertainty told me she would navigate this tunnel and come out the other end. It was as if testiness had morphed into something else, a kind of acceptance that she had a right to be testy but wouldn't be. In some ways Nikki Phillips reminded me of Linnie—that kind of "things are tough all over" attitude, and I instantly liked her. And because of that, my opinion of the man who had deserted her diminished even further. We can't always trust first impressions, but we make them anyway and I usually stand by mine. I wiped more moisture from my eyes with the cool cloth until I was able to focus again.

"Let me get rid of this," I said. She pointed to a hallway.

"First door on the left—just leave it in the sink."

When I came back she had turned on another light—a saucer shaped overhead with what looked to be vents radiating out from the center. It was one of those fixtures that people tended to ignore because it was too hard to dust and leaving it dark hid the fact.

"Better?" she said. "Your eyes?"

"They are. Where I come from the weather is a little more moderate."

"It would be difficult not to be." She winked, mimicking my answer. "From the states, huh?"

"New York City. Actually just outside it."

"Not even from Canada? You've come a long way," she said. "Manitok sent for you?"

"She...apparently a lot of people are worried...."

"Don't worry about hurting my feelings, Mr. McNally. I know the score, as you Americans like to say. Manitok looks so young that sometimes I want to cut her some slack—admit she doesn't know any better—but she does."

"I'm not sure what you mean."

"Soul mates. It's one of those expressions you can think, but you don't say out loud. You married?"

"Yes."

"Your wife, is she your soul mate?"

"She's my wife."

"Well," Nikki said with a dramatic sweep of her arm, "that's never going to work out. You didn't marry your soul mate? Why even go on?"

The bitterness in her humor was oddly refreshing—I like people who question bullshit—but I didn't want her to get ahead of herself.

"Can we back up for a minute?" I said.

"We can, but then I wouldn't think you were much of an investigator. It's pretty obvious that she and my husband have something going on. Derek claims he never had sex with her, but there's more to a relationship than sex."

"Soul mates."

"Yes," she said, clasping her hands in mock prayer and looking skyward. "Now Manitok is pretty straight and probably keeps married men out of her bedroom. But there have been others for Derek—some up at Autumn, some here in town. Plenty of blame to go around."

"Is that why you're not interested in getting him back?"

"What? Why would you say that?"

"You're not part of the fund-raising group at the co-op."

"Yes, Mr. McNally, I'm going to chip in a few bucks to get my husband back so that everyone in town can say I value my husband at ten bucks, or a hundred, or a thousand. Whatever figure you plug in makes me sound like a bidder at an auction."

"So you do want him back?"

"He's my husband and he's the father of three children—I hope not more than three. No, forget I said that—he's always been very honest about his dishonesty."

"That's not really an answer."

"Yes, I want him back."

"With the infidelity and all, do you stay married just for the kids?"

"No. And it's *maybe* on the infidelity."

"Then why?"

"He makes me laugh—or used to anyway—and he is good with the kids, especially our oldest. As long as he doesn't expect anything from me, I can live with him."

"Expect anything like what?"

"The physical part of our arrangement is over—he knows it and I know it. He's even free to pursue such things elsewhere, of course, but that's up to him. I hope he doesn't get someone pregnant or contract some disease, but again, that's his responsibility. I mean I can't expect a man that young to stay married to a woman who won't put out. Am I right?"

"I've never entertained that question before."

"Squeamish about sex? I said *put out*. I could have been more graphic."

"Either way I get the point. As far as your being right, I would think if both partners agree on no sex, then there's no problem."

"It was unilateral. Eventually he'll leave me—if he hasn't already. In the meantime there are plenty of willing ladies around."

"And men?"

"He's not gay and I don't cheat. Willing men don't matter. Guys like Derek, they aren't looking for a better woman: they're looking for a better self. Ten years ago he was young and probably in love with me. There were no kids. No responsibilities. He liked that Derek."

"Did you?"

"Of course. What's not to like? But he's not that guy anymore, at least not to him."

"And to you?"

"He's different, of course, but I was willing to change along with him. I figured we'd accept each other's changes because that was our agreement. Turns out he was okay with me, but not with himself. That's why I don't mope around wondering what I did wrong. I didn't do anything wrong."

"Unilateral?"

She laughed. "Just catching up? Did I shock you?"

"Were you trying to?"

"Not at all. And I don't go handing out information like this either, but if you're willing to look for Derek, then I'm willing to let you know what the situation is."

I was grateful for Nikki's openness, but one of the results was that Manitok became a less likely culprit. That's a good thing—it makes the job more satisfying when you don't feel disdain for the person who hired you.

I asked Nikki if the kids were sleeping: the house was silent other than our somewhat subdued conversation. She said one of them was, but that the other two always needed some convincing and would almost certainly show up in the next ten minutes. She left, presumably to hunt down those kids, but instead returned with a decanter on a tray. She left again—need some glasses, she said—but returned this time trailed by a decidedly unsleepy looking girl in blue flannel geometrically patterned pajamas. She was seven or eight, no more, and as close-cropped as her hair was, it was still a mess until she crawled onto her mother's lap and Nikki straightened it. She never took her eyes off me; her mother said nothing to either of us.

"I'm Mac," I said, to break the silence. It didn't work. I looked at Nikki and silently asked her to say something.

"This is my daughter Regina, my high-maintenance child. Every house should have one."

The little girl continued to stare at me, occasionally rubbing her eye or poking a finger into a nostril. Both received equal probing.

"High maintenance?"

"First one up, last to bed. Eats whenever she decides to, bullies the other two who, I'm pretty sure, sleep late to get some peace. Regina, say hello to Mac."

She didn't, but her mother's command at least got her to stop staring. She slid to the floor and walked into another room where I heard dishes clattering.

"She's angry," Nikki said. "She heard a man's voice, thought it was her father. She'll stomp around out there for a while, but she knows enough not to break anything."

"Until she stabs you again. Do you want to go and, you know, keep an eye on her?"

"She doesn't respond well to surveillance. Leave her be. Would you like some brandy?"

She lifted a bottle from a small glass tray and turned over two snifters.

"It's nice to have a dram or two before turning in," she said.

Yes, a dram, I thought, whatever the hell that was. Some Canadian measurement I didn't understand. I took the smaller glass and sipped at it—it was awful. To me brandy has always belonged in eggnog or in the bottle, but I tried not to wince. Nikki seemed to enjoy it though, so I just kept my opinion to myself—I'm capable of doing so. No, really, I am.

Regina sauntered back in before I was halfway through that dram and demanded to be put to bed for what I assume was the second time.

"Already did that," Nikki said. "Now you'll have to wait."

"Now," Regina demanded. She was a young lady of few words—all challenge and indictment. Her mother, more practiced in the art of combat, shook her head but said nothing.

Regina eyed the decanter, which suddenly looked more fragile than ever. I waited. Instead of a shattering attack, the child sidled over to the TV remote and hit a button. Nothing.

"Sorry, sweetie, TV's off for the night," Nikki said, her apology blatantly insincere. Then we both watched with perverse pleasure as Regina tried every button on the remote, none of which caused anything other than the little girl's fingers to move more spasmodically. Even then, she seemed to have a good handle on what constituted an acceptable response to frustration, for when she slammed down the remote—she chose the couch where it landed noiselessly and undamaged. Then she was back to the kitchen.

"High maintenance," her mother repeated.

"She knows her limits...and yours."

"Let her stew for a moment," she said, then finished her brandy in a gulp and poured another.

"Hope I remember to put the batteries back in the remote tomorrow. You know, I found her here one night about 3:00 a.m. watching some home decorating show. So now I disable the remote, at least when I remember. And she hasn't figured out yet that there's an on/off button on the TV."

"Neither did I," I said. That drew out a cautious smile.

"Now, what can I tell you about Derek," she said, "or has Manitok told you enough?"

"Nobody ever tells me enough," I said. I kept watching the kitchen door, expecting Regina's re-entry with an appropriate selection from the knife block.

"Ask away," she said, "before Regina enters for act two."

CHAPTER 13

Martin Wilkes would have been disappointed: I didn't begin by asking for a list of Derek Phillips's former girlfriends. Instead I kept it traditional—had he given any indication of his leaving? Had he been depressed, manic, nervous, distracted? Had he begun talking about final arrangements: burial, cremation, a living will? Had he exhibited any radical changes or unexplained mood swings? Nikki reminded me that she saw him but two days out of seven and, since there was no longer a sexual component to their lives, they didn't talk as much as they had before. Then she said there was that *one thing*—and proceeded to tell me the same bizarre story about her husband having some ability to work outside the realm of time. I listened as if I hadn't heard it from Manitok, but the narrations were remarkably similar. She didn't realize she was confirming a story more than telling one, and even though Derek Phillips could have been lying to both women, the whole time-out-of-time thing began to take on a semblance of credibility.

"Obviously I'm not from here," I said, "but is this one of those extreme weather phenomena?"

"What do you mean?"

"I mean in the desert there are mirages. They're visual. Does the extreme cold mess with the other senses in the same way?"

"You mean freezing time? I like the concept," she said. "We should call it a freeze frame?"

The drams were working.

"We could."

"Bad joke. Unfortunately you're about two-thousand miles from home, not light years beyond the sun. So no, time up here is a lot like time on your planet."

"Things slow down in the cold," I said. "Machinery, nature. I suppose it's possible."

"I don't know exactly what's possible," she said, "but I've never heard of it. Maybe Manitok has a better idea of things like this. She's a little more aware of all that myth, the spiritual side of things. I mean she accepts it, promotes it."

"Lives it?"

"You'll have to ask her. She'd probably say there's a better chance some local mythological creature is fucking with him than the cold scrambling his brain. Or maybe the lack of regular sex makes the days longer. It hasn't affected me, though. *My* days just fly by."

The sarcasm was hard to miss, but I asked anyway. "You believe that?"

"About the sex?"

"About the gods."

"I try. Whenever Derek talked about the Inuit and their history, I paid attention and tried to be receptive. I thought, if that's what drew him to Manitok, well I could be pretty damn spiritual too. But it wasn't just her. Besides, in the end it's still the twenty-first century. I think the days have passed when gods and spirits exercise control over our lives."

"Do you believe in God?"

"Are you planning to baptize me?"

"I don't think this brandy is an acceptable substitute for holy water."

"Oh believe me, it's the holiest of holy waters. More?"

"Not just yet. All I meant was...."

She didn't let me finish. "I believe that there might be a God, or two, and that maybe they even created the world. But then they just said *adieu, mes amis, it's yours to fuck up*...or something like that."

"Not a statement I'd associate with God. Maybe the local gods swear more."

"Local gods. Kind of a contradiction, isn't it? Something all-powerful restricted to a little community?"

I went along with her because I knew she knew the alternative. If these things were happening only in her husband's mind, then that kind of imbalance could have led to his disappearance, some ill-formed decision to just walk away. And if that were the case, his chances of his being alive just fell to zero. Before I could point that out, Regina rumbled back into the room and plopped down on the couch next to me.

"What's your name?" she said.

Reminding her I'd already told her would have accomplished little, but before I could respond, Nikki stopped me.

"That's all hon—you've used up all your points. Go to bed."

"I want to know his name."

Nikki looked at me and shrugged. "Whatever. If he wants to tell you."

I nodded. "It's Regina," I said. "Just like yours."

"That's a girl's name," she said, "and you're not a girl."

She may have thought my response was silly, but she never even approached a smile. I hate to think ill of children, but I did scan the room for sharp objects with which she might poke out an eye. For a second or two she remained motionless, then slid onto the floor.

"It's Mac," I said.

"Mac and cheese," she said immediately, then repeated it a few times. The wooden expression never cracked. She left without saying anything else.

"She used up her points?" I asked. "Like with a credit card?"

"Like with a parole board. She puts her toys away, she gets points. Washes her hands, points. Act like a little shit, lose a few. I keep a tally in my head and when she uses them up, she has to start over."

"How many did she lose tonight?"

She shrugged. She didn't really keep count—didn't have to. She'd found a useful maneuver to keep her daughter in line and didn't want to foul it up with details like some idiotic chart. I remember thinking if Derek Phillips was irretrievably gone, at least his kids had a chance with a woman like Nikki who, no matter how disjointed her life had become, relinquished none of what was important. Even the brandy seemed a justifiable crutch—I could not imagine her drunk all day and ignoring her kids. The occasional boozy escape wasn't going to do anyone any harm.

When I told her I had plans to visit Autumn, she handed me a wallet-size picture of her husband—old habit I guess—I mean who else was going to be wandering about alone in that barren landscape? I told her I'd do what I could, that the next morning at Autumn should give me a better handle on things. I didn't see any confidence or reassurance in her eyes, but in truth I didn't hear any in my voice either.

"You'll meet Hal Whitton," she said. "That's Derek's boss. They got along pretty well until Derek started to...whatever. I don't think Whitton is popular with the workers. A lot of men consider him a little bit...well, we used to say effeminate."

"Is he gay? Did he ever come on to your husband?"

"I don't think Derek swings that way. I'm not sure if Whitton does either. Maybe in that environment the guy just isn't manly enough."

"Then why do I need to know that about Whitton?"

"There are a few women who work there," she said, "some even on the factory floor. But it's a rough-and-tumble environment where everyone is supposed to obey the same set of rules—men with women, women with men. Same-sex relationships don't fly at the mines. Neither do men who don't swing their dicks to prove their manhood."

"You're speaking metaphorically, I hope."

"Yes," she said with a smile. "They won't make you swing yours while you're there. Just wanted you to know the ambience."

"I guess if Whitton were missing that would explain it—some rough-and-tumble men didn't want the gay guy around. But Whitton isn't the one who's missing. Who were some of Derek's friends?"

"At Autumn? Not many. A few acquaintances. Guy named Jeremiah Queen. Yes, don't say it, a Queen in a rough and tumble manscape. Anyway, that was one. Maybe a few others."

I wrote down Queen's name, and Whitton's. I asked her if she'd ever met either one. She hadn't.

"Whitton seldom leaves the site, and Queen—he's kind of a weird guy—not only never leaves the plant, but Derek used to say he never left his room, but I don't know about that. I don't think he was much of a company man though. I mean company with a lower-case c."

"Unlike Whitton."

"That's what Derek said."

"Why don't you come with us, Mrs. Phillips. You seem to have a good handle on the place."

"With you and Manitok? Hah! First off, I wouldn't set foot in that plane."

"Just me. No plane."

"Don't tell me you're going by snowmobile."

"I am."

"Charter a plane. At least you won't die slowly."

"I don't plan to die at all."

"Few people plan it. But going solo increases the odds. Take somebody."

"But not you."

"I can't."

As if by way of explanation, Regina returned for her curtain call.

"Are you going to find my father?" she said, staring directly at me. She was brandishing a teaspoon that she'd just licked clean of something: Nikki held out a hand and disarmed her.

"Do you want me to?" I said.

"Yep."

"Why?"

"He's supposed to live here."

"Uh huh, would you be sad if he lived somewhere else?"

"Sad?"

"Would you cry?"

"No."

"But you want me to find him?"

She nodded.

"Okay then, I'll find him. You smell like peanut butter."

"I know."

I was tempted to feed her some cliché like "you take care your mother now" or "you'll have to be a big girl until Daddy returns" but I thought she would see through it quite easily. *I'll find him* must have been satisfactory.

"Nice job on the spoon," I said after Regina had again left us. "Probably couldn't find a paintbrush, huh?"

"Keep them in a high cabinet now. Hey, how about taking Regina with you? I'll help you strap her in."

"Only you can handle her. One more question before I leave—gotta get up early and hit the road. Not much daylight, right? And even when there is...."

"The question?"

"Oh, yeah, what are you not telling me?"

"That's it? That's the question?"

"Yes."

"I don't understand," she said, but her eyes shifted a millimeter—less, a scintilla of a millimeter—enough for me to know that she had told me the truth without enhancement, even though there was some. There always is, either by omission or by design. I wanted to think that Nikki Phillips was willing to do anything to get her husband back, but that whole sex thing bothered me. If you love somebody you don't arbitrarily decide to push him away, and what kind of husband acquiesces?

Speaking of sex, there was Whitton. In a place like Autumn where, according to Nikki at least, same-sex relationships are verboten, maybe someone like him would be less loyal if he felt oppressed. That supposition turned out to be wrong on more levels than I care to count, but I was a day and many kilometers away from knowing that.

I told Nikki I'd be in touch. She nodded, then stoppered the decanter. Her imbibing was over and she was back on guard duty again, waiting for the next insomniac to drift in—perhaps armed.

CHAPTER 14

For the record, not that anyone is keeping one, I work alone. Never had a partner. Never needed or wanted one. Never lived in that noir world of shots and beers with just a sympathetic bartender as my audience listening to me confess my disgust with people, with life, with the world. Never walked under bug-fouled streetlights and into forbidding back alleys, never been asked by some slithery young thing with a plunging neckline if I wanted to kill an hour or two. Actually never met any slithery young things with a plunging neckline at all unless I was snapping photos of them from a distance with a telephoto lens—which, it now occurs to me, is pretty much the same job description as a voyeur. Oh well.

But basically I worked alone because the paperwork was never so overwhelming that I needed someone to file forms. I had mastered alphabetical order as a child, and as long as the sequence remained the same, it worked quite well for me. Then cell phones came along and I hardly needed an answering machine in my office anymore. It's also true that I had no office. Now you could say with some degree of truth that Linnie was my sounding board, because at times she provided insights I might have overlooked. But she also understood that I would frequently ignore her advice. There were times when I could have, maybe should have listened. But all in all I knew how to approach situations, geographical latitude and temperature extremes notwithstanding.

But my conversation with Nikki Phillips about dying spooked me a little.

About those temperatures: it's January in northern Canada—it's supposed to be cold. Even so, I don't think I ever felt intimidated by any weather until I first stepped onto that airfield. Every once in a while in Westchester the temperature will get down pretty low, and if you go a little farther north and west up toward the Catskills, it'll drop below zero several times in a winter. Where I live, ten above is about as bad as it gets. It's uncomfortable. It means warm clothing. There's no swimming or picnicking or cavorting in a tank-top and shorts. I get that. But ten *below* zero, or twenty below is a completely different animal. It's more than cold you can feel. It involves all the other senses—even hearing: the grinding sound of bone-dry snow crunching underfoot drives home the fact that this isn't some New York flurry. You can even smell the cold because, really, you can smell nothing— as if odors themselves have been frozen solid, chopped into fine particles, then tossed to the side of the road where they await the thaw...which wasn't happening anytime soon.

Maybe that's one of the reasons I stayed and listened as long as I did— without laughing—to Manitok's plans for our proposed partnership. It was warm in the co-op where I returned after my visit with Nikki and her little assassin. Manitok was ready to close, but I convinced her to hold off for ten minutes: the more I stood by the wood stove, the less chance I had of being reduced to some fine particles lying by the side of the road.

"Autumn has its own investigative staff," she said, "and they've even brought in some help from out west. They're not going to like having another investigator on site."

"That's their problem," I said. "A family of someone who goes missing has a right to hire whoever to pursue the matter, exclusive of any formal police investigation. You're right—they're under no obligation to let me bop around their complex, but they might not want to give the appearance of being inflexible either."

"But if they don't cooperate?"

"There have been times," I told her, "when cops sometimes didn't want me nosing around, but they learned to live with it, mainly because if I ever spotted the hint of criminal activity, I let them know. We didn't necessarily go out for beers afterwards, but it worked."

"Symbiosis?" she said.

"Survival. These security personnel can learn the same thing."

"You don't understand," she said. "You're thinking in terms of a crime. Autumn doesn't see it that way—their official statement lists someone who wandered off into the night."

"*Wandered off* isn't an official anything."

She shrugged, her way of saying she agreed but couldn't do much about it.

"So that happens a lot? People just go out for a pack of cigarettes and forget to return?"

"It happens."

"Look," I said, "I'm not asking for names here. I just want to know if there have been other...wanderers."

"Three," she said. "Derek and two others, as far as I know."

"Over how long a period of time?"

"Maybe six months."

I told her that if three people went missing in New York City, that would fill up about three seconds of news time. But from an isolated work site with heightened security—that's well past the national median unless you work for, or run afoul of, some drug cartel.

"And they've all been officially reported missing?"

"In a way. The other two aren't from Baker. They're from out west somewhere, maybe B.C. They had no family around, so when they took off, the story wasn't quite so big here. Of course Derek said the story was made up to get rid of them."

"What! You mean they were killed?"

"Shipped off."

"Companies fire incompetent workers. They don't disappear them."

"Tell you what, when you find Derek, bring the other two home with you."

I told her that probably wouldn't happen. Low on the priority list of most major corporations is the idea of being forthcoming: it may be listed in their PR releases, but they're more likely to drip out information that they feel will keep people from asking any truly probing questions. Last year in Westchester there was a chemical spill in an electronics outfit. The fire department, a few ambulances, a hazmat team, everyone but the NRC arrived for a situation that never breached the walls of the company and could have been remedied with some Mr. Clean and a sponge. Of course when the news got out, the company looked like conscientious neighbors who would turn themselves in if anything went the slightest bit awry. But I kept wondering what happened on the days they didn't make the call? Or, with Autumn, what was happening on the days they weren't *searching for* missing employees?

"That's why," she said, "it'll be good for us to go up there together. I have a better handle on how things work."

"No."

"Just like that?"

"Yes."

"Just like that."

"Yes again. I work alone. I don't want a partner or an associate or a sidekick."

"A sidekick?"

"Yes, that's someone who...."

"I know what a sidekick is. If you don't want my help, fine. Go to Autumn alone and they won't tell you a thing. If you even make it there. And by the way, how do you plan to do that? A hundred kilometers is a long walk. Taking the Interstate?"

"If I can use my E-Z-Pass."

She knew what it was, though she seemed unimpressed by the sarcasm. Again.

"I know I can rent a snowmobile," I said. "Seen posters right here in the store."

"Snowmobilers in the Arctic know better than to travel long distances alone. Sometimes they don't come back."

"Nikki said we aren't actually in the Arctic."

"Then take Nikki with you. Her keen grasp of latitude will keep you from taking a wrong turn. She can be your sidekick."

So maybe the word *was* demeaning. I admitted it. It didn't change anything.

"When I take a job," I said, "it's because someone has hired me. Not me and a partner, or a driver, or a guide. Me. If something goes wrong, I take the blame. If I fail, I take the blame. It's true that I also cash the check, but I've earned that by accepting the responsibility."

"And the danger."

"If my job is done right, the danger is minimal."

"Okay, Mac. I get it. What's seventy miles from New York City?"

"What do you mean?"

"Name me a city that's seventy miles from where you live."

"I don't know, somewhere in Connecticut. New Haven."

"All right," she said. "New Haven. Let's say a case takes you there. Seventy miles from home. What do you do?"

"I go."

"You mean you get into your car, start it up, strap on the seat belt, get on some highway, and drive."

"Sometimes I turn the radio on."

"Well then you're really screwed. There are no stations up here. No airbags either. We have some cars but no highway to drive them on. You're not in Kansas anymore, Mac."

"Ugh, please."

"All right, Dorothy. If you want to make believe you are, go ahead. The chances that a snowmobile will break down are low. It's a simple machine. But if it does, you'll die."

"And if I'm not alone?"

"Your chances of survival are ten times as good."

"Ten? Really? There's a formula for this?"

She glared at me. I guess that was her answer.

Linnie claims I have a stubborn streak that often displays itself in a kind of know-it-all attitude which, she says, is all the more annoying when I don't know it all at all. I usually say she's wrong, but sometimes I catch myself living down to that assessment. This was probably one of them—worsened by the fact that I was confronting another know-it-all. I relented.

"You're probably right," I said, "about the danger."

She didn't respond. Didn't even move a facial muscle.

"So you're waiting for me to remove the word *probably*?"

She nodded.

"We go as a pair," she said. "Less chance we'll fuck this up."

"That must be some Inuit expression. Let me ask Mason to translate."

"*Akaugunniiqtuq* might come close to an Inuktitut term, but sometimes English works better."

CHAPTER 15

There are two kinds of people who hire a PI: those who want questions answered and those who want the answers to disappear. I've always been partial to the first kind, but I also know that every case encompasses both. I was wondering if Nikki Phillips and Manitok were, at the present time, both sides of this particular coin. I could consider that possibility later; first I had to deal with Manitok's warnings about going it alone. It turns out she was right about the danger—I learned that when she and I stood next to a crippled snowmobile the next day—thirty miles from the nearest anything.

But the evening before, still bent on going it alone, I returned from the co-op to find Mason asleep in his chair at the hotel. He stirred to full alertness even before the door closed behind me.

"Ms. Austin was looking for you," he said. "How do you know her?"

"Rode in from the airport with her."

"She's RCMP—know what that means?"

"Mounties."

"Right, but she's MPP too. A degree in public policy, kind of like a representative. Got everything going for her."

"You should avoid drooling when you say her name. Don't forget, there's a Mrs. Mason. Tanny, I believe she's called?"

He nodded, the smile became a little less pronounced. "Good memory," he said. "Too bad."

"Consider it a favor. I don't want her calling me some day, asking me to investigate you."

"Tanny's not the type to call a PI if she thought I was screwing around: she's more the swift kick in the nuts type...which is why I'm out here and Ms. Austin is in the lobby."

"You have a lobby?"

He pointed to a small alcove where a few chairs, a table, and some magazines were scattered—and Austin was waiting.

"She likes older men," I said to him. "Sorry."

"And I believe your wife's name is Linnie?"

"We'll just keep each other honest," I said.

I left him to his fantasies and found Austin pecking away at a laptop. She was no longer bundled up in layers—a fact that made it much easier to defend Mason's right to be smitten. Marianne Austin was one of those women who probably worked hard to appear average, and average is a pretty good status for a cop. Just be there, do the job, move on. They don't all look like Angie Dickinson or Kim Delaney (I guess I'm dating myself with those names) but back when I watched TV a little more, those were the faces behind the badges. Marianne Austin certainly would have held her own against those two and any one of the current crop of beauty-pageant detectives if she had wanted to.

"Settling in?" she asked.

"A little. Meeting some of the locals."

"Found Manitok okay?"

"I...did I tell you I was looking for her?"

"Yep, in the taxi."

"No I didn't."

"You must have let it slip."

"No I didn't. It's not in my makeup. Now you could have seen me go into the co-op and assumed I'd gone to meet Manitok, but I'm just as likely to have forgotten a toothbrush and stopped in to buy one."

"And stayed a while."

"Had a coffee, some cookies. Talked with some of the locals about polar bears and icicles, you know, Arctic stuff."

"Oh well, busted," she said. "My elaborate reconnaissance plan has exploded in my face."

"It happens in our line of work. Now if you *didn't* assume I was coming to see Manitok, I'd have been shocked. Apparently hiring me was no secret. And how was your day?"

"I know about Derek Phillips."

"At this point there are South Sea Islanders who know about Derek Phillips."

"Probably, but Nikki Phillips is supposed to consult with me before she does anything related to the case...like talk to a reporter...or any investigative type. You know clients, they don't always follow directions."

"She's your client?"

"There's a case open. Her reporting is not mandatory, but with a missing person, she's supposed to keep me in the loop."

"So you're more of a lawyer. I thought you said at the airport...."

"Solicitor. I have a lot of functions. Nikki called me after you left. I hope you're okay with that."

"Why wouldn't I be? I didn't swear her to confidence. We just talked, and if you've been doing the same, you know as much as I do."

"About Derek losing track of time?"

"Unless I miss my guess, he's lost track of more than that by now."

"You think he's dead."

"I'll tell you, Ms. Austin, when someone goes missing where I work, there's about six million square miles where he could end up and survive. Up here there's about six and I don't think he found one of them. You talked to Nikki—did it seem to you she thought he was suicidal?"

"No."

"Of course that daughter of hers might drive me a little nuts."

"Reg? She's a handful,"

"All of that," I said. "The smug observation here is that she needs a father, but that's too obvious. Makes me glad I never had children. Do you have kids?"

"I was married once," she said, "but no, no kids. With Regina though, it's just a phase—her turmoil just reflects the turmoil in the home. Give her time to come around."

"It won't be on my time. I'm not here that long. Anyway, this police matter—for what it's worth I don't plan to interfere. I've always turned over evidence whenever there's been a crime. I'm not going to stop now."

"That's good," she said. "And I have to ask, since you're semi-retired, are you still licensed?"

"Renewed for two years," I said. I reached for my wallet—Austin waved me off.

"Found you on the register. I know you're legal."

"But you asked anyway. That's duplication of effort. You must have a lot of free time."

She smiled.

"No such thing as semi-retired," she said. "I make you out to be under sixty—kind of early to throw in the towel."

"I didn't actually throw it, just sort of lobbed it. Tell me again why Nikki Phillips is *supposed* to consult with you?"

"She wants law enforcement involved in this situation, in case it ends badly and Autumn is liable. So she has to meet us halfway, keep us apprised. If she goes off and hires her own PI, then I need to know, so that when I see someone poking around in Derek Phillips's affairs, I don't associate him with a crime."

"Even though there may have been one."

"Right. I don't want to confuse curiosity with guilt."

"Then let me say right now—I didn't kill him."

"I'm crossing you off my mental suspect list as we speak," she said, as her eye went to someone behind me. I thought it was Mason eavesdropping or leering. When I turned around, it was a Mason-and-a-half's worth of person. Had to be six-five, weighed maybe two-fifty.

"Olin," Austin said, "come in. Francis McNally this is Olin Nadeau."

"Nadeau?" I said. "Are you related to Manitok?"

"She's his sister," Austin said. Olin still hadn't spoken and I wondered if he could. Or maybe the constant glowering restricted his mouth muscles. A foreign language speaker perhaps? I wasn't sure what the language of choice was in Baker. French? Some native dialect? Just as I was becoming immersed in the linguistic mystery, Olin Nadeau waved a massive finger at me and told me to stay away from his sister. Stay the fuck away, actually, which I recognized as neither French, nor native dialect, but more NYC.

I didn't have a ready response, so I asked him if he was a cop. I knew the answer, but I wanted to keep him a little off balance. I also didn't want my first words to be some reference to his size. He knew he was huge. He knew he could squash me like a bug. I didn't need to enhance the idea already brewing in his head.

"No cop. You ain't either."

"You're right."

"I know I'm right."

Austin cut in. "Olin here is available, he's a local, he knows who to rent from, he's even a good mechanic if something goes sideways on the trip."

"What trip?"

"To Autumn," Austin said. "Aren't you and Manitok going there?"

"Somebody post that on Facebook? I don't remember you and I discussing this."

Olin's expression grew more ominous: I don't think sarcasm was his forte, so I backed off rather quickly.

"But look," I said, making eye contact, "this is no secret. I had planned to go alone. Your sister said I would die. She wanted to come along. We're leaving in the morning."

"That's not the way I heard it," he said.

"That's unfortunate," I said. I wasn't going to ask him the way he heard it when I already knew the facts. "Truth is, that's the truth."

"I don't want her going up there."

"Neither do I."

"Then leave her be."

His voice wasn't as thunderously low as I'd expected, but he was an imposing figure, even seated. And with the layers of winter clothing on, I was surprised he could fit through the average doorway. He was too clean-shaven to look like some mammoth lumberjack, but a tangle of straight black hair stuck out from the edges of an earflapped blue baseball cap, the interlocking NY unmistakable even in Nunavut.

"You a Yankee fan?" I said. Out of the corner of my eye I saw Austin shaking her head.

"No."

"But the hat. Why do you wear it?"

"Keeps my head warm."

"Then you must follow the Blue Jays," I said.

He folded his arms and moved an inch or two closer. "What are you talking about?"

"The baseball team in Toronto. You should have a Blue Jays cap."

"That's the name of a baseball team? The Blue Jays? Baseball sucks anyway, but that's still awful."

"I like your hat better. The Yankees are my team."

"You own them?"

"It's an expression. It means I follow them."

"I know what it means, and they aren't your team. And I didn't come here to talk about baseball."

"Just talk to your sister," I said. "She'll explain what's going on. Just talk—nothing physical."

The accusation was a risk, but not a big one. In one of my vetting extravaganzas, I'd checked Manitok's family and found that Olin had been involved in several altercations. His first wife had accused him of threatening her but not of physical violence.

"I don't hit women," he said.

"You threaten them though—it's kind of a step in the process. Plus she's your sister—family members fight all the time."

"You wouldn't be running your mouth if a Mountie wasn't here."

"Yeah, I would. Your sister looks old enough to make her own choices. Same with you. And me. Why don't we all choose to let me do my job so that I can leave every one of you alone and get back to my wife?"

"He's right, Olin," Austin said. "It's your sister's choice."

"Not with Phillips it isn't," he said.

So that was the problem. It wasn't me leading his sister into danger, and he didn't think I was some pervert luring a young girl into the wilds so that I could, you know, watch the two of us freeze solid.

"He's got a wife and kids," I said. "If something happened to him, they deserve to know."

"Then let her go look for him," he said. "If she was that interested, how come my sister had to hire you."

This was not the time to reiterate my original suspicion that Phillips and Manitok were, to put it genteelly, an item.

"I can't answer that," I said. "But you're welcome to come with us, I think. Unless Manitok...."

He didn't let me finish.

"My sister doesn't make choices for me," he said. "You two go, find Derek Phillips, if he even wants to be found. But leave me out of it."

"But you *were* out of it until you showed up here to tell me to leave you out of it."

His glare softened a bit—there was the trace of a hint of an indication of the beginning of a truce. He may have thought I was a pain in the ass, but he also realized that this little confrontation was his own doing.

"All right," he said. "You think you're clever."

"Actually, I don't. Right now, I think I'd like to keep you from punching me in the face."

"I don't hit people anymore."

"Anymore?"

"Like I said."

"Look, Olin is it? Manitok isn't going to be controlled by anyone—that's my opinion. I could be wrong. If she decides to come along...."

"Yeah," he said. His face was so wooden that I couldn't tell what emotions were festering beneath the surface.

"You worry about baseball," he warned, "and you're not gonna survive here. One more thing, Mr. McNally: my sister always has an agenda, but nobody ever knows what it is."

"I think she wants to find Derek Phillips."

"Do you?"

"Yes—she hired me."

He laughed. "In two months," he said, "your Yankees will be playing. Take care of yourself so 'your team' won't have to get along without you."

And then he was gone. And the room seemed much larger.

"Sorry about that," Austin said. "I thought he wanted to talk."

"And he did," I said, "but he was maybe a little drunk."

"He does have an alcohol problem."

"And a threatening problem. Although he said he doesn't hit people anymore. That's probably a good thing, judging by the size of his hands."

"I can lock him up if you'd like. Threatening is still a crime."

"Not worth it. How does Manitok put up with him?"

"Two strong willed people: they don't get along."

"Somebody must get along with somebody if he knows our plans."

"Well," she said, and there was a loud exhale as she prepared to confess. I stopped her.

"Say no more. I get it."

"Sorry," she and, "but I thought he might be more helpful than his sister on the way."

"Not to me," I said. "What's Manitok's agenda?"

"Like Olin said, no one ever knows until after."

"Until after someone disappears?"

"I don't think Manitok would allow anything bad to happen to you."

Austin said that with confidence, and I think she actually believed it. But if she had faith in Manitok's good judgment, then why had she tried to employ the services of Olin the Giant, especially since she knew of their sibling feud and that Olin would respond with anger at the very mention of his sister's involvement? Marianne Austin's confidence was forced, contrived, something to make me feel better about what lay ahead. She reminded me once again that the Arctic was a hostile environment, and that much of what Olin Nadeau had said was little more than typical advice.

But I'd heard every word: it didn't seem merely typical to me. And the next day, staring at a crippled snowmobile, it seemed even less typical.

CHAPTER 16

"We leave tomorrow" I told Mason after my "guests" had both left. He pulled out a bottle of whisky from behind the counter.

"None for me," I said.

"Half a one?"

"Half."

He poured a double shot into the glass and handed it to me.

"I'll finish what you don't," he said. "Austin tell you about the fight on the plane?"

She hadn't; he did—a story so bizarre and convoluted that I was drinking without realizing it: a flight home from Autumn on the Greyhound, some pre-flight drinking, a sucker punch from Phillips, a rejoinder from Olin, the rest of the passengers choosing sides, a shot fired through the fuselage by the first officer trying to keep the riot from affecting the flight of the plane.

Then the damage: a broken wrist, at least two broken hands, countless contusions and bruises, more than likely some unreported concussions, and a man hospitalized for months while doctors tried to straighten his back so that he might walk upright again.

"Phillips started it," Mason said. "No doubt."

"For sure?"

"That's what they say. I don't have a reason not to believe it."

"I hate those sentences with two negatives."

"I don't disagree," he said, smiled and refilled his glass. I covered mine.

"Is there anybody in Baker Lake who wants him returned?"

"Must be someone," he said. "Sleep well. You'll need it."

"Manitok and her brother. What's their issue?"

He took out a piece of paper and scribbled a word I'd never seen: *Tuniit*.

"You got me," I said. "What is it?"

"You mean 'what are they?' Part of the mythology," he said. "Long story. Manitok will tell you. She believes it. Olin doesn't. There's your feud."

"Over...how do you say this?"

"Too-nee-it. Religion and politics—families come apart over those."

"Tuniit is a religion?"

"I can't do another long story," Mason said. "Tanny'll think I'm screwing around. You ask Manitok. She'll give you the details."

"From her point of view."

"That's all any of us are doing," Mason said.

He cleared the glasses off the counter—the bar was closed, but like that last hanger-on with no reason to go home, I stayed put.

"I'll vouch for you to your wife," I said. "Come on, you know the customer is always right. Explain Tuniit."

"They're just people," Mason said hurriedly. "Some claim they were the first people."

"You mean like Native Americans?"

"I mean like Adam and Eve, though the culture that produced them sprang up about a thousand years ago. Most of us believe that there's no mystery attached to them at all—that they were a race of giants that rose and flourished and died off. Simple as that."

"And others believe..."

"That they're wandering about, trying to protect their land."

"Theirs?"

"Ours. I may not have been born here, but...yes...ours."

"Will I see them on my trip tomorrow?"

"Their ghosts, maybe. Besides, they're shy, rather keep to themselves. But if you insult them, they may come after you."

"And they're big. So they're like the Hulk."

"The what?"

"American comic book character—quiet guy becomes angry and turns into a...well, a hulk. Green—but not in the ecological sense."

"Sounds familiar."

"So in order to see them, I'd have to call them bad names?"

Mason laughed, then assured me it would not be that easy. Common knowledge pegged the Tuniit as having died off in the fourteenth century. The Thule Inuit, the current group's ancestors, moved into the same territory at about the same time, but there's always been controversy as to whether they lived in the same place at the same time.

I didn't think that mattered, but Mason disagreed.

"If Inuit settlers actually saw these giants, then the legend has more credibility. I mean if Jesus had lived before man took over earth, who'd buy that story? If he'd walked among the dinosaurs before man arrived, he'd be in the same conversation as Mars and Hercules."

"Which brings us to Derek Phillips. He believed all this."

"Or he exploited others' beliefs. Whether he was making it up or just losing his mind, weird shit was going on and he was at the center of it. Ancient beings? Mental illness? Too much booze? Your call."

He pointed to a painting on the wall above the lamp—some emaciated and wild-eyed creature with ribs showing through its blue-tinted body, long stringy hair reaching down below its waist, and nails a footlong pointed menacingly toward some unseen adversary. Under it on a small brass nameplate was an inscription: a combination of letters and symbols—what looked like an *L* but probably wasn't, a tilted triangle, an *H*?

"Mahala," he said.

"I don't see an *m*."

"Looks dangerous."

"Not a gentle giant. We have our nemeses too." "But we have Lucifer."

"Ah, *Paradise Lost,*" Mason said. "I was, let's say, *motivated* by a professor to read that once. So dreary. But we don't hold with Milton up here. Nobody burns forever in the darkness. In fact we don't have a hell, but we do have a kind of afterlife I guess—two of them. One is up in the sky; the other deep in the tundra. They're both reserved for people who have endured the pain of life and done so with what the elders like to call *energy and vigor.*"

"What about the people who don't live their lives like that? They aren't given the opportunity to burn forever?"

"I think you know, Mr. McNally—despite your little joke—that the threat of hell scares very few people past the age of ten. Once the fear of dying takes over, hell becomes less threatening. And by the time they're old enough to do really bad things, it's a distant memory, or for some a reprieve."

I smiled at the cynical observation, mainly because he lacked all cynicism—happy as he was with his wife and his job. We talked a little more, but he was getting nervous. I asked him if he wanted me to write a note to

Tanya explaining where he was and what he wasn't doing, but he said no, it would not be an issue. He had an odd look on his face and I knew he wasn't worried about explaining where he was, but he and Tanya had some bedroom plans and I was delaying them. He closed up. I left.

Maybe that bromide about older people becoming less flexible was working in reverse. A lifetime of laboring in my monochromatic world had led, circuitously, to this opportunity to become more expansive. Or maybe I'd been changing all along. I had never set foot in a voting booth without choosing a Republican, not until 2008: I didn't care what Obama's policies were or if he even had any—I wanted to be part of twenty-first century history, to say I voted for the first black president. But then there'd been gay marriage, and climate change, and guns—and all these topics that I wasn't quite so comfortable with—topics I was always able to push aside when I was working regularly. In 2012 I voted for him again. It was easy once the grey started showing up and he reminded me of me—an old guy with a wife who looked half his age.

Whatever was going on among Manitok and Derek Phillips and his wife, I didn't know. It probably wasn't political, but if it was philosophical—or even theological—I could understand the strong feelings and entrenched positions. It was then that I remembered that when Wilkes was here a decade before searching for his wife, he'd had some spiritual event—a local holy man of sorts with whom he'd had an actual fistfight but who, in the end, had made his passage easier. I'd have never thought of him—and I had no idea what his name was—but for Mason's excursion into myth and legend.

I wondered if Marianne Austin was still awake. Public servants keep weird hours, so I called. She said she was in her office catching up, but I was welcome to stop by.

It was cold. I know that goes without saying, but night-cold is a different animal. You walk out of a building and it's like walking into a wall. This might have been one of those. A few street lights, countless stars, and a thermometer flashing -31.

"That's Celsius," Austin reminded me when I clumped into her office. "So in your language, maybe 24, 25 below zero."

"No wonder it seemed so balmy," I said. She smiled.

"Most nights the wind dies and everything seems almost tolerable. That's when you have to be careful: it's not tolerable. What time do you leave tomorrow?"

"Ten," I said. "I wanted to ask you something, but I think it goes back before your time here. When my friend Wilkes was here in 2009, he met this guy...I don't know...a shaman maybe?"

"Do you remember his name?"

"I could find out. I can call...."

"Was it Auguste Demarais?"

"I think that's it," I practically shouted. "You know him?"

"Wilkes must have been in Repulse Bay. That's where Demarais lived until a few years ago when his sister-in-law moved him down here. She was afraid nobody other than her would ever check on him and he'd die in some old house he owned. Nowadays he seldom leaves his room over at the center."

"An assisted living center?"

"Heavily assisted."

"So no point in looking him up, right?"

"Why would you want to?"

"Oh this conversation I had with Mason before. The Tuniit and some other mumbo-jumbo."

"Which you think may not be mumbo-jumbo after all?"

"I keep an open mind."

"No you don't," she said, stifling a laugh.

"Okay, how about I like to think I keep an open mind?"

"Better."

"And I'd like to see this guy."

"Too late tonight. They button that place up pretty early, and they're not keen on visitors other than family in the morning. But he's there. Beyond that, I don't know much."

"You said heavily assisted. Does that mean he's non-communicative?"

"People say he has a touch of dementia, but others say that's just Gus, that he's always been off-kilter. Not that I'm comparing, but Jesus probably had people ready to institutionalize him, too."

She had an electric teapot ready to go and dangled a teabag in front of me. Mason's whisky had already lowered my body temperature, so I accepted the offer of anything that might raise it before setting off again. Besides, I liked Austin. She was one of those people caught between—responsible for a new territory moving forward in a modern technological world, but carving out a space for surviving traditions and mythologies. A place where someone might call her on her smartphone to discuss Sasquatch. And she was busy at it: her office, small as it was, held a dozen small tables, and every one of them was piled high with papers, folders, forms, and various supplies. I gulped the tea quickly so that she might actually get some work done without any distractions.

"Early start for me," I said. "Gotta go."

"You and Manitok," she said, a tinge of wariness in her tone.

"Yes. You sound uncertain. It's not a good idea?"

"She knows her way around. Just be careful. You know what her brother said before is the common opinion. She always has an agenda."

"I thought everybody liked her."

"Everybody does. Everybody understands. Her family is first. Always. But Baker Lake and everything that comes with it is right behind."

"You mean I'm third?"

"That would probably be optimistic."

"You're not building my confidence, you know."

"You don't want to have that anyway, not traveling in these parts. You'll be fine. Stop by when you get back. We'll grab a coffee."

"Or a tea," I said, pointing to the teapot still spewing steam.

"So much for auto-shutoff," she said.

"Technology," I said, then moved toward the door. "I'll let you make a dent in that workload."

I left. I was heading for bed. She wasn't...not for a while. Late-night assignment: I almost felt some nostalgia.

CHAPTER 17

Sometime after 10:00 the next morning, Manitok led me over to Ricard's Rentals where I learned that yellow was the preferred color for snowmobiles: it made them more visible for helicopters searching for the missing. I asked him how long before the missing became the dead.

"Ten minutes," he deadpanned, then got us outfitted in our monosuits which were pretty much what it sounds like: a kind of onesie for polar masochists. And a helmet with a shaded visor. No part of my body was in contact with the air when Ricard was through with me, and even though I felt like a primitive robot in a 50s sci-fi movie, he had the balls to ask if I was comfortable. I nodded; of course even though my head moved, the helmet stayed pretty still.

When I asked Ricard where the nearest chopper was, you know, for a rescue, he said that, other than Autumn which owns several that could be anywhere between Vancouver and Halifax at a given time, his best guess was Churchill. He might as well have said Tucson—the difference between an hour in the cold and a day in the cold would only matter to the coroner waiting for the body to thaw, the specimen itself having long since stopped paying attention to such matters. When I shared that thought with Ricard, he agreed with me. I'd have been happier if he had laughed at the complete absurdity of an accident on a snowmobile, but he was too serious for that sort of thing.

We left shortly before 11:00—later than we'd anticipated—in weather that remained cold and calm, though I noticed a hint of a breeze and some high clouds on the northern horizon. A long sweeping turn to the left brought us out of Baker before the trail ducked behind a series of hillocks that rose like randomly scattered throw pillows. When I looked back briefly to where we had been, the town had vanished behind one of them, effectively ending the pleasant section of the trip for me: from then on I remained in too high a state of anxiety to think about anything other than how many feet in a mile, what exactly constituted a kilometer, how much fuel it was to some topographic landmark Manitok had mentioned, and why I had ever left Linnie to fend for herself while I ran off to do the same. As the mileage accumulated, my anxiety dropped incrementally, but I never contemplated a safe arrival without inserting some condition—*if* we don't crash, *if* we don't hit weather, *if* we aren't attacked by wolves. Wolves can run just under forty miles per hour—Ricard relayed that information right after he told me we'd be traveling about forty miles per hour.

Manitok had prepared me well enough, comparing the trail to a race course without the turns: flat and straight. The dangers, unfortunately, were more subtle than hairpin bends and sudden rises. A few months back a young girl visiting Baker was almost killed when, riding with her father on a trail only a few kilometers out of town, she flipped the machine and wound up with a leg pinned underneath it. If her father hadn't been right there, the ending would have been more tragic than a few bruised toes and some dented machinery.

"So every minute or so," Manitok said before we set out, "whoever's in front turn around, make sure your partner is still with you."

"That'll be you," I said.

"You want to smell the fumes all the way up, that's fine," she said. "Better to switch off once in a while."

"How trustworthy are the machines?"

"They're machines," she said. "You push down the toaster, you get toast...until you don't. It's just a machine."

"Sometimes I burn the toast."

"That's negligence, not malfunction. So keep alert. Ricard is a mechanic—keeps things in good working order. And snowmobiles are very simple devices—you start, you steer, you go. You can eliminate negligence by using common sense. Once you realize it's dangerous out there, it isn't so dangerous."

After several miles on the trail she dropped back and let me lead. At first I turned around to check on Manitok so often that I kept losing partial control of the machine—drifting left like a drunk driver. I didn't even trust the rearview mirrors at first, but as we got farther along, I gained a modicum of confidence, especially on some areas that were completely flat and wide as a football field—a Canadian football field, I thought, enjoying my own joke more than anyone else ever would.

There were in fact some hills too at which I slowed, but even those became less daunting after a while and I became, if not reckless, at least a little less timid. Eventually I was able to avert my eyes from the road once in a while, not only to check on Manitok but also to catalogue all the wildlife I had anticipated seeing. That didn't take long: there was none. I guess it was true that animals stuck to migration trails, very few of which intersected the snowmobile routes. Or maybe something in caribou DNA warned them to stay away from noxious fumes and the machines that produce them. It's a strand mankind has somehow missed.

And so, like an airplane flight when the scenery never varies and there's seldom anyone to talk to, the trip became a bore—a smelly and somewhat noisy fifty-five kph jaunt through a basically barren landscape. I remembered a trip that Linnie and I had taken not that long ago—cross-country in a rented Lexus (a luxury car that spoiled me: thus my current car payments). We had laughed at the agrarian monotony of Illinois and Iowa, but not even that prepared us for South Dakota. Nothing but land and mileage markers on either side of the Interstate for twenty, thirty miles at a time. No off ramps except for the occasional ranch exit: we wondered how gigantic these ranches must be, but were never curious enough to hop off and check.

But even in the tedium of plains there was, if not beauty, then at least majesty on either side of us. In New York the "horizon" tends to be the next building; in the Dakotas, and in Nunavut too, the horizon lies so unimaginably far from the eye, that it's easy to imagine there really isn't one. Linnie would have gotten it—maybe even joked about it—but instead she was at home. I started playing it all out in my head again: her insistence that I come up here and finally erase all the guilt. My objection to her being alone. Then I began counting the days until I could see her again, planning little things that might lie within her—our—realm of expectations: some short trips, some matinees, a little shopping. I remembered a new Brazilian restaurant opening in Scarsdale and I wondered if I could make reservations online right from Baker Lake, then surprise Linnie when I got back. Of course her condition changed hourly and one of my sportcoats was at the cleaners and I'd have to ransom that first, but if I could call the restaurant certainly I could call the cleaners...and that's the way the mind operates without external stimuli, and that's how it helps you forget that you're on a trip with another person whose well being is partially your responsibility. I'm not sure how far along in my musings I got before I turned to check on Manitok.

She wasn't there.

I don't panic, but my mind could produce nothing other than a mental picture of a woman pinned under a snowmobile, shivering while she tried to maintain at least enough body warmth to keep her heart from freezing, her organs from seizing up, her bones from shattering. I eased off the throttle and swung around in a wide arc—I remembered the story about the girl and her father and I was fearful of tipping over—and started rehearsing in my mind how I would try to get her out from under the machine that was crushing her, then onto my machine and somehow back to Baker—or on to Autumn. I didn't know exactly where we were geographically, but Manitok would, if I could find her and she was still conscious—still alive.

I think we've all pretty much grown accustomed to pulling out the mobile phone and trusting our wellbeing to some cell tower. Maybe back home I could have done that—called Manitok and asked her where she was, or maybe used some app to triangulate her position. But here, the time it would have taken me to retrieve the device would have been valuable minutes lost; besides, no call was going through. I sped back full throttle in the direction from which I'd come: I was feeling more confident in my ability to handle the machine, and less confident in the ability of anyone, even Manitok, to survive out there with an injury that might be serious enough to have rendered her unconscious. I tried to remember what happened when people went into shock—if their body temperature went up or down. I'd heard EMTs on television telling people to keep the victim warm, and that seemed all but impossible given our surroundings.

And all the time I was hanging on to the steering wheel more than guiding it. A minute. Two. Then the snow came—a ground blizzard that spun up out of nowhere, obscured everything, then vanished just as quickly. I slowed down when it started, then went full throttle again and seconds later there was Manitok, standing next to her machine which was, to my surprise, not lying on its side or on top of her, but simply parked slightly off the trail. She did not appear injured, or if she was, she was hiding it well, standing by the silent snowmobile. I pulled up close, left my machine running, and jumped off.

"What the hell?"

"If by that you mean am I all right? Yes, I am."

"What happened?"

"Out of fuel," she shouted.

"That's impossible."

"Not if some asshole doesn't fill the tank. That sound about right?"

"Ricard? You said...."

"There's your burnt toast," she said. I could tell by her tone and her language—seasoned judge of emotions that I am—that she didn't want to talk about it any further. On the other hand, we had a problem.

"How big is the gas tank?"

"It doesn't matter when it's empty."

"It does if we can split up the remaining gas."

"Well," she said, "that'll work if the asshole who failed to fill my tank threw in a syphon in case he failed to fill my tank. Now if you thought to bring a length of tubing...."

I shook my head and I wondered if maybe we could MacGyver something together, but at the same moment I realized that's how Nunavut thins the herd. People plan everything to the last detail and some flaw occurs and then they die because they're looking to fix it when you should be looking to get the hell out. So instead of figuring out how to lift one of the snowmobiles and pour the fuel into the other or something equally inane, I unscrewed the cap on mine—the tank looked full, at least full enough to match the gauge on the dashboard.

"Grab your bag and squeeze on," I said, "if this will hold us, we'll just plow through."

"No," she said. "I know where we are. There's an outpost on the right, maybe three kilometers. I recognize the trail marking. We can get fuel."

"An outpost? Here?"

"Yeah. Five, ten minutes that way." She pointed, well, east I guess if we'd been heading north. There was nothing anywhere in that direction.

"What kind of outpost?"

"Some construction Autumn is doing. Leave the bags here—no one's going to happen by and steal anything."

"You're sure?"

"You already asked me that. Come on, it's dangerous to waste time arguing," she said, "and I don't want to ride all the way to Autumn squeezed onto one snowmobile."

Again I looked off in the direction she'd pointed. Nothing. In fact, since we'd been traveling through nothing already, this was less than nothing: not even a trail. But she was adamant, confident. Having been here for a day did not provide me with any authority, especially in a life- and-death situation, with a local.

She climbed aboard and off we went toward the hidden outpost. I'll never know if she was right, because maybe a minute or two onto this new route, we met two oversized chromium yellow snowmobiles, each with armed men—or maybe women—coming toward us.

"We should stop," Manitok said. I didn't bother to compliment her on her keen sense of the obvious.

CHAPTER 18

One of the new arrivals, his voice deep with concern, asked if we were in trouble.

"Ran out of gas in the other machine," Manitok said. "We were hoping to borrow some fuel."

The other two looked at each other and said nothing at first. We waited. The sun, drifting westward was already low and I wasn't sure how much daylight was left.

Another one of the armed riders stepped forward.

"There's nothing in the direction you're heading. Why'd you leave the trail?"

It was a woman's voice, not accusatory, more curious I guess. I let Manitok answer because the detour had been her idea, but she mumbled something about having seen tracks and thinking maybe there was an outpost of some sort nearby. The story she told that woman didn't align with the one she has used on me, but by this time I could feel (or maybe sense?) the cold starting to work down through the layers and yearned for the meager protection of the snowmobile.

"Nothing down there," the woman said. "We can give you some fuel. Where's the other machine?"

Manitok pointed back in the direction from which we'd come—an unnecessary gesture: where else would it be? We led them back toward the trail. Minutes later the same woman was pouring fuel from a two gallon container—at least she was until she shook her head and stopped a few seconds later.

"This is more than half full," she yelled. "It certainly isn't empty."

Manitok came over to look. "That can't be. Why would the thing just stop?"

"Could always be water in the fuel line," the woman said.

She said it with as much credibility as she could, but she didn't believe it and neither did I.

All I could think of was her brother's observation and Marianne Austin's agreement—Manitok was less a guide than a woman with an agenda. Their warning became even more credible when the rescue woman turned the key and pushed the starter: the machine struggled a bit, searching for fuel, then roared back to noisy life.

We let the snowmobile idle for a few seconds while the woman gave us an ETA—less than thirty minutes to Autumn. I don't know how many times I thanked these people, though what I really wanted to know (but what seemed inappropriate to ask at the time) was if we were headed nowhere on that trail, where were *they* coming from? Were they out on routine patrol, looking for sightseeing visitors who had wandered off somewhere? That would be a humanitarian act of the first order, and a consummate waste of time...except for today. I was, of course, happy to have been rescued (mostly from the trail, partly from Manitok), and suppressing my skepticism was one way of expressing my gratitude.

We took off waving like a family that had just spent a vacation at their relatives', but once we were out of their sight, I pulled over.

"Sorry I didn't keep an eye on you," I said.

"By the time I realized that the motor wasn't merely sputtering," she said, "you were out of earshot. But we're three quarters of the way there. That outcropping over there—that's eighty kilometers from Baker Lake."

She paused for a moment, then added, "fifty miles."

"Thanks," I said, and nodded. I began to feel better about our survival prospects, began to feel that maybe the engine wouldn't seize up from lack of oil, or some belt snap from too much tension, or one of those polar bears I had hoped to spot wouldn't come by and maul us both. I was afraid to check the gas tank, but I did it anyway. Three-quarters full. Just like Manitok's.

We'd survived.

But I never felt good about the rest of the trip. Everything had suddenly become tenuous, like driving without a spare—a situation that centered on one of my most prominent childhood traumas. Once, traveling with my parents somewhere (memory will not release the destination so readily) we had a tire go flat. It wasn't a dramatic blowout of any kind, just a car drifting to one side, a souring expression on my father's face, and a gradual deceleration to a stop on the shoulder of the road. Now Dad—who would never have abdicated his responsibilities to something like AAA—wielded the jack and tire irons like a circus juggler and had us back on the road in ten minutes. He was quite pleased and there was some acknowledgment of his expertise from my mother, but the rest of the ride was misery for me: I realized (was I the only one?) that in the trunk lay a useless ring of rubber. If another tire were to go bad or some broken beer bottle lay waiting in ambush, we were screwed, stranded, left for dead on the shoulder. Manitok and I had, in effect, lost our spare, and rather than trying to put a positive spin on the situation, I drove silently with one eye on the fuel gauge, one eye peeled for nails and beer bottles, and both eyes watching Manitok for any untoward or inexplicable movements. I wanted her and her agenda—if there was one—in front of me.

And when I say I never felt *good* about the rest of the trip, I should qualify that. Maybe five or six miles from our destination we were met by two different but equally large snowmobiles driven by two unarmed drivers. The machines were, like the others, chromium-yellow.

"You're from Baker Lake," one of the drivers yelled. "Had a little trouble on the way up?"

Manitok explained the situation to him, after which he signaled us to follow him while his partner brought up the rear.

Only then did I feel slightly more *good*. I didn't watch anybody the rest of the way, not even Manitok. Let these two Autumn folks deal with it.

CHAPTER 19

Despite all that would occur in the days to come—much of which will remain with me forever—the sight of that mining complex in an otherwise lifeless and desolate setting was—and I don't know any other word— thrilling. It was like being in a sci-fi movie set on some remote and barren planet where one massive, anomalous structure dominates, maybe even absorbs the landscape around it. It wasn't the Death Star, just Autumn— sprawling, gleaming, massive, and shockingly out of place.

It was then, with our engines still running, that I first heard—or maybe felt—Autumn Mines: a low metallic vibration whose pitch occasionally rose and fell slightly but whose noise level—which seemed at times about to disappear, remained constant. My helmet dulled some of the sound, but I wasn't about to remove it for a better appreciation. Bad enough that I lifted my goggles for a second to have a better look. Immediately I snapped them back down before my eyes froze open and I wound up like Jack Nicholson at the end of *The Shining*.

"You seem surprised," Manitok shouted. "What did you expect?"

"Something...smaller. This is...this is bigger than your town."

"It's bigger than many of our towns combined."

She pointed to the left where a ten-story monolith sat, it's maw continuously consuming and spitting out trucks themselves the size of small buildings. No signage identified it—it could have been a FedEx shipping depot or a jumbo-jet hangar or the largest Motel 6 on earth—but the chromium-yellow trucks bore a large blue tepee-like letter "A" on their doors and beds, visible even from this distance; and though neither Manitok with her younger eyes nor I with my fading ones could actually read the smaller print, we'd both seen that logo often, even back in Baker.

Autumn.

We were motioned toward a set of doors where a worker in a makeshift uniform wearing a clip-on badge waved us forward. As we approached, they lifted and we saw a sign advising all small vehicles to drive in. We were an exceedingly small vehicle compared to what I'd just seen, so we did. As soon as the door began to drop behind us, a warning sign flashed "Turn Off All

Engines in __ seconds" and the numbers clicked back from 15. We didn't need that long to push a button. I even risked lifting my goggles again: the inside temperature was endurable.

"You can't be serious about 70 people working here," I told Manitok.

"More like 200," she said, "when you include engineers, drill operators, explosives experts, administrators, clerical workers, maintenance staff. But Baker Lake sends only a percentage. The rest fly in on overlapping shifts from places even farther away, stay for longer periods, maybe a month or two. Some are here permanently. The more highly skilled you are, the more money you make of course, but also the more likely you're here for the duration."

"And is there a good mental health plan for those people?"

"I didn't say Derek Phillips lost his mind."

I hadn't said that either, but it seemed more plausible now. Of course I used to hear stories of my grandfather working in a factory—the same factory at the same machine—for thirty years or more, and for all the years I knew him, he was in control of his faculties. People adjust, and just because I was fortunate enough to have a job that almost required movability, didn't mean everyone else was insane. Still I found the prospect of being cooped up in this complex for months at a time in semi-darkness troubling, if not maddening.

And even if Phillips had retained his sanity, who was to say someone else didn't and just murdered this weird guy with the time problems. Funny how murder crept into my thoughts. Nothing like searching for foul play, though murder is at the extreme edge.

I had seen a few of my subjects end up in prison; but despite what most people think about the investigative profession and its day-to-day activities, I've never caught a murderer, at least I don't think so. I investigated a borough bigwig in Queens once—caught him skimming most of the neighborhood's profits and stashing it in the Caymans. When the cops came to arrest him, he barricaded himself in his house and threatened to kill himself and his wife, probably not in that order. He didn't do either, but that would have been my first and—as it turns out—my last murder. And obviously, even though I was licensed to carry a handgun, I seldom did and never shot anybody, never even discharged the thing except on the range a few times. Taking a human life changes a person—look at the PTSD epidemic in America if you don't believe it—and after a lifetime of avoidance, I didn't want to wind up here—or anywhere—worried about finding a murderer or a murder victim. Or becoming one. That kind of crime tends to raise the stakes and the danger.

But given that, I knew that an area this vast, this remote, this unforgiving could guard an endless trove of secrets—murders among them. I couldn't help thinking about Martin Wilkes searching for his wife years before, searching because he believed that one man could somehow distill this expanse down into something manageable...and then turning out, beyond all logic, to be right. Yet even then, to find her in a condition from which she could never recover—that was the payoff for being right?

While I was considering that question, a man in white coveralls approached, an unlit cigarette dangling from the side of his mouth.

"You the two from Baker?" he asked. I nodded. He pulled out a small tablet, made a few finger sweeps, walked over to what appeared to be a miniature printer, and gave us each a strip of paper. "Come on," he said, "let's get someplace warmer."

We followed him into a room the size of a small gymnasium minus the bleachers. One side was filled with shelves and benches on which lay the apparel of survival: coats, parkas, anoraks, and boots, along with a large array of goggles and helmets; the other three sides were lined with small machinery and other equipment, crates, boxes, even what looked like discarded office furniture. We were then handed off to another worker—a guard of some sort (the name tag read Emil though he never introduced himself) who casually dragged his rather small frame up to us.

"Three-sixteen," he said to me, then looked at Manitok. "I had to give you 401—we don't have consecutive storage anymore. Stow all your outerwear in them. Keep the bags. That strip of paper has the code to open the locker. Three tries then you're locked out. Don't drink too much or wear mittens when you punch in the numbers."

Punching in numbers with mittens, no doubt, was Emil's best joke: I wondered how many times he had used it, and for that matter how tired he himself had grown of the routine. But he left us to find our new spaces, which we did, then came back when we had stowed everything.

"You ready?" he said.

The question was a mere formality: he wasn't waiting for any authorization. "Come along," he said with neither enthusiasm nor insistence, and we took our bags and followed him through another door, beyond which sat a middle-aged man in similar white coveralls, the color exacerbating his pallor and greying blond hair. As ashen as he looked, he seemed energetic and animated.

"Hal Whitton," he said, and reached out for my hand. "So you made it. And Emil took care of you in the storage center?"

I held up my strip of paper, proof that Emil had performed his assigned function and I had fully acclimated myself to the traditions of Autumn.

"Hear you had a little trouble on the way up."

"Bad news travels fast," I said. "Francis McNally."

"Frankie Mac," he said, as if correcting me.

"All news travels fast I guess. We did have some trouble—thought we ran out of gas," I told him. "Guess the fuel line was blocked."

"That can't happen," he said with an authoritative tone that fell flat in a situation where he had no authority. "Someone's got to get his ass kicked. Store gas properly and you don't get water."

"It was sabotage," I said. "Someone screwed with the machines."

In the unplanned silence that followed, I'm not sure who looked more stunned, Whitton or Manitok, whom Whitton had still not acknowledged. Then as if she had suddenly appeared he called her by name and told her it was good to see her again. His tone, acerbic despite his attempts at cordiality, told me all I needed to know about the relationship between Whitton and my new partner.

"So you two know each other," I said.

"We've met," Whitton said, looking at me. "Who sabotaged your machines?"

"I have my suspects."

"What are you talking about?" Manitok said.

"I'm talking about your great big giant brother," I said. "He came to see me this morning."

"You told me that."

"Then he left and messed with the fuel line on the snowmobile. "

Whitton leaned in.

"Should I report this?" he said. "We have people in Baker Lake. If we need to make an arrest...."

"My brother wouldn't do that," Manitok said, her pitch rising. "Kill his sister? Are you crazy?"

"Most murders are committed...,"

"...by family members, I know." she said. "Not this family member. He wouldn't know how to do anything mechanical anyway."

"Maybe he hired somebody, paid off Ricard."

"Or maybe Ricard decided he didn't like *you*," she said, now hardly able to control herself, "and decided to be rid of you once and for all."

I won't say Whitton was enjoying the show, but he was at least absorbed, which was basically what I wanted. If he thought Manitok and I didn't like each other, he'd be more likely to play one against the other, and one of us would become a pseudo-confidant: that's when more information usually slips out. Of course I hadn't anticipated a previous antagonism between them, but I figured, what the hell—go with it.

"Well," I said, quickly dismissing the entire argument as nothing more than a difference in perspective, "the point is we made it."

Whitton had not quite caught up. "So...I shouldn't alert the authorities?"

"Nah, why bother. Damage is done. Couldn't prove anything. Maybe it was somebody else." I looked at Manitok, inwardly happy that no weapons lay nearby.

"Don't worry," she said, "someone's ass will be kicked."

Whitton nodded. "Luckily we had some people in the vicinity or you'd have been trudging along on one machine. As it is it's kind of late in the day to be traveling."

"Could have turned out worse," I added, my response so blatantly understated that I don't think he knew how to respond. (*Having one's organs freeze solid one by one is worse than being late? Thanks. I didn't know.*) He hesitated momentarily, then said it was time to get us settled and asked us to come with him. I was surprised he trusted us walking together without punching each other like two middle-school combatants. But I wasn't ready to go, not while he was off- balance.

"Why were your people even in the area?"

"Patrols," he said.

"That far out?"

"As far as Tehek if they have to. We'll talk. Come on, my offices are in back."

"Wait," I said. "Patrols for what? Do a lot of people wander off the trail that way."

He looked at Manitok to save him—the enemy of my enemy and all that. She was silent.

"It happens," he said. "We knew you were on your way. Sometimes the trails get a little tricky."

"How so?"

"Well," he said, floundering, "these little mini-blizzards pop up and obliterate it, you lose the scent, and the farther you go the greater the error becomes."

"We had one of those little blizzards," I said, just to loosen the screws a little. I had learned what I wanted to learn: there was no reason for any patrol to be looking for us, and even less reason for them to be off the trail coming from nowhere. Which meant they'd come from somewhere that didn't concern us.

I wondered if *as far as Tehek* was a Nunavut expression like *from here to Timbuktu*, but Whitton, determined to end this sidebar, motioned us through another doorway and down a short, brightly illuminated corridor uncluttered by anything other than recessed lighting fixtures and exit signs and the occasional emergency alarm box. Then it was on to a larger space where I recognized the mien of the clerical worker—there were maybe a half-dozen or so in a windowless cluster of cubicles, laboring away at all the incidentals that keep a business from going belly-up. The prestige—the decision-making and organization—came from what Whitton referred to as *in back*.

But even that prestige seemed modest when we saw his office. A matted and framed panoramic photo of the excavation stood on the wall opposite his desk (in lieu of a window, Whitton joked) and provided the only smattering of realism among with the poster prints of some French impressionists— Monet or Renoir—I never could tell them apart no matter how much Linnie counseled me. Against my better judgment but with a fifty-fifty chance of getting it right, I pointed at one and guessed Renoir.

"Cezanne," Whitton said. "*The Seine at Bercy*, like it?"

I did, even though my guess had been dead wrong. The painting was an appropriate addition to the industrial environment, though the nineteenth-century task portrayed in the print—a small sailing vessel with a davit lowering some goods while a dispirited pack animal waited to haul it away—provided a dramatic contrast to the colossal machines and immense landscape into which we had been admitted. Or maybe Autumn was the inevitable result of little machines that grew into bigger ones and eventually into enormous complexes. Maybe we had traded dispirited pack animals for dispirited workers—or maybe I shouldn't philosophize until I actually know what the hell I'm talking about. Those office people weren't necessarily sad—I would be, but projecting my own feelings on to others isn't the same as empathy. Sometimes it's merely projecting.

Whitton moved some furniture so that we could all sit in some proximity to each other, then, better at small talk than I ever was, gave us a brief history—not of him or Autumn, but of his office. Apparently it had not always been this particular shade of blue—and not cerulean, he pointed out, as if that underscored his own personal revolution. He had ordered all new furniture—lots of metal and glass—and demanded that the grey carpeting match the grey upholstery perfectly.

"It can be a little dreary up here—I couldn't tolerate a dreary office on top of it," he said, then before either of us could comment, picked up a phone.

"What can I get you folks," he asked. "The commissary is open and they're always at it. And don't say you don't want anything—I've taken that snowmobile junket from Baker Lake and all I want to do when I get here is eat something."

"Maybe coffee," Manitok said.

Whitton glanced her way long enough to let her know her order had been recorded, and to let her know he didn't care, then turned to me.

Now the old PI in me doesn't like to be beholden in anyway to the people he's investigating, but the new McNally—the retired version doing a favor for a friend—thought he should probably not feel that way, nor act that way. Besides, I had to separate myself from Manitok.

"Coffee," I said, "and anything you have that's handy to go with it."

"Everything's handy," Whitton said, then laughed, pushed a button on the desk phone, and instructed someone named Jody—we may have passed her on the way in—to send up the *usual pastry selection*.

"Up here," he said, "the cold saps your strength like nothing you've ever known. It's not like New York City."

"And pastry helps?"

"It doesn't help your cholesterol or your blood pressure or any of the other functions you're gonna need to live another fifty years, but it'll keep you alive until you straighten out your diet. Agreed, Miss Manitok?"

It was his first open recognition that she was in fact seated among us, but it was a begrudging one. Worse, *Miss Manitok* sounded silly to me, like Mr. Eminem or Mrs. Madonna, or maybe more appropriately, Ms. Sacajawea, and I wondered if it was intended to annoy her, or even diminish her choice of an Inuit name in his modern world. Or maybe, because there appeared to be a subtle antipathy between them, I was reading into things that weren't there.

And I wasn't likely to live another fifty years: maybe he meant Manitok, maybe himself. I'm not going to see 110 unless my car payments extend further than I thought and the bank won't let me die.

"So you've come to investigate our little disappearance," he said, and I was immediately annoyed. Again.

I don't like it when a potential suspect dismisses a possible crime as a little inconvenience. I don't mind when I do it, though I try to know what I'm talking about first.

CHAPTER 20

Whitton's efforts to control the conversation worked well, until he slipped and mentioned that his guys would check out the snowmobiles—which allowed me to ask again why his people were in the area.

He looked confused, as if my question were so completely off-base that no reasonable answer was possible even though I'd asked the same thing only a few minutes before. He was so bad at dissembling, I was surprised he had withstood an earlier investigation, unless it had been so scattershot that he never felt pressured.

"To be honest, whenever we're expecting people...."

"You weren't honest before?"

I laughed when I said that, of course, I wanted him uncomfortable but I didn't want to spend my time at Autumn under lock and key.

"Go ahead, Mr. Whitton...I was kidding."

"I knew that," he said, not returning my laugh. "Like I said, we send out a few...well...I guess you'd call them scouts. They check and make sure any expected arrivals are okay. No accidents," and he winked, "No frozen fuel lines."

"But they weren't even on the trail. I mean we had turned off...."

"Which was not smart," he said, his voice betraying a little pique for the first time. "This isn't the kind of place where you can look off to the side. I'm surprised your companion here didn't make that plain. You're supposed to have each other's backs when you travel."

Your companion here—apparently she was no longer Miss Manitok. And me, I was meant to feel like a three-year-old who had just knocked over his glass of juice—careless, foolish, but harmless in my innocence. Unfortunately I had in fact knocked it over and couldn't very well defend myself without sounding unrepentant; on the other hand, I couldn't let the question drift off.

"She did tell me that," I said, "and until I went into a little trance, we were okay. Are there people out there now?"

"What do you mean?"

"Scouts, or rescuers, whatever—are there some out there now looking for other potential victims?"

"I don't think we're expecting anybody, so I would say no."

"And that's what they do, these...these scouts? They're on the payroll to guard against mishaps?"

"They have other responsibilities—mostly security."

"Who dispatches them?"

"In your case I did—I was the one you were coming to see. I was responsible."

"Thanks for that," I said, and I must admit I sounded sincere. I even saw Whitton look relieved that he had dealt with me. But he hadn't. Not yet. And then there was the obvious antipathy towards Manitok—another matter entirely. It made me wish I had unlimited time to pursue it all, that I was still at the peak of my investigative skills, that I was still thirty years old and Linnie was still feeling well. That's a lot of conditions, none of which were going to be met.

"What about when people leave? How far do you accompany them?"

"Usually we don't."

"Makes sense," I said. "You can always check out the equipment here and at least be certain there are no mechanical issues."

I had saved him the trouble of explaining the seeming contrast between arrivals and departures, mainly because it really didn't matter: Derek Phillips didn't borrow a snowmobile and tell Whitton he was going for a ride. There'd have been no need to monitor his trip.

Whitton may have been ready to explain that and more, but the *usual pastry selection* arrived and saved me from needling him any further. Or just distracted me. Back in New York at some overpriced hotel coffee shop, a croissant, maybe a cinnamon bun, a small pot of coffee, and a tab of twenty-five bucks went together. Plus tip. I knew: I'd been there shadowing high-class clientele who weren't good at finding the inexpensive shadows. But a pastry selection for three at Autumn, though it did include croissants—three of them, also featured three cinnamon buns, oversized corn and blueberry muffins (and muffins of yet-to-be-determined composition), pedestrian-looking donuts that Whitton assured us were anything but, and some gooey concoction encased in honey and nuts. The coffee arrived in a large carafe with a bowl of various sweeteners, some non-carcinogenic, others just fattening, and three small pitchers of dairy products of different consistencies and caloric content—all settled neatly on a cart that I knew would later be used to transport files, reports, and various machines from one office to another. There was no sterling silver teapot, but it would not have been out of place.

"And all this stuff," I said, "is flown in from...where?"

"We have a pastry chef and a rather large kitchen staff."

"And your workers eat this well?"

"Better—omelets, flapjacks, real breakfasts, full-course dinners. Up here the workers need those things. I can have somebody cook you up something if you'd like. Just say the word."

"No," Manitok said. "This is already a bit overwhelming."

Whitton ignored her. "Try a little of everything. I expect that when you leave you'll tell everyone back in the states that the workers eat well."

"Of course," I said, though the request seemed bizarre. Of all the information I hoped to gather, it seemed unlikely that anyone "back in the states" would care one iota about the workers' eating habits; besides, with a man missing and Manitok and I having barely escaped with our lives, the menu choices seemed, at the very least, trivial.

We were being bribed, or at least I was. It had happened before when a client actually told her husband she'd hired me to tail him. There was a another woman involved: I guess the wife saw this as a preventative measure, perhaps forgetting that it was too late for that or she wouldn't have hired me in the first place. So of course the guy picked me out—when you know you're being followed it isn't difficult—and asked what it would take for me to stop. I told him that if I were in fact following him, then the person who was paying me to do so would have to stop paying me. Fair enough, he said, and offered me twenty-five grand for the next thirty days—all I had to do is report no suspicious activity. I declined—it was especially easy since he and the other woman were locking arms at the time. I was always amused by the time frame—thirty days: wealthy as he was, a thousand dollars a night was high-priced-hooker range—he could have enjoyed a wide variety of sexual experiences with a myriad of partners, especially since his wife already knew he was screwing around. Even more intriguing was that he considered this woman, for whom he was about to end his marriage and spend a small fortune, more or less a rental. Next month there'd be another twenty-five grand, and on, and on. It will come as no surprise that I could have "used" three-hundred grand a year, but I turned him down and reported everything except the bribe attempt to my client. I learned about the actual divorce settlement later—he was right to propose paying me 300k a year: it would have been a lot less painful.

Whitton's attempt to cajole us was less lucrative and more subtle. But it was also easier to ignore, so we nibbled—a bite here, a forkful there. The whole experience felt odd, accustomed as I was to not being the desired or desirable part of any gathering—at least in any official capacity. Being catered to was something I realized I might be able to live with. Maybe if I had been a PI in Nunavut, I'd have eaten better. But selling my soul to Autumn might have been a deterrent.

Eventually Whitton grew more talkative—he was in his element now, not having to explain or justify anything, but rather revel in the extravagances of Autumn Mines—the showpiece of the Arctic. Whitton himself was born in Ontario but grew up everywhere. I did like the way he phrased that, and I think he did too—just enough fact tinged by just enough mystery. If Hal Whitton had looked a little more elegant and maybe even sinister, his verbal self-portrait would have been more compelling—like that Gatsby guy maybe. As it was, he had accomplished a great deal in his forty-some years, but not enough for any jaw-dropping skepticism. He'd simply moved up the corporate ladder—just another retelling of the American dream north of the border.

"And you Mr. McNally," he said at the end of his narrative, "what are you going to do about Derek Phillips?"

Whitton's phrasing made Phillips sound more like a skin condition than a missing person, but I answered honestly that I just wanted to find him, that I'd been contracted to do a job, that I understood the odds diminished daily—the usual disclaimers I enumerate when people wait too long to hire me. I made no eye contact with Manitok.

Me and Whitton: buddies. Manitok: what's her problem?

I had nothing to lose from that approach. I already knew that Whitton was not going to help me find Derek Phillips or anybody else. He was too heavily invested in Autumn to confess some misdeed that would malign it; that meant I had to make him think the opposite—that he was source number one, that I'd be talking with others but only his opinion really mattered. Sure, he might see through that, but there was just enough ego in his earlier résumé to indicate he might buy some of it if I could soft pedal it enough.

After we'd poked around the food a little more and he'd ordered the cart removed, everything in the office—from the croissants to the Cezanne—began to quiver slightly. I stared at Manitok, then at Whitton and noticed his fingers curled slightly around the edges of his desk. He wasn't holding on for dear life, but he was holding on.

"Try at least a bite of that honey-nut bun," Whitton suggested just before the earth settled down again. "It's outstanding."

That seconds-long event, to me, still defines Autumn—where the pastry is fresh-baked and arrives on functional carts...which then roll away during earthquakes that go unacknowledged.

CHAPTER 21

When I was a kid my father took me to the movies often. The theater was a bus fare away and, whenever my mother had something important and car-worthy to do, Big Fran was tasked with entertaining little Franny. The destination of choice was always the Strand, an art-deco structure from the 1930s and the most elegant movie house in town.

Generally the experience was more entertaining than the movie: my father knew everybody—or at least everybody who worked there. Sometimes that meant free butter on the popcorn or even a box of Jujubes for "the boy." One time we were allowed to sit in the balcony, which was seldom officially open because the theater (razed years ago and replaced by a self- storage center) hired only one usher whose main responsibilities were twofold: keep the younger loge patrons from throwing Jujubes at the others, and curtail the slightly older patrons from experimenting with diverse sexual positions while squeezed into the narrow space behind the back row. It was worse in the winter—the only alternative until drive-ins reopened in the spring. It was quite cramped though: it's unlikely any pregnancies ensued.

My childhood comprised the hey-day of science fiction movies, most of which centered on the advent of the atomic bomb and the resultant genetic mutations which would rise from the depths and, in short but logical order, befuddle, terrify, then eat us. Japan suffered the most—monster after monster trampled Tokyo—but no country was immune.

I mention this because, even though I've forgotten the name of most of these "epics," the one with the goofball title *The Day the Earth Caught Fire* has stayed with me. In my scientifically underdeveloped, Cold War brain, the plot made perfect sense, centering on the Soviet Union and the U.S. spending their off hours testing bombs they would ultimately never use. Thus was the nature of the word *deterrent* back then. In this particular movie scenario, however, the two countries inadvertently tested their doomsday devices at the same exact moment and, unbeknownst to them, at the same general location on earth—Russia somewhere in Siberia; the U.S. somewhere in Alaska (at that time not even a state, so blowing it up couldn't possibly have mattered). The simultaneous blasts tilted the earth off its axis, resulting in meteorological mayhem for all until someone devised a plan to repair the damage by—of course—exploding two bombs on the other side of the world to...well you get the idea.

I don't think I—or anyone else who ever saw the movie that day— actually believed that something as insignificant as man could ever screw up something as big as the earth. Nowadays with rising oceans and boiling summers and typhoons the size of small planets—with California burned and Texas flooded and Florida leveled, I'm not so sure anymore. Nowadays when someone mentions the coming apocalypse, I don't hark back to the nuclear-spawned *Godzilla* or the societal collapse in *Planet of the Apes*, but *The Day the Earth Caught Fire* still resonates whenever I feel the earth shake, maybe more so when a tremor affects something with the immensity of Autumn.

"Blasting," Whitton said, finally admitting that *something* had happened as the pastry cart came to rest against my knee. His first lie, or at least the first one I recognized as such. I'd experienced blasting: the house shakes and just as suddenly it stops. This was different—the sound, the duration, the subtlety of it—a natural phenomenon as opposed to a synthetic one.

"Kind of powerful, wasn't it?" I said.

"We're blasting mountains, tons of rock. Pick-axes aren't going to do it."

"Mountains?"

"I was speaking figuratively," he said, "Mountains as in quantity."

"So you use dynamite?"

"We use all kinds from black powder to slurries," he said. I had let him back in his element and now I had to pay the price in babble.

"I can't keep up with all the names," he said, "but I order it and they use it. I've got an expert who can tell you all about them, chapter and verse, blasting patterns, you name it. Jeremiah Queen—he has the licenses, certifications, everything. He could blow a golf ball off a tee and leave the tee standing."

"Professional golfers do that every weekend using only a golf club," I said, "but I get your meaning. Actually Queen is on my list—one of your people I'd like to talk to, but let me settle in a bit first."

"Really? You have a list?"

Well that struck a nerve. I don't think he liked the idea that I might have arrived with some preconceived ideas or, and this bothered him more, a list of suspects or witnesses. Time to add on.

"Some folks back in Baker who had some familiarity with the situation. There's a Marianne something I spoke with...."

"Austin," he said, trying unsuccessfully to mask his disdain. "She's been here."

"Oh I know. She's an investigator too. She was a big help."

If Whitton didn't like her, then I liked her even more. And that made two women he seemed put out with. Misogyny? Annoyance? Or just protectionism toward anyone who wanted to screw with company autonomy?

"Amateur," he said, then laughed. It was one of those laughs intended to cover up or dilute what was obviously a slur. If I'd laughed along with him, I'd have been complicit, and because I liked Austin well enough, I refrained.

"What I meant was," he said quickly, "she has so many responsibilities that she can't be an expert at all of them."

"None of us can," Manitok said, ending her moratorium, "otherwise you'd have been able to give us more information on explosives."

That little jab didn't go over very well either. Whitton was growing increasingly uncomfortable, as do most con artists when there's the slightest possibility that the con will unravel.

Time for more unraveling.

"This Jeremiah Queen," I said. "Any idea where I could find him?"

"Tell you the truth, I don't even know if he's on site. He may be out west at an excavation."

"But you said before...."

"I may have misspoke. He travels. Like I said, he has the expertise."

"How far *out west*?"

"Probably out in Calgary."

I didn't have to look at a map to know that "out in Calgary" in the present context was equivalent to "on Mars."

"Can you check?" Manitok said. "We don't have a lot of time."

"Absolutely," Whitton said. There was no anger with Manitok. There didn't need to be.

Whitton was going to pick up a receiver, punch some numbers—or no numbers. I couldn't see—then inform us with regret that Queen wasn't picking up, or Queen was on assignment, or Queen was at a driving range blowing golf balls off a tee. I waited dutifully while the sad truth emerged. Jeremiah Queen, in fact, wasn't picking up.

"Let me ask around," Whitton said. "I'll see when he's scheduled to return."

"What's your receptionist's name again? Jody? I can check with her on the way out."

Of course I knew the name, but even though I had no intention of questioning her, I wanted Whitton to try to figure out a way to ask for her discretion before Manitok and I left the office. He must have known it would be futile: he didn't try.

"Well, Mr. Whitton," I said, "we'll get out of your way. Thanks for the food and the information."

"I probably won't even know you're here," he said, immediately pawing at some paperwork on his desk, an action which drew me to the screensaver on the monitor behind him as it changed from a panorama of Autumn to derricks and drilling apparatus. I nodded toward it.

"Oil?"

"Oh, that. Autumn has many subsidiaries. Out west it's oil."

"Out west where Queen went. And here?"

"Minerals. Will there be anything else?"

"Not after you tell us where our rooms are."

"Of course," he said, laughed at his pretended embarrassment, hit some key that hid the screensaver, then pushed a button on his desk and Jody entered. She never uttered a word, but silently led us back in the direction from which we had come, then into another part of the building that looked like a hotel guest area. She dealt with Manitok first, mumbled a few words, let her in and gave her a keycard, then asked me to follow her a few doors down and went through the same routine.

"Jody," I said.

She turned slowly and said nothing for a moment, then responded.

"I generally go by Ms. Brackett."

"Oh, sorry. Ms. Brackett. Can you just tell me the easiest way to get to Jeremiah Queen's room?"

"Did you ask Mr. Whitton?"

"Forgot. I was so busy stuffing pastry in my face that I..." I had no ending. I was hoping she might smile and not require one, but apparently I didn't know Ms. Brackett.

"Forgot?"

I nodded.

"He doesn't have a room in this area," she said, turning away.

"Wait, please. Does he have an office?"

"Down below," she said. "I never see him. Is that all?"

"Ms. Brackett?"

She sounded exasperated—never a bad thing.

"Yes, Mr. McNally."

"Do you like working here? Do you like Whitton?"

She shook her head. "I'm not going to engage in...."

"I'm not looking for evidence or trade secrets. I'm looking for somebody—not you. You're in front of me so I know where *you* are. Do you like it here?"

"Here, standing in front of you answering questions? No."

"How about when I'm not around?"

"It's better."

I'd fed her the line, but she enjoyed saying it. Buried under the protocols of being "Whitton's girl" was a sense of humor, and maybe more.

"And Whitton? I notice he didn't ask you to come in and share all that food with us."

"I don't like sweets."

" 'Jody, come in and have a coffee with our guests.' See how easy that is? And don't say you don't like coffee: I saw the mug on your desk."

"It's tea."

"Of course it isn't," I said. I knew I was smiling. She wasn't, but at least she hadn't left...yet. "I guess I can't tip you for showing us to our rooms, but if I see you in the commissary, I'll buy you a...tea."

"Don't," she said. "I earn a salary that covers taking people to their rooms."

She turned again and this time kept walking, her knee-length black skirt swishing silently away as her heels tapped to a deliberate, somehow unfriendly rhythm. But before she turned the corner and left my field of vision, she turned back and pointed at me.

"Maybe a beer."

"You got it," I yelled. I thought she was joking until I learned later that the croissant and donut commissary actually had a bar.

And because of that, I finally got a smile out of Jody. No, I can't see around corners, but I knew: I had found a possible ally at Autumn. A source.

I was pretty sure I wouldn't find many more.

CHAPTER 22

My room, Manitok's too, was more of a dormitory than a suite, but there was a bed with enough surrounding space for an easy chair and a desk, even a microwave and a large-screen television. On the walls hung nondescript paintings of nondescript places, heavy on the tropical reds and oranges, light on anything that could be construed as a cooler shade.

And a window—I had that over Whitton—though it merely overlooked the same barren landscape I witnessed on the way up. I think my room faced north: I could see long shadows stretching away from me. More important, the shadows seemed thin in the waning daylight. In a sense I'd wasted what there was of that daylight—something to which I'm not accustomed—and I felt almost panicky, deciding right then to conduct my own investigation of the place. But before I could get my shoes back on, there was knock on the door. Whitton.

"Thought you might want to see the place before it gets completely dark," he said. "We'll pick up your partner on the way."

When we did, she didn't look pleased, though Whitton seemed to take no notice.

"We'll get right down to the work level," he said, as if he were promising two excited children a ride on the water slide.

His attitude had reverted to the original greeter and glad-hander. I wondered if maybe he was afraid of my giving him bad marks for the company and wanted to undo any harm he'd done in his office. Which meant he was hiding something, but since most people are, I figured I'd take advantage of his newfound cordiality. We followed him once again through another well-lit hallway and past an exercise room, some other small offices, and a string of supply closets before arriving at an elevator.

"We'll get you two fixed up," he said, as if there'd been no recent flap between us. "Maybe you'll feel better when you see how this place functions."

As if I had been the one to make us feel not better. Well maybe I was, but since feeling better wasn't really a priority, I ignored his pep talk and we followed along, arriving at the *welcome to Autumn* level where we'd already been, where Emil still patrolled (or made himself look busy), and where the temperature was appreciably lower, but not yet uncomfortable.

"We leave the building in phases," Whitton said. "They tell me that extremes in temperature require some gradual acclimatizing, so we have this place—we keep it about five Celsius and use it as an intermediary step to the outdoors. Wasn't this pleasant when you arrived?"

"Felt like Miami," I said. It wasn't much of an exaggeration, but even though I didn't doubt his gradual temperature theory, I doubted very much that Manitok would install a little moderation chamber at the entrance to her co-op. I offered the suggestion just to get a word out of her. I did. No.

If it had been Linnie in a snit, I'd have nudged her gently to break her out of it, but I was afraid if I nudged Manitok, she'd nudge me back by punching me in the mouth, after which the Autumn vigilantes on snowmobiles would arrive to arrest us.

"You came up on a decent day," Whitton said, oblivious to the tension. "It's worse much of the time. All the excavating and building around here creates air currents—channels—and sometimes the wind finds one and you have these little mini-blizzards where the snow and the dust get picked up and the visibility drops from unobstructed to zero in seconds, right where the work is being done or a vehicle is being driven. It's not unusual for a supervisor to sound the alarm and get the men off the floor, then seconds later signal the all-clear."

"What's it like now? Do you know?"

"I always know. I can't get readings from any weather service, but we have our own instruments and I get it sent to my phone. Right now," he said, tapping his cell, "the wind is about ten knots—annoying but not dangerous."

"And the temperature?"

"After a while we don't ask. It's cold—then in the summer it's not. Isn't that right, Miss Manitok?"

He was still trying to include her: I admired his tenacity, and in a way, her hostility. She condescended a slight nod.

"Of course," he said to her, "the cold keeps you in business, right? Parkas. Boots." He didn't wait for an answer since he probably knew by now there wouldn't be one. "Another thing," Whitton added, "the initial excavation cut off the sun angle, and the buildings block it further, so it may seem even darker than usual. Bright enough to see, but gloomy."

"Through the dust?"

"You saw that coming in, right?" he asked. "We have special breathing apparatus so nobody takes in any of that stuff."

"Special breathing apparatus? You mean masks?"

"A little more complex than the ones you get at Home Depot."

"That stuff floating around, is it toxic?"

"Smashing stone all day, grinding it up, you get a lot of airborne particles. It's not toxic, but even so you don't want to be breathing in dust all the time. Hell, asbestos isn't toxic until you fill your lungs with it. And in truth, the engineers don't always know what's in a blasting site until they open it up. We don't take chances."

"Sounds as though you take a lot of them."

"Our safety record is good. Not spotless, but damn close. Last week a truck blew a tire and the driver cracked his head on the side window when the truck tipped. A day later one of the maintenance staff underestimated the kick from a nail gun and added some colors to his chin. Things like that impact our record, and every report comes across my desk."

If all that was true—minor incidents in a place this size—then their record was tremendously impressive, but then Whitton was not above lying—or maybe reformatting the truth. As for toxicity, the chances were pretty good that something being blown out of the earth after lying undisturbed for millennia was going to be a little more troublesome than tree pollen. But after we each put on an Autumn-issue official breathing apparatus—as I said earlier, a mask—I didn't feel apprehensive going out there.

Whitton may have been playing with semantics a bit, not including Derek Phillips in his safety record; then again in actuarial terms Phillips had not been a true accident victim. I wondered if there existed a constantly updated electronic sign somewhere reading *Days without a Disappearance* with Whitton tending to it daily. And what number day were they on? He said he was in charge of everything, except dealing with local cops of course, why not that? I didn't blame him for sugarcoating the activities at the mine—he'd be foolish not to show the shine and gloss to the world, especially a visitor.

Clients lie about themselves all the time, could I really expect anything more from the face of Autumn?

Hal Whitton is a type. I guess we're all *types*, but he was representative of one I never much cared for. Spewing out flattery so fast, there was never an opportunity to contradict, and always smiling so that you feared you missed the joke somehow; and while you were trying to figure out what it was, the bullshit kept mounting until it was piled so high you had no idea where the facts ended and the fiction began. Eventually you smiled at everything because, well, there may have been that joke you missed and didn't want to look slow. He's the kind of guy that, when we're teenagers, we feel privileged to be acknowledged by. Then we grow up. Don't get me wrong: I didn't find him repulsive. I guess that's damning with faint praise, but if I had to be under his supervision for a day, finding him not repulsive would make it all easier. A client once told me he didn't find his cheating wife as repulsive as he thought he would. Now *that's* damning with faint praise.

But he and Manitok—that was another story, one which I'd yet to hear.

We stepped outside into the Arctic dusk, one illuminated to daylight by a stadium's supply of lighting, and I caught my breath. Apparently, having ridden that convertible over seventy miles of icy tundra was not enough preparation. Maybe it's age—maybe that's why Linnie's parents always hated winter and eventually had one gigantic garage sale, then phoned Goodwill to pick up the rest. They spent their final years watching the sun dip into the Gulf of Mexico every night. I remember how she admonished them for going someplace where there were no seasons. Turns out they were onto something.

"You all right?" Whitton said.

I nodded. I would have said something but I wasn't sure my mouth would move. And the worst part was—technically we weren't really outside at all. Instead we stood in a massive enclosure—like an oversized major league ballpark—filled with gigantic machinery, the most impressive of which was a rotating drum attached to a series of motors and belts with gauges the size of barrel hoops: the drum itself would easily have housed Linnie's SUV and the garage where we park it. The entire monstrosity produced a constant din, but one whose smoothness belied its size—as if each ball bearing (did it even have ball bearings?) had been smoothed and polished so as to remain as noiseless as possible. Most of the equipment bore Japanese names—Komatsu, Hitachi, some names too far away to decipher, each tagged with the distinctive yellow logo.

"Chromium yellow is our shade," Whitton said with an odd combination of sarcasm and pride. He was probably satiated of the color, but aware also that its owners were paying him handsomely. "This is where the stones eventually get crushed."

I didn't think the explanation was needed: there's something unmistakable about the sound of rocks being tossed about inside a seventy-ton metal apparatus. Also unneeded was my snarky question about anybody ever having ridden inside it: I was, after all, seeking a missing a person and that point would not be lost on Whitton, who didn't answer. On the opposite side of the structure, an overhead door lifted and one of the trucks came through, towering over a pick-up parked nearby. It backed up to some bin near the rotating drums, lifted its bed, then dropped in another selection of rubble—maybe from an exploration—before returning to the outdoors.

"Come along," Whitton said, leading us toward an area dominated by a massive pool that would have put an Olympics venue to shame. A leaching pool, he called it, the final step in the extraction of gold from its source. Then came his brief introduction to hydrometallurgy, which reminded me of college and brief introductions to calculus and Keynesian theory—which I also failed to grasp.

Then the mandatory joke: "Nice pool, but don't swim in it."

"Liquid at ten below? That might put the average person on alert."

"It starts as water," Whitton answered, "but it's nothing more than a big chemical soup at this point. It has to be concentrated enough to pull one element from another. But I'll tell you, we have it balanced so perfectly that if you were to swim in it—and didn't die of exposure—a quick shower would clean you up. No permanent damage."

"Define permanent," I said.

"We have a normal pool for that and bathing suits for sale. Free for guests."

It was not an answer.

"I sell them for profit at the co-op," Manitok said.

"I'll put a notice on the bulletin board," Whitton said. "Throw some business your way."

I subtly moved between them and asked some question about chemicals, neutralization, all kinds of other things I didn't care about. These two really didn't like each other and it was killing me not to know why. It wasn't killing Whitton—he just sped along.

"Well that's the beauty of some of our processes. In a lot of mining operations the leftover chemicals need to be stored or dammed up or carted away somewhere—up here the sun neutralizes them. Yes, the sun. It does get higher and stronger as the year goes on," Whitton said, "and we do get a lot of it—enhance it with mirrors and reflectors. Before the cold returns all chemicals have been neutralized."

If he weren't already on the outs with Manitok, I'd have called him on that. It happens in all industry: *Last year POISONCO recycled 100 million gallons of water for your use!* (Yes, and hopelessly polluted 900 million more. I may not be an environmentalist, but I have a keen grasp of bullshit, personal or industrial.)

To his credit Whitton admitted it wasn't potable, but reusable in the same process. Manitok, of course, asked what kind of chemicals, knowing that he was not about to give away secret formulations; but he seemed okay with individual components like cyanide, sulfuric acid, and various heavy metals that screamed *carcinogen!* though Whitton never used the term. Maybe if something can kill you fast—like cyanide—getting cancer is moot. Either way, I didn't want to be washing down my morning pills with any water that flowed through Autumn's pipes, just in case.

Then it was on to some radioactive materials, but I'm sure if I had asked Whitton about them he'd have told me how the dangers of radioactivity had been grossly exaggerated and we'd be having it for dinner. I wondered if stockholders knew all that—and how much it would dull the luster of their dividend checks. Probably not much.

Somewhere around then the casual tour took a decidedly unpleasant turn: the wind sprang up and workers began racing around in the general direction of buildings.

"Now we're in for it," Whitton said. "Good thing you hadn't planned to return to Baker this afternoon." He turned us around and waved us after him. There was no panic, but there did seem to be a common purpose—to get the hell out of there.

"Looks like you get to enjoy another meal or two," he said once we'd gotten out of the weather. "And we have plenty of sleepwear. I'm certainly not going to let you travel in the dark."

We'd already planned to stay the night—did he somehow miss that? He seemed more interested in how much time this little windstorm was going to cut from the workers' day. As for the workers themselves, I had some factory jobs when I was young, and I know that people react differently: some take the interruption as a blessing from on high—a chance to have a smoke or grab a coffee; others—especially hourly wage-earners—immediately agonize over lost time and pay adjustments. I saw both reactions on the workers at Autumn, but I saw another one too. At first I thought it was fear, but it was more complicated than that.

I asked Whitton what was going on and he reiterated his spiel on the weather.

"Not that," I said. "Some of the men looked upset."

He gathered Manitok and me into a little intimate triangle. "No offense," he said, looking squarely at her, "but we have some old-time believers here—always looking for signs and omens. Everything *means* something."

"Old-time believers in what?" Manitok said. She was posturing: she knew the answer.

"Myths. Legends. I don't follow them that much."

"Because?"

"Because they're myths," Whitton said dismissing her, then looking to me for verification. I was, after all, not a local: how could I possibly believe what he considered to be nonsense? I probably disappointed him when I said that a lot of myths have a basis in fact. He shrugged, said something about arranging for me to speak with the staff meteorologist, and reminded us that there was a scientific explanation for everything.

"Not for Sedna," Manitok said, interrupting him. "She can be a bitch."

"Science, wind shift fronts," Whitton said, the rebuttal obvious but feeble, "not ghost stories."

But the concern in his eyes was unmistakable, and the glee Manitok felt over having put it there was just as obvious: she'd notched a little victory in what seemed like an ongoing war. They both smiled as if it were all a big joke, and she got it because she was Inuit, and he got it because he worked in Nunavut, and I didn't get it because I didn't fall into either category. But it did occur to me that if a little windstorm could be caused by an angry god, how about an earthquake? And that little smile that passed between Manitok and Whitton—there wasn't much joy in it.

CHAPTER 23

Whitton deposited us in one of the lounges, informed us of the dinner hours, and left.

"Okay Miss Manitok," I said to her, mimicking Whitton when we were finally alone, "what did the man do?"

"The man? Whitton? He's an asshole."

"Language, Manitok, please."

"He's a fucking asshole."

"Not the revision I had in mind. How does one earn such a revered title?"

"We have a history."

"I hear that expression so much these days, I don't even know what it means anymore. You and I have a history too, a short one. Certainly you're not secretly berating me. Not secretly, anyway. So what is this so-called history, aside from the fact that you've been here before."

"How did you know that?"

"Wild guess. And since you want me to be honest, as big a pain in the ass as you can be, you two could not have developed such antipathy so fast. You both had a head start. I'd say you were here shortly after Phillips' disappearance. Probably rode in demanding answers that nobody had, then let your distaste for the company dictate your attitude. How am I doing so far?"

"They stonewalled us."

"I'll take that as 'you're doing well.' Who was *us*? You, your brother?"

She was silent.

"Don't tell me, Marianne Austin too. You got her involved?"

"She's the law. She should be involved."

"Yes, she should, as the law, not a partner with some civilian vigilantes. No wonder Whitton has no use for us. I should have come alone."

"It's too dangerous."

"Seriously? We were marooned in the middle of whatever with a dead snowmobile and heading off in the wrong direction, and you're warning me now about danger?"

"If you'd been alone...."

"It wasn't my snowmobile that crapped out."

"It could have been."

"I don't believe that. And I don't believe in destiny. I do believe in conniving though. What say we talk about that?"

Her expression wavered between anger and shock. Mine tended more toward a grin.

"You know," I said to her, "you can't hire a PI and expect him to honor privacy, or simply refuse to observe. I'm not going to say with 100% certainty that your fuel line didn't freeze, or that there wasn't some bad gas in there that fouled things up, but I place those chances as almost negligible. How about you?"

Her anger and shock both vanished, and I was hoping some shame might nestle in, but she seemed more defiant than embarrassed.

"You were never in any danger."

"Noted."

"The people who stopped us—that fact told me we're on the right track."

"I don't disagree, and I'd disagree less if we were actually on the same track at the same time and not headed in opposite directions. Did you expect to find Phillips out there in some outpost you made up, or living in a pup tent with a little camp stove for heat?"

"I didn't make anything up."

"Then where exactly were we going?"

"Out toward Tehek. But I don't know exactly."

"Tehek. Whitton mentioned that. It's real?"

"A lake off to the east. There's been some chatter about it recently."

"By whom?"

"People, just people. It's a sacred area, parts of it. Rumors about it always stir people up."

"And it stirred you up. And Whitton finished the job. What did he do to piss you off, and what did you do to reciprocate?"

"He said he had always counted on the Inuit women to keep their men in check, not contribute to the problem."

"Yes, and?"

"You're okay with that?"

"It's paternalistic. No I'm not okay with it, but I don't know the circumstances under which he said it."

"You want *specifics*? Let me be blunt: we're supposed to kiss them goodbye every Monday, greet them with a blowjob on Friday evening, then fuck them more or less continuously until Sunday night. Is that *specific* enough?"

"Yes, it is. Vulgarity always helps me piece together facts," I told her. "Now let me check with some of the other people here who might expand upon what you just said."

She hadn't noticed, but the empty space around us had disappeared and we'd become the new entertainment.

"Dirty jokes," I said to a gawker nearby. "Little contest we have. Most foul-mouthed buys the beer."

"Your wife just won," he said, gave her a thumbs up, then turned back to his companions.

It would have been the right time to mention that Manitok was not my wife; then again, it didn't matter to anyone there, and if it pissed off my new "wife," all the better.

"So Whitton's a dinosaur," I said in a near-whisper. "The world is full of them. My country is run by them."

"I wasn't male-bashing. I was pissed off at him. And not just for thinking that—I don't care what he thinks—but for putting it out there for me to quietly agree with. Like *yes sir I willingly abdicate my role as an Inuit woman.*"

"As an Inuit or as a woman?"

"Both."

"Did you say anything to him?"

"Nothing. He knew I was pissed."

"Well, if you want, I can beat him up for you."

"This isn't funny."

"Let me tell you something else that isn't funny. Deliberately flipping the fuel shut-off valve to make it look as if your snowmobile was out of gas. Is that pretty much the way it happened?"

"Pretty much. How did you know?"

"The schematic for that machine is online. The shut-off valve is pretty accessible, so you did it in one of two ways. Either you stopped, quickly flipped the switch, and stayed close while you were burning out the gas in the line, or you just waited there with the machine idling until you got the same result. Now I don't care how you did it. But don't do it again. I don't have any use for a liar."

The word was, admittedly, a little harsh, but I'm not sure if there's a suitable euphemism for a person who lies. If I can shame a person like Manitok, there's a chance she can become better. It's the pathological liars that are beyond redemption. She wasn't saying anything: I thought maybe I'd made an impression.

"Are you mortified?"

"I'm embarrassed. Is that good enough?"

"Because I figured it out, or because it was a god-awful unbelievably irresponsible and stupid thing to do?"

"The second, I suppose."

"That's good, Manitok. That's a big giant step toward mortification. Now when you remove the *I suppose*, let me know."

"Consider it removed. It was stupid. Don't you want to know why?"

"I know why it was stupid."

"I didn't mean...."

"I know what you meant, and I know why you did it. Phillips isn't missing—he's somewhere and you have at least a vague idea where. So you declare him missing, get his wife to go along—I don't know what you've got going with her and maybe I don't want to—but either way, finding him would be difficult...unless...and this is where I come in. I give the search legitimacy. Now it's not some spurned lover trying to get even; now it's a serious search for someone that something awful must have happened to."

"Nikki and I—we're not lesbians."

I didn't want to laugh, but I couldn't help it. "You mean I went through that elaborate scheme to indicate some collusion between you two, and all you come away with is that you aren't gay? If you were, how would that change where we are or what we're doing?"

She shrugged.

"Let's do this," I said. "Let's back up to a point where we agree. Nikki said her husband is on a kind of special assignment. Is that much true?"

"We should talk in the room," she said. "This is too public."

"Until I have a chance to sweep that room, we'll talk here in the noise and chaos."

"You think they're spying on us?"

"Spying? Even in the best of circumstances I expect to be heard, or recorded, or both, every time I leave my house. I don't even like to sing in the car anymore because someone at Sirius is laughing hysterically. I'm pretty sure every drive-thru order I ever gave is on file with the NSA. The NSA is...."

"I know what it is."

"A place like this with lots of security and something shady going on—they want to know everything. So do I. Let's hear it. Just lower your voice."

She did, to a whisper I could hardly hear, though my lip-reading skills helped too. Derek Phillips had been singled out by Whitton to work on some new project. For a company like Autumn, new projects came out of R&D at a rapid pace, though not all the ideas reached the working stage. This one had, whatever it was. She couldn't be more specific because, the last time she spoke with Phillips, he himself didn't know. Neither did Nikki.

"He told her he'd be gone for a month," she said.

"It hasn't been a month, has it?"

"No, but he told me something before he left, something about the project. He didn't think he could be a part of it."

"But he already was."

"He said he might tell Whitton he couldn't do it—that it would be too hard on his family."

"Why the change of heart?"

"That I don't know. When he told me, it was as if he'd had some spiritual awakening, some epiphany."

"Is he religious?"

"I never thought that."

"So he came back here and, what, begged off the job? The normal reaction from a supervisor would be disappointment, maybe a little frustration, probably a little more coaxing. But even if that didn't work, I don't think the next step is abduction or murder. Something happened between the time he said he'd take the job and the time he wanted out. What was it?"

"I don't know."

"He tells you everything. I'll bet you know stuff Nikki doesn't know. He didn't tell you this?"

She shook her head.

I looked around. No one was paying any attention to us: I wanted to keep it that way.

"Let's eat," I said. "At least look like we belong."

We found the commissary and went through the buffet line—for whatever influence the Inuit had on the place, the spread looked like every other all-you-can-eat extravaganza anywhere in the U.S. It was good, but neither of us was particularly hungry.

I told her about my brief conversation with Jody Brackett, the reluctant tour guide who had verified that Jeremiah Queen was somewhere inaccessible.

"We have to find him," I said. "Queen. I don't believe for a second he's off site."

"That may not be easy."

"I know, but I'm getting the distinct impression that Phillips was not the most popular guy here. Other than Queen, Nikki didn't seem to know many friends' names. I wonder if anyone else here is really lamenting his absence."

"Queen is an oddball," she said.

"I can assume you got that from Phillips. But an oddball is in charge of the explosives?"

"He's probably good at his job."

"Let's finish up here, and find out."

I shoveled in the remainder of some mashed potatoes, or at least enough to make it look good, and I was just ready to stand up when I saw Whitton not looking at me. You know what that's like: someone is staring your way until you notice, and then it's as if you never existed.

"Wait," I said to Manitok. "Let's have a beer."

"I thought you were in a hurry."

"I am, but I don't want Whitton to know that."

I took Manitok's card and mine and got three beers—my limit and half of hers, then brought them back to the table. "Three?"

"Be right back."

I took the third one and walked over about three or four tables to where Jody and two other women were seated.

"For helping us out," I said. "We appreciate it."

She nodded, almost smiled I think, squeezed out a thank-you, and then turned back to her friends.

"What was that all about?" Manitok said.

"Bribery and coercion," I said. "And charm."

"Better stick with the first two," she said, sipping at her beer. Whitton was still seated where he had been, but he seemed less interested in us.

And then the fight broke out.

That sounds very much like something a middle-school student would share with his parents at dinner, but this was a little scarier than that; and I'd be surprised if it concerned who was taking who to the snowball formal. Not only that, although Autumn had a strict firearms policy, cafeterias are flush with utensils that can puncture and slice quite effectively. The escalation was lightning fast from words to fists, and although my view was partially blocked, I saw at least two haymakers thrown, either one of which would have knocked me on my ass. Manitok backed away—something I didn't even notice until I turned to tell her we should move back and found her pressing against a wall, the color drained from her face. I'd seen her angry, disgusted, concerned—but always in control. I put my hand on her shoulder as the fight raged on, now limited it seemed to the original two combatants and a few who, like officials at a hockey game, were trying to subdue them. The brawlers—one black, one white, both about the same weight class—seemed equally matched. The victory would have eventually gone to the man with better skills had not security personnel finally pushed through, separated them, and led them both away. One of them—the black man was bloodied pretty well—he'd probably lost a few teeth or suffered a broken nose and, if one of those punches landed hard enough, might be airborne in the Greyhound pretty soon, off for some facial reconstruction. The white combatant was still yelling as he left—still threatening, still angry. I didn't hear any racial slurs—I don't think the fight was over being too black or too white.

I got their last names—Cotton was the white guy (appropriate? ironic?) and Danforth his opponent. Someone nearby referred to them as a pair of hotheads; others agreed that they sniped at each other daily but, up until then, had not allowed their hostility to escalate to blows. But someone else claimed they'd thrown down before and that this little disagreement would violate some probationary period Autumn had placed upon them. In short, there'd be a new job posting soon: I didn't plan to apply.

As things calmed down, Whitton began mingling, going from table to table, ostensibly gathering statements. He looked like a flight attendant walking through the cabin assuring the passengers that, even though all the oxygen masks were dangling from the ceiling and one of the engines had come loose from the wing, everything was going to be okay.

On the off chance that a safe landing actually was possible, I started moving toward one of the exits with Manitok right behind. And though I wasn't cognizant of individual faces or appearances at the time, it was hard not to notice this one: a huge man dressed like a fat scarecrow.

I had just made eye contact with him when Whitton stepped into my path.

"As fights go," I said to him, "that was a pretty good one."

"It happens," he said. "You get people cooped up, give them a few beers, probably some woman they both…you know."

"I usually let Manitok here handle the descriptive language, but I know."

"Not funny," she said. The fight had shaken her.

"Sorry about that, you two," Whitton said. "Hate to see our company look bad."

"Those things happen," I said. "Now tell me, who was supposed to win?"

"What do you mean?"

"I probably would have bet on Danforth—he looked more like a heavyweight. I guess he was out of the loop, didn't get the memo."

"I still don't know what you mean," Whitton said. "Those two have been at each other's throats for a long time."

"Maybe. And they love to fight. I'm sure that convincing them to put on an exhibition was easy. Who did it?"

"Exhibition? Do you know something I don't know?"

"I don't think so."

Whitton was trying hard to remain the gracious host, but I had just made that project more difficult.

"You have some imagination, Mr. McNally." He tried to make it sound like a compliment, but failed.

"Actually I have very little. I have trouble making shit up. I'm much better at figuring shit out. Can I talk with the two actors?"

Whitton shook his head.

"They'll both be in the infirmary, and in about an hour they'll both be on the Greyhound heading for Baker Lake, or beyond."

"Will they be arrested?"

"No, but they will receive further medical attention if necessary along with their pink slips. We can't allow things like that to happen. Boys will be boys, but not here. As far as your implication that this was somehow staged, you can be sure I'll look into it."

I was sure he wouldn't. And when I once again looked over his shoulder, the mammoth figure in the doorway was gone. Whitton stepped aside and let us pass with an exhortation to get a good night's sleep or something like that. There was something peculiarly smarmy about that comment, even for Whitton—the implication that Manitok and I would be sharing a bed. I could easily at that point have begun the second bout of the evening and laid him out where he stood, but I think Manitok got the same vibe. She led me away.

"Asshole," I said in the corridor.

"I like when you borrow my words," she said.

We turned the corner and, to my surprise, found Jody standing alone. Before I could ask why she was there, she slipped me a scrap of paper, then silently turned to go.

"How was the beer?" I said before she could get too far down the hall.

"A little flat," she said, pointing a finger my way. "You still owe me."

I looked at the piece of paper: *Room B-8.*

"Talk about charm," Manitok said. "You must have more than I imagined. Do all women throw themselves at you like that?"

"Only one."

"Your wife."

"Right, but sometimes she needs a beer too. Let's go find this Jeremiah Queen."

CHAPTER 24

B-8 sounded more like an airplane or a vitamin than a location, but that's what Jody handed me. It should have been a basement room, but I'd seen no stairwells leading down from the main level, and no B on the elevator. The prospect of wandering about Autumn like two drunks trying to find their way home while being monitored by a dozen security cameras spelled nothing but trouble, but then I remembered that this was not Manitok's first trip to Autumn.

"Where's B-8?"

"I would imagine...."

"Don't imagine," I said. "Where is it? If you've been before, then you know."

"I never got to meet Queen," she said, "but maybe...follow me."

I did, silently hoping that if she didn't know *the* way, she at least knew *a* way. Finally, at the end of one of the few unlit hallways—B-8.

A windowless door with no writing—no indication of its use or its user.

"Gotta be it," Manitok said.

"Before we go in, are you okay?"

"Why wouldn't I be?"

"The fight before, you looked a little upset."

"I was. I'm better. Let's see what this guy has to say."

"I'm serious. There was a lot of blood, a lot of anger."

"I've seen blood and anger before," she said. As dismissive as she tried to appear, I didn't think she was being honest with herself or with me. We tried the door. Nothing.

She repeated the action a few more times until it finally swung open and we stood staring at the large man from the commissary. "Julie send you?" he said.

"Julie?"

"Thought you were a PI. Julie. She sent you?"

"You mean Jody?"

"Like there's a difference," he said.

We followed him into a large space more fit for storage than human habitation, past a door ominously labeled *Neutralization*, and finally to an oversized control panel next to which he took a seat. I said earlier that Manitok's brother was large, but next to Queen—and I assumed this was Queen—Olin could have been one of the seven dwarfs. Except Grumpy: that was Queen's domain.

His appearance didn't help. Linnie has sometimes accused me of having a fat bias, but over the years I've added a few pounds myself and developed an empathy for people with obvious weight issues. And to be honest, I never had a fat bias. My younger brother Davis was always heavy and underwent his share of name-calling by what he called the skinny hordes. Some of that came, indirectly, from my folks who would strongly suggest to him that he lose weight at a time other parents were begging their sons to get a haircut. I guess I got caught up in the routine, though I know now it was none of my business. But Jeremiah Queen—well he wasn't going to elicit any empathy, not at first sight. He looked like a slob, but he would have looked no less like one had he been stick-thin. Autumn may not have been a shirt-and-tie environment—lots of jeans, collared shirts and blouses, a preponderance of sweaters and fleeces, and seemingly ubiquitous vests. Queen had probably tossed that Arctic Casual memo into the neutralization tank, then took from the same tank his overcoat, which he wore over a pair of plaid Bermuda shorts and a Harvard sweatshirt in requisite crimson. The oversized fur-lined slippers flopped comically.

"So you found me, now what?"

I pointed to a board, maybe ten feet square with all the lights off and all the gauges registering zero.

"Nothing running?"

"She runs at night," Queen said. "We rest her during the day."

"So you work at night?"

"Is it nighttime now, 'cause I don't appear to be working?"

"No, I only meant—Whitton says everything runs 24/7."

"Who's Whitton?"

I shook my head. "You wanted to see us, Mr. Queen. So, here we are."

He denied ever having said that, and he was right of course. But in a show of partial cordiality, he pointed to some chairs in the other corner and we dragged them closer to the one he now occupied.

"My name's McNally," I said to him. "And this is Manitok from Baker Lake."

"I know who you are."

"But we're starting over because the first time didn't take. And Whitton?"

"He's some kind of boss. Not mine."

"Right. And who's yours?"

"I am. Who's yours?"

"She is," I said, nodding toward Manitok, "and right about now she's getting pissed off because you and I, sir, are wasting her time and money— her money."

Queen looked unimpressed.

"So you're the gumshoe, right?"

"Gumshoe?" I said, smiling. "I've never been in a Mickey Spillane novel before. How about shamus or Sherlock or private dick?"

"Whatever," he said. "And this Whitton, did he give you the buyer's tour?"

"The what?"

"The buyer's tour. How much of this mine are you fixing to purchase? Because if you got the buyer's tour, you're probably going to miss the good stuff. But enough about me. Whitton is a liar, you know that right?"

"The man you said you denied knowing?" Manitok asked.

"My powers of analysis are very good," Queen said. "And Manitok, you're the Eskimo in the room, right?"

She ignored the jibe and redirected the conversation.

"I figure Whitton for a company man," she said, "one who likes to exaggerate the greatness of the company that issues his checks."

"That's what I meant," Queen said. "A liar."

He turned away from us and back toward the panel, still dark. I moved my chair closer.

"All these switches," I said. "Will you be flipping one soon?"

"If you want me to. Curious? Pick one McNab."

"McNally."

"So pick one. Maybe a light will come on."

"Mr. Queen," Manitok said more quietly "I can vouch for Mr. McNally."

"Because you have an Inuit name? Who vouches for you?"

"As the Eskimo in the room, I have credibility. You're in my territory."

"No ma'am, you're in mine. You could be a Jew or a Muslim or maybe a Hindu. Names don't mean anything in my territory. Did *you* want to choose a switch instead? I'm not particular. Man. Woman. Anglo. Inuit. Don't matter."

"I don't want to flip any switches," I said. "Nikki Phillips told me that you and Derek were friends."

"Were? Is he dead? Am I dead? Do we know when we're dead, McNab, or do we just wander around in our lives wondering why everybody ignores us?"

We were dancing now, the three of us, and Queen was having fun choosing the music, exercising control. I didn't have time for that, so I reached across him, flipped up three toggle switches, then sat back down.

Queen shook his head, looked somber. "That's the destruct routine for the entire operation. Sixty seconds from now this whole place will detonate and everyone here will be dead."

"Including you?" Manitok asked.

"I have a safe room below ground."

"Then we'll tag along."

"Not enough space," he said, though he made no motion toward moving.

I was willing to humor him for another minute. "And this detonation— there would be no way to stop it?"

"Not without the code. It's a twenty-number randomly generated combination that I've memorized. Of course I know lots of codes. I know the best codes. But my memory really isn't what it used to be."

"Oh well," I said, "better give it a try. It's almost a minute."

"Is it?" he said, then flipped down the switches. "That also works. To do any real damage, McNab, you'd have to flip five more and enter a password. That would neutralize one of the acids that get used in the process. Of course since there's nothing to neutralize at the moment, the light will just flash for a while until the sensor realizes the tank is empty, then shut down."

"So there's no doomsday device here, is there?"

"This whole mine is a doomsday device. Isn't that true, Manitok?"

She hesitated, started to speak, then stopped again.

"See?" Queen said. "She knows. Doomsday comes in many shades and colors. For most people it's the day they die. It doesn't matter if the rest of the world continues on—they're dead and that's what counts. Now the real doomsday—the day of doom—know what that is?"

He didn't wait for an answer, though I guess he wasn't interested anyway.

"That's when God comes down and lists everyone's sins—yells them out nice and loud for everyone else to hear—then when he's done everyone goes to hell...'cept God. It's fun—you should read it."

"Read what?"

"*The Day of Doom*—written about four-hundred years ago by one of *your* pilgrims. Now our little doomsday device—Autumn and all the others like it—it's a lot simpler and a lot slower and much less dramatic, but just as effective when it comes to our way of life."

"*Our* way of life," I repeated. "Do you mean the mine? The company?"

"Ask your *Eskimo* friend here what I mean."

A knee-jerk reaction to *Eskimo* would have been playing into his hands, so I figured what the hell, this conversation isn't going anywhere. I turned to Manitok.

"You're the Eskimo in the room, what does he mean?"

She smiled, and when I looked at Queen, his scowl had diminished. Of course nobody had answered the original question, so I tried again. This time Queen seemed less hostile. "Where're you from, McNab? Toronto? Winnipeg?"

"Nope."

"New York, Chicago? L.A.? Paris? Are you a *gendarme* and this is all just semantics?"

"New York," I said. I was starting to like *McNab*—I wondered if Linnie would be amenable to changing her name.

"Well folks," Queen said, "you came a long way for nothing. I can't help you."

I tried a different approach.

"Whitton says you're a whiz with explosives."

"Hal Whitton isn't the best judge of anything," he said. "And don't worry about security in this area. The corridor cameras picked up your tortured and tortuous approach. So did I. Get a GPS for God's sake."

"Explosives? Whiz?"

"Oh yeah. I'm a whiz because an ounce of common sense and an instruction book are all you need to handle them, but since most of the crew up here has neither, including Whitton, I guess I'm the whiz."

"No accidents."

"None so far."

"Not even in storage? I mean that's where they're most susceptible."

"This isn't some fireworks factory in China where there's a kerosene heater in the corner next to a hotplate. First off, I'm licensed, and that gives me the right to authorize a facility for storage. Second our storage is free-standing and metal-sheathed, including its base so that no one can slither through from underneath. The floor is some kind of neutral composite and there are so many electrical redundancies built in you couldn't generate a spark if you dropped your hairdryer in the bathtub. Nobody has access except Whitton and me, and he's scared shitless to go in there for fear his scuffling feet will create static electricity and blow up Canada. Of course the flooring makes that impossible—which I've told him a million times, but that's Whitton for you."

"Is there an inventory?"

"I'm not showing it to you, but of course there is. I do an audit twice a month, and if my figures don't jibe with the Explosives Act, I'm out of a job. Are you looking to blow somebody up?"

"No," I said. "I was just wondering if you actually *had* constructed a doomsday machine."

"I'll give you plenty of notice before I detonate."

He was smart, and getting him to talk about what he knew convinced me he was neither a mad scientist nor an asocial lab tech. I figured...one more chance to be forthcoming.

"Again," I said. "I'm McNally, this is Manitok from Baker Lake. I'm an off-white American. She's, well, sort of a beige Inuit. Last chance to start over. You know why we're here."

He exhaled loudly.

"Hard to find anyone with a sense of humor anymore," he said. "All right, someone is missing. Derek something or other."

"You're still screwing with us."

"Derek Phillips, yes."

"Nikki says you know him," Manitok said.

"Nikki isn't the best judge of anything."

"You said that about Whitton," Manitok said, her patience wearing thin. "No one is compared to you, but I'm not convinced that you're any better. Maybe I'll ask Whitton about it."

Queen was silent for a moment, then swiveled his chair around to look at us directly.

"You can do what you want, Missy. Just don't confuse me with someone you can bully with Whitton's name. You see, Mr. Whitton and I have a good relationship: we each think the other is a douchebag. Only one of us is right, and it ain't him. So definitely go squealing if you want: it'll only confirm his theory; and when he comes down and accuses me of being uncooperative, that'll confirm mine."

"I think what Manitok meant," I said, risking her wrath too, "was that we have all our territories clearly marked and we didn't even have to urinate around the perimeter. Now Derek Phillips—tell me about him."

"Is he dead? I noticed your employment before of the simple past, usually indicative of a completed event. But not to bust your balls over verb usage, yeah, I know him. Knew him. I know a lot of people. Now I need to get back to my job before I no longer have one."

"Did you like him?"

"Decent guy," he said, "until he wasn't. I'll tell you what people are saying—there may be some truth mixed in with the rumors and lies. Use your own filter."

"Make it easy on us," Manitok said, "which truth do *you* subscribe to?"

"Here's the company line: he got fed up with his job, his wife, his kids, started drinking too much, found a way out of here one day and that was it. Somewhere out on the horizon there's a frozen body waiting for the thaw."

"But that's not your line?"

"No, McNally, not mine. He has something going."

"With a woman?" I asked.

"Just one?" Queen said. "Are we talking about the same Derek Phillips?"

"Answers like that...."

"All right. Jesus, you two are gloomy. Let's just say he had a reputation—more a womanizer than a cheater."

"There's a difference?"

"Womanizers just love women. Even so, I don't think he had anything going on here. Anyway, that's not what you need to know. He didn't run off and elope or abandon his wife and kids. He just left. Acted strange for a while, kept to himself for a while, then he was gone."

"And you know why."

Queen was silent.

"Gumshoe that I am," I said, "and have been all my adult life, I can ID a reluctant witness, and you, my friend, are the quintessence."

"Big word for a cop to be using."

"I know my audience—I heard your *tortuous and tortured*. Where is Derek Phillips?"

"That's not important," he said. "Chrissake the Eskimo here knows the answer to that. It's *why*. Without the *why*, you have no chance."

"Maybe we know why," I said. "His wife said Derek was having some weird experiences. Know anything about that?"

"Only what he told me, that the frozen gods were fucking with him. I guess there's not much else for them to do. Did you ever think about that? Those old gods? Neptune? Jupiter? What do they do now that nobody believes in them? What does anybody do when nobody believes in them?"

"You're digressing again."

"That wasn't rhetorical," he said. "What do you do when nobody believes in you?"

"I guess it depends on whether or not you believe in yourself," I said. Only after the words were out there did I realize how much they sounded like some online collection of suggested yearbook quotes, or an inspirational speaker trying to sell a book. Queen knew it too and smiled. Point for him. Sometimes people like that need a little victory to open up. And he was ready to, I think, when another voice from behind me interrupted.

"Mental health is sketchy in a place like this, but we do our best."

It was Whitton, I didn't even have to turn around. I could feel the chill.

CHAPTER 25

I hadn't heard him arrive, but then that was the point.

"Sometimes," he said, "someone slips through. Sorry, Mr. Queen, I was walking by and heard voices...."

"And since nobody ever comes down here," Queen said, "you thought I was one of those mental health issues?"

"I have no worries with you," Whitton said. "Everything under control?"

"Always," the large man said. "Isn't that why you hired me?"

"And why I keep you," Whitton said with just a hint of menace, then turned to Manitok and me. "If this guy gives you a hard time, you let me know. He doesn't like to have company, but nobody does their job better."

"I could do his job," I said. "I know where the doomsday button is."

"Don't share that secret," Whitton said, trying his best to joke along. "Of course we mine for gold—we're not developing nuclear warheads or missile defense systems. And it's not as if there's another mining outfit across the street that's going to steal anything."

Whitton had answered a question nobody asked, an easy tipoff that he wanted to control the topics of any ensuing conversation. And he did, filling the next minute with a veritable infomercial on Autumn Industries, of which Autumn Mines constituted only a small part. A rousing verse of *O! Canada* in the background—maybe the maple-leaved flag waving— would have completed the picture, but I'm sure Whitton saved that touch for more formal venues.

"Not much very exciting around here, and that's how we like it, right Mr. Queen?"

It's the kind of statement you make just before you say. "Well, gotta run" or maybe "I'll let you poke around a bit." Whitton said neither—just stood in place like a sentry until I realized we were the ones who were supposed to make one of those statements of departure. There followed an uneasy silence punctuated by some throat clearing and a few shifts from one leg to the other before Whitton finally acknowledged that if we didn't need his assistance, he had no reason to be there.

"I know you want to leave in the morning," he said as he approached the door. "Just want to make sure you don't get bogged down in anything. Same for you, Mr. Queen. Don't let these visitors crimp your style."

He smiled and left.

"You two," Queen said when the door slid shut, "can't you take a hint?"

"Meaning?"

"You should probably be on about your business. I have some things to attend to."

Manitok had seen what I saw.

"He threatened you," she said.

"He's my boss."

She didn't let up. "You're a skilled worker. He's a company shill. You can't let someone like Whitton threaten you. Why did you even ask us to come down here if you were going to knuckle under as soon as a boss said something?"

"Maybe you're your own boss in your comfy co-op. I'm not. And I'm not going to be stocking your shelves after they fire me up here. Now maybe you two should leave."

He still hadn't answered the why's of Phillips's disappearance, and I was pretty sure Queen knew them. He was within a hair's breadth of sharing them when Whitton arrived. but he would need a compelling reason to share it or, lacking that, a damn good reason not to. You work for people, you take their salary, you enjoy their benefits—only something serious would make a person turn against them. It wasn't me. It wasn't Manitok. But it was something that had shifted Queen's allegiance. And Whitton—or whoever was eavesdropping—must have heard it too and sent Whitton by to terminate the conversation. The threat to Queen was simple but effective: shut your mouth, keep your job. That little hideaway of his wasn't nearly so secure as Queen thought, not if Whitton had casually dropped by when we were beginning to break through. I was angry with Queen for giving in, but I felt bad for him too: he had things to say—important things—but he didn't want to lose his job in the process.

We let ourselves out without any goodbyes, and Manitok and I—who were becoming less rather than more communicative—traipsed silently down the corridor and past the theater. On the electronic bulletin board outside the lounge, the posted movie listed *American Sniper* as the entertainment for the evening, then offered some other standard diverting options. I dragged Manitok into the theater—it probably seated fifty or so—and there was another couple there already along with one or two singles. She told me she didn't want to see a movie; I told her we wouldn't be there long.

We sat near the other couple—I didn't want to look too secretive, but I also thought that, because they were talking loudly, anything we said would become part of a general jumble of words. I was sure at that point that we were being watched, monitored, recorded—whatever a company with unlimited means could do if it had the desire. As soon as we sat down I whispered as much to Manitok, whose reaction was the same as most Americans when they hear that: *of course those things happen but not to me.*

"Yes," I said to her, "you and me."

And then she did the next normal thing and looked around to see the devices. I let her—at that point it didn't make much difference—but I wanted her to be aware that whatever we had said up to that point was probably shared with Whitton and others.

"At least in here," I said, "we're less likely to be overheard."

"About what?"

"About Queen. His room is bugged."

"He said it was clean."

"He said he knew how to clean it. Everything he said in there after a certain point was for someone else's benefit."

"Whitton's?"

"Maybe," I said, "but I don't believe for a second that Hal Whitton is the brains behind anything big. He's a bit player. This is bigger than Whitton. And Queen knows way more than he said."

"We're not talking about a disappearance, are we?"

"Only as part of a larger picture. In fact, while we're all hopped up looking for your buddy, a lot is going on. He's a great diversion, but he's also the problem. And another thing, it's *cramping.*"

"What's *cramping?*"

"It's *cramping* your style, not *crimping* like he said before."

Nobody more obnoxious than an atheist who found religion. Same for a converted language wrecker. Linnie will tell you that I had accumulated a lifetime of malapropisms—enough of them so that I had learned the word *malapropism*. But over the years I'd reduced the number, mostly because Linnie always caught me on my mistakes so that I wouldn't make them again. *Crimp* was on the list; and even though it was considered acceptable, it wasn't acceptable to me. Manitok was unimpressed. A perfunctory "good to know" was all I got.

"Speaking of good things to know, maybe this is the time to tell me why you sabotaged your own snowmobile: where exactly is Derek Phillips?"

"I don't know," she said. "I mean I really don't. East of the trail, probably about ten kilometers out."

Then she told me everything—which is to say maybe three-quarters of what she laid out in the next few minutes was accurate:

1. She was sure that Phillips was still alive.

2. She was sure Jeremiah Queen was helping him.

3. She was sure that Phillips was still working for Autumn in some capacity.

Now multiply each of those by 75% and there have to be a few kernels of truth mixed in.

"You know," I said, "sometimes you have to pay attention to the people you don't work for. Like Marianne Austin. You don't like her much, do you?"

"I have no problem with her."

"That's what people say when they don't like someone. She pegged you as a person with an agenda. Of course, I figured I knew what it was—finding a friend, maybe a lover. No moral judgments, just observation. But now it appears my safety wasn't on the agenda. Just so you know, I quit people who lie to me and I don't give refunds. And before you say it wasn't really a lie, I quit people who say that, too. So we're done here one way or the other. I'm stuck in this place until tomorrow, and I'll observe mostly out of curiosity, but I don't have much of that left either."

"Can I say something?"

"No, because I won't believe you. Tomorrow we leave. Someone will check out the snowmobiles and fill the tanks, and I'll bet if I ask Whitton for someone to tag along with us, he'll provide that."

"I won't interfere," she said.

Some domestic scene was unfolding on the screen when Manitok and I left and returned to our rooms. We made tentative plans for the morning—eat something and leave right away. She was so amenable that I should have known something was up, but maybe my skills and powers of observation really are diminishing. Maybe it's time to remove the semi- from semi-retired.

But I wasn't considering that an hour later when, still awake, I heard a knock on the door and saw Queen standing in the hallway.

"That girl can take care of herself, McNally," he said. "I don't think she needs you to defend her. If she wants to sleep with some divorced guy who wants to sleep with her, it's none of my business and, I might add, none of yours either. And yes, Derek was a good pupil, learned fast."

"And you are?"

"Don't be funny."

"It's just that I usually start a conversation with *hello*."

He walked past me and into the room. I eschewed the sarcastic "come on in."

"Who's divorced?" I said. I had at least picked up the gist of his unsolicited rant.

"Derek Phillips. You didn't know?"

"Neither does his wife I'm quite sure."

"He told me they were split up."

"They may be going through a rough patch, but he's not divorced. You know he has three kids, right?"

"Yeah, I guess, I mean I knew."

The confident Queen looked frustrated, but he recovered.

"Well," he said. "Maybe Derek was a little deeper than I thought. Or more devious. Maybe he told people he was divorced so that he could be part of this new team. Make a few bucks extra. Nobody would be the wiser. And Autumn played along with the disappearance because they needed him."

"New team?"

"Son of a bitch had me fooled—I made him an expert in explosives. I should have known."

"New team? What new team?"

"You don't need more than one expert up here," Queen said, ignoring my question again. "I didn't figure he was trying to take my job, and he wasn't. That sneaky son of a bitch."

"You already established that. What new team?"

"Let me ask you something," Queen said. "Ever eat pistachio nuts?"

I didn't answer.

"See, when I eat them," he said, "I put them all in a bowl, then throw the shells back in the same bowl. When I begin, everything I pick up is a nut, but as I go along, I find more and more empty shells until after a while, just shells. You keep picking them up, but there's nothing there. Mining for gold is like that—lots of nuts at first, then just shells."

"You could have just said that. So you're starting to find more shells than nuts up here? When was the tipping point?"

"Hasn't come yet, but it will. And a company like Autumn can't afford to let that happen, not if they don't want a stockholders revolt and a new board of directors. In the months leading up to Phillips's disappearance, there was talk. Rumors. Promising seams failing. Lack of purity. More expenses. It's the cycle of mining—like your nuts and shells."

"And so there was an alternate plan. A new team."

"Yep. I got no gripe with the company," Queen said, "but that Phillips. I got a gripe with him now."

His cellphone beeped, and there couldn't have been a soul north of Montreal who didn't know who was on the other end. Queen gave out a few yes and no answers, then hung up.

"Whitton," he said needlessly. "Nighttime. I gotta go to work."

"Checking up on you," I said. "Doesn't it piss you off when someone cramps your style? Come on, best guess. Where's Derek Phillips?"

"Your partner probably knows. Of course, she's gone. By the way, it's *crimping* your style."

CHAPTER 26

When Queen said, "she's gone," I thought Manitok maybe had trouble sleeping and decided to patrol the corridors or maybe hang out in the lounge—maybe pick up some more information. But no. *She's gone* meant she was gone—from her room, from the building, from Autumn. I was dumbfounded.

"They let her go alone? At night?"

Queen shrugged. "She's a grownup. They couldn't stop her if they wanted to. How much do you really know about her?"

"But a woman making that trip at night? Alone?"

"Women make trips at night these days. Alone. Some of them even have driver's licenses. Did you sleep through the revolution?"

"You know damn well what I mean."

"It may be seventy miles back to Baker, but I doubt if that's her destination."

"Right. Phillips."

"And if it's not some romantic liaison..." Queen said.

"You don't know that. I mean, locked up here far away from Baker, how would you have any clue as to what goes on there?"

"Phillips and I, we were buddies, like you thought. Were. I don't have many of those. I'm like a...let me use something an older guy like you can relate to...I'm like a colonoscopy, medical specifics aside. You don't like me, you don't want anything to do with me, yet I'm standing between you and cancer."

"Can we dispense with any future comparisons? The pistachios were bad enough."

"You get the point. Now Phillips treated me pretty well, at least well enough to talk about women. You know his wife is frigid?"

"For someone who knows so much, you are a wellspring of inaccuracies."

"All right, I'll be PC: she has frigidity issues."

"He told you that?"

"I told you, we're friends."

"I have friends too; I don't go around telling them personal details about my sex life."

"Maybe you would if you didn't have a sex life. Like Phillips."

"Then maybe he's the one with issues," I said.

"Whatever the case, Manitok didn't do it for him...maybe because she can be a pain in the ass."

"Don't tell me she's like a colonoscopy too."

"Good one. But now that you mention it, to Autumn, yes she is. She didn't like it when they came here, hasn't been thrilled with them since. Every once in a while she gets her little group together in the co-op of hers and pretty soon there's a protest or a letter or a visit from your local Mountie to check on some violation or discrepancy."

"Like a watchdog. So they knew her up here."

"You knew that. You think Whitton developed that instant a dislike for her? Absolutely, they knew her, my man. And I'm sure when she volunteered to leave in the middle of the night, they probably threw her a quiet little going-away party. Probably still going on."

I started hunting around for warmer clothes. Queen advised against it.

"You go out there, it'll be like tossing a non-swimmer after a drowning man," he said, then added, "sorry, another comparison."

"That one I get."

"Look, it's two hours on a dark trail with just a headlight. If she's already out there and headed for Baker—which she isn't—but if she were, she'd be home before you were halfway there. If she's off for some hidden rendezvous, then you'll never find her anyway."

"I know where she turned off last time."

"In daylight maybe. Not at night. You have a wife waiting for you at home. Don't send her a frozen corpse. It's distressing to the recipient...in most cases."

"I can't just sit back and let her...whatever."

"Yes you can. A suicide mission for you is a calculated risk for the locals. They understand the risks. Besides, like I said, she may not be going home."

"But if they follow her, then what?"

"I think she's smart enough not to let that happen."

"Let's say you're right. She's somewhere right now with Phillips. What are they doing?"

"That I don't know, but if he's working on a project for Autumn, you can be damn sure she's trying to screw it up or convince him to quit it. Bet you're glad you took this gig, huh?"

"You'd be surprised how much like every other *gig* this one is."

"Lies and deceit—I understand."

"Of course you do. You're a contributor."

"Well," he said, and he looked proudly embarrassed, "I guess I am, but listen Mac-whatever you're called, if you have a few minutes..."

"Where would I be going?'

"Good, then let's put this in perspective. In a hundred years this will all be jungle. You'll be fighting off mosquitoes and knocking down coconuts."

"And I'll be turning 160."

"With medical advances...well, that may be a stretch."

He took out an electronic cigarette and switched it on.

"Isn't this a non-vaping room, Queen?"

"I don't see any signs. This is how I'll live to 2100."

"Then puff away. I never figured you for a climate change type."

"Why? Because I'm fat?"

"My exact reason. Your insights are spot-on."

"Facts is facts, that's all. Take off your clothes."

"I don't think so."

"Go in the bathroom, remove your clothes, and toss them out here. Your room is clean—I checked—but I'm not sure you are. Do it."

"What if you run off with them and I'm stuck here forever?"

"Consensus is I'm a pervert—and I do have some strange...let's say...appreciations. But seeing some old guy's junk is not one of them. Hurry up."

"Your admissions do not put my mind at ease," I said, but I did as he requested—down to my boxers—and watched him scan everything and feel around like the pervert he claimed not to be.

"Can't even trust scanners anymore. Here." He tossed me my clothes.

"Now listen," he said. "Eventually they'll be coming for me. Derek Phillips is alive and working on another project about twenty kilometers east of here."

"A new mine?"

"Yeah, an oil mine. There are areas not far from here that are as oil-rich as the sand in western Canada. For that matter we may be sitting on some, but that's for a later date. Right now the building has begun."

"At the end of that turnoff?"

"More than likely."

"And Phillips?"

"He has a talent for some weird shit...I don't know, but Whitton wanted him."

"So they hired him and covered it up with a story about his disappearance? I don't know much about Canadian law, but lying to authorities, making a false complaint, that can't be allowable."

"It's not. But who made the complaint? His wife. As far as she knows, he's missing. They're not going to arrest her."

"Is she in on it?"

"Your guess is as good as mine, but I'd say no. If secrecy is key, you don't tell anyone. You don't risk it."

"These are amateurs, Queen. I say they lack that wisdom. And why the complexity? Phillips works for Autumn. If the company wants to strike a deal with him to begin some new project, then you let him sign off. That's it. Done."

"It's like putting up a garage," Queen said.

"Please, no more analogies."

"They're more like similes, don't you think?"

"Yeah, and it's *cramping* your style, not *crimping*."

"Hmmh, didn't know that. Where was I?"

"Garage?"

"Right. You want to build that garage, you get a permit and build it. However, if you want to build that garage in your neighbor's yard, the process is a little more difficult."

"Especially if you don't tell the neighbor."

"Hey, you're a PI after all. I was beginning to doubt..."

"So this new project is occurring on land that Autumn doesn't own. Who does own it?"

"It's public land."

"Did Autumn bid on it?"

"It would be like...."

"Please. No. Did Autumn bid on it?"

"May I continue?"

This time his simile/analogy was perfectly sound. It would be, he said, like putting a steel mill in Yellowstone National Park. The place is so big that the site could probably be hidden away and be completely unobtrusive.

"But it would still be there," he said, "and there's a spiritual factor to a place like that. Same with Tehek. It's sacred land."

"You mean like an ancient burial ground?"

"No. I mean I don't think so—that could be part of it. Mostly there are tales of extraordinary events, all centered on the lake."

"Name one."

"Later."

"How does a small town like Baker Lake stymie a company like Autumn?"

"Want an analogous situation?"

"No wonder you have no friends."

"Then I won't mention how Vancouver—your Vancouver not ours—thwarted an oil export terminal. It happens all the time. Problem here is, a company like this one building in the middle of nowhere would go unnoticed. Then once it's done, the chances of its being undone will be nil. Court cases would last forever, and Baker Lake itself—with the chance to raise its standard of living—would be split."

"And then there's Manitok."

"Always. Phillips could have befriended almost anyone else in Baker and the company would have been fine. But he chose a social activist with strong beliefs in cultural history and traditions."

"What about Phillips?"

"He may have started off the company man," Queen said, "but I'll bet something changed him."

"Manitok."

"Maybe. But it's more than that."

"But he's still on the payroll."

"That I don't know. I don't think Autumn would be so brazen as to have him killed and fake a disappearance. That's not Whitton, wuss that he is. Still, Whitton may answer to less, let's say, sensitive individuals."

"So if I'm following this maze of bald-faced lies and cryptic clues, I was hired to find a missing person by someone who knows the person isn't missing."

"Yes."

"That's it? Just yes? No qualifiers? No comparisons?"

"If we're right, you were supposed to do the grunt work, gather information, make it look as if the desire to find Phillips was so great that they went all the way to America to find a PI."

"And now Manitok is off doing this on her own?"

"She's already begun."

"And where do you figure in?"

"Let me tell you something," Queen said. "It used to rain in August."

"Could you skip ahead a bit."

"No, I won't do that and you're not going anywhere. It used to rain in August. True, you may not see many trees here, but to the west out toward Yellowknife and the Yukon, it's a different landscape. In '17 it was 29° in Yellowknife—Celsius—call it 90° in the states. And that was the official report—who knows how hot it was in some of the valleys. Ninety degrees as close to the pole as Baker Lake. Stores are selling air-conditioners. Fucking air-conditioners! Twenty years ago that would have been a joke—*like selling a sandbox to a camel driver.* Just twenty years. These climate-change people talking about eons and 'by the year 2100,' yet you get changes like this in twenty fucking years? We have no old sea ice this season. Just new ice."

"What does this have to do with...."

"New ice melts faster, more open ocean, more heat absorption and more melting. I don't believe in God. I don't go to church. But nature can be a bitch, and there's a whole lot of stuff we don't understand. I mean, how would you have explained a smartphone to your grandfather? And yet here we are. How much don't we know?"

"You're talking about science. That will always expand."

"I'm talking about what we don't know, beyond science. What if nature does seek a balance? What if she gets pushed to the point where the natural flow of things doesn't work anymore, and so we get some pandemic that destroys half the world population? All it needs is heat as a boost, and we keep supplying it."

"Can we get back to Derek Phillips?"

"This is about Derek Phillips. This is about exploiting land too close to Baker Lake, right on top of Tehek. If this continues...."

There was a knock on the door. Queen smiled.

"My time with you has come to an end," he said with a flourish. "I have enjoyed our little talk. When you get back to Baker Lake, look up Auguste Demarais."

"Why?"

"You wanted to know about the myths surrounding Tehek. Demarais's your guy. Find him."

Another knock.

"What's your role in this whole deal, Queen?"

"My role in this? If you're any kind of detective, you already know. And you are. And you do. Now let the bastards in," he said, "before it gets ugly. Have a good flight home."

I opened the door. A man and a woman I'd never met exchanged pleasantries with Queen—something about having looked everywhere—a problem with some neutralization chemical—it all sounded pressing and scientific but it was all bullshit. I got the point and I'm sure Queen did too. I wouldn't be chatting with him about global warming anymore. As for Auguste Demarais, I had heard that name earlier in the day from, unfortunately, Manitok: she wasn't there to elucidate.

At that moment I began questioning my own decision to stay, to not let this become another strike against me. If it was going to be simple pride keeping me there while my wife lay ill, then I was the fool. And to learn what

I had just learned and remain there on the job—when virtually everyone I'd spoken to, including the complainant, had lied in some way, then *fool* was an understatement.

I tried to call home but I couldn't get through. After fifteen minutes of frustration, I threw on some clothes and headed off to find Whitton and ask him why his zillion-dollar operation wouldn't allow me to make a cellphone call...when my cellphone beeped.

It was a text from Linnie: *Pretty good day, no rush coming back, find the guy, you da man.* Linnie is seldom wrong, but this time she was. I was not "da man," that much I knew.

I found Whitton and joined the fun: I lied—said my wife was ill and I needed to get home immediately. He told me the Greyhound was leaving at 6:00 a.m. I set my alarm. In the morning I was going back to Baker. I would, as Queen suggested, look up this Demarais guy, but unless he could put me in a limo and drive me to whatever hidey-hole Derek Phillips was skulking about, Linnie's *man* would be back home sooner than she thought.

And once again, empty-handed.

CHAPTER 27

The flight in the Greyhound reminded me of using a leaf blower or a chainsaw. After a while you don't care if leaves are being herded or the wood is being cut. You just want the goddamn thing to shut up...which the Greyhound never did even after we'd landed. An old colleague used to say that any flight that ends up in an airport is a good flight, so this was an exceptionally good flight I guess.

Once I got back to the hotel, I found Mason in a supply closet, taking care of the duties that had once been handled by the young man he had fired an hour or two before. I explained to him whatever I could, told him I might need an extra night's accommodations, then went off to find Marianne Austin. Funny how we turn to law enforcement when nothing else makes any sense.

She was surprised to see me.

"Thought you'd be back and gone by now," she said.

"You're correct. I'm back and Manitok is gone."

And so another explanation, though unlike the philosophical acceptance of Mason at the hotel, she quickly shifted from disbelief to horror.

"I can get people here," she said.

I pictured red-clad Mounties riding in on horseback to save the day, but I had no idea where they were supposed to ride into. I mentioned my conversation with Queen.

"Tell me," I said to her, "What do you know about the new Autumn project? Something involving oil."

"You're thinking of their western projects."

"No, I'm not. You haven't heard anything?"

"Nothing. They have no rights to any exploration off their own property."

"I don't think 'rights' have much to do with it. But that property of theirs, how far does it extend?"

"They own two-thousand acres, so that's about maybe three square miles. The buildings themselves...."

"Fill the area, I know. So nothing extends over to that lake up there, Tehek ?"

"God, no—nowhere near. Why?"

"I don't know. I think I need to speak to Demarais."

"Of course you do."

"What does that mean?"

"Every time something weird happens, Demarais becomes chief consultant. On other days he's an old guy with a little too much vodka in his bloodstream."

"If people believe him...."

"First we need to let Olin know about his sister," she said. "He's not going to be happy."

"That's a given. This Demarais, is he legit?"

"Most of that depends on what you want to believe. There's a story about him when he was a teenager. You can figure out how long ago that was. He's supposed to have rescued a kid from a house that no one knew was about to burn. He had some sense of it from a mile away, called the authorities, they went there and found a piece of furniture smoldering. Of course they questioned Demarais, thought he was some kind of arsonist, but he hadn't been anywhere near the place. There was just a baby with a babysitter who fancied a cigarette now and then, just didn't fancy putting it out."

"How did Demarais know?"

"He just did. Couldn't explain it. Of course, as with most people like that, the myth gets all wrapped up with the truth, and after a while you can't tell them apart."

"It happened here, in Nunavut?"

"When Demarais was a child, there was no Nunavut. Anyway, he's from Denver."

"Denver? Colorado?"

"Apparently. No one knows how he wound up here, or why."

"He's a mystic from Denver? That doesn't sound very sinister."

"I'm not sure it matters where he comes from. He's always known things, divined things, however you want to say it. And he's always tortured himself because he hasn't been able to prevent tragedies. He used to live way up in Repulse Bay, north of here."

"I've heard of it," I said, without elaborating.

"He had a brother-in-law killed in a plane crash a few years back. Never found the plane nor the body. For all Demarais's psychic abilities, he couldn't get a read on it at all, blamed himself for the death. He said if he could have located the plane...."

"Brantley. That was the pilot's name."

"Yes! How do you know that."

"We all have a back story," I said, and gave her the highly condensed version of mine, all of which came by way of Martin Wilkes who had known him—flown with him.

"So this is redemption for you," she said.

"It was until Manitok left me stranded."

"And now all you have left is Demarais. Let me tell you something about the guy: it's never been an easy life for him. Whatever gift he has is every bit as much a curse. The gods may provide the powers, but they extract payments too. Loneliness, isolation, guilt, remorse—and now this final...imprisonment.

"But you still believe in him?"

"I believe in exhausting possibilities. So do you."

"And Olin?"

"Olin may be more receptive than you think. One way or the other, he has to be told about his sister. Seems like my official duty," she said, pointing to her badge. "You're welcome to come along."

An hour later the four of us occupied one corner of a large common room in the assisted living center: Austin, Olin, me, and at long last Auguste Demarais. By my math his birth and mine probably occurred only a few years apart, but though I can see and feel aging daily, Demarais looked to be involved in a much faster process. He looked like an ancient whose deterioration had spread to every area of his existence—whose whole demeanor seemed suffused by grayness and decline. *Assisted living* seemed inadequate to what he needed, yet the facility where we found him advertised such and nothing more.

Olin had taken the news well, blaming Manitok more than me. Maybe his response had been tempered by Marianne Austin's standing by as a witness with a badge. Or maybe it was because he himself had been employed by

Autumn that he had some understanding of what an inconsequential status individuals maintained in Autumn's day-to-day activities.

And he hated Whitton, which helped.

The three of us had gone through some minor protocols to retrieve Demarais from his room, but when one of the orderlies brought him out, everyone else stopped what they were doing, at least momentarily, as if they expected him to perform some magic trick or feat of prescience. He didn't. He just sat in one of the five chairs that had been put in a small circle for us.

"Five," he said, counting them, "and four of us. Who am I conjuring today?"

"Must be Sedna," Olin said.

Gradually Olin had managed to transform himself from furious to angry to impatient in the time since Austin broke the news about his sister. Fortunately very little of the fury had been directed toward us; that he split fairly evenly among Whitton, Derek Phillips, and every manager/supervisor/executive at Autumn. His vow to rip them all to shreds was probably overstated bluster, but I was just as certain that once we were through with Demarais, Olin Nadeau was heading north to do some damage.

"Which one of you is Derek Phillips?" Demarais said.

Austin was having none of that.

"You're not senile, Gus," she said. "Don't screw with us."

"Such language," he said, then motioned toward me. I told him my name before he asked, then reminded him that he had helped my friend Martin Wilkes years ago.

"Almost ten years."

"Right," I said.

"Does he say hello? I just wonder because he didn't like me very much."

"He didn't like himself very much," I said, "and you saw him at his worst."

"He was a desperate man," Demarais said, "and a foolish man, thinking he could get his wife back somehow when she was already gone. He punched me. And that was only 2009? I was still on a snowmobile patrolling the shacks in Repulse Bay; now I have to rely on others to boil my tea water. Did you say he asked for me?"

"I think so," I said. "I talked to him..."

"Poor man—he was embarrassed afterwards but I wasn't. Now you're here and again we're looking for someone."

"That's true," Austin said. "Derek Phillips. We want your help."

"Derek Phillips the time stopper?"

"The what?" Austin said. "What's a time-stopper?"

"A little trick," Demarais said. "I've seen other magicians do it."

"Phillips is not a magician," Austin said. "I think you know that."

Demarais sighed. "It's always the same—people like magic but never really believe it. You can buy that trick in any magic supply house. Of course you have to learn to do it. It's practice that makes it work."

"Tell me about it," I said.

"No, no," Demarais said. "A magician never gives away a trick."

We waited. When he seemed to have exhausted the topic, I spoke up.

"You're messing with us, we know that. When you're ready to be serious...."

"Phillips came to me," he said. "He told me about this power that he had. The more I listened, the more I thought he wasn't joking. I'd heard of it before. It made me think if he can do that, he can do anything. But if nobody can find him, maybe he's turned."

"Turned?"

"Black magic. White magic. They don't usually exist in the same person. One always wins. So let's start searching," he said, feigning an energy he really did not possess. "If we each get a snowmobile and spread out...."

He stopped and waited for us to grasp the absurdity of his plan—five snowmobiles to cover 800,000 square miles—and when Austin accused him of faking senility again, we all relaxed a little.

"So," Demarais said, "you don't need me for a search party, which can only mean you need to know things you think I know but probably don't."

"We just want to talk," Austin said in a voice softer than I was accustomed to. "You're the expert in these parts."

"Not anymore."

"I don't believe that," Olin said. "You are no different than the man who came to my school and talked to us."

"About the old ways," Demarais said, studying Olin. "I don't remember you."

"I'm bigger now," Olin said, and we all smiled. Even Demarais. "I'm Olin Nadeau. Jackie is my sister."

"Manitok," Demarais said. "Why isn't she here with you?"

"Busy," Olin said.

Demarais raised an eyebrow.

"If you want my help...."

"My sister is with Phillips, we think."

"Uh-huh. She visited me recently," he said. "She seemed different."

I asked him when, but *recently* was the best he could do. I intended to check the log before we left.

"What did you talk about?" I asked.

"She was worried about Derek," he said. "I think he was with her."

"What does that mean?" Olin asked. "Either he was or he wasn't."

"I felt he was there. That's all."

The *when* had become more important, so I went to the main desk and asked for the visitation records for Demarais. Since the young man on the job seemed rather busy drinking coffee and shoveling pieces of muffin into his mouth, I rephrased the request by inserting Austin's name and rank and the possibility that her formal request not honored was a misdemeanor. The new approach did little to dilute his surliness, but it got me information: two weeks since Manitok had visited. Alone. Before Phillips had disappeared.

"If I did that now," Demarais said, "I'd be arrested."

"Did what?" Austin said.

"Talked about the old ways in a school. Today I would need permission from the Prime Minister to do something that subversive," he said. "I would be offending someone."

"You're wrong there," Austin said. "After all these years your lesson is still taught, passed on from instructor to instructor. But today we need a historian, not a psychic."

"And we need a cop? That's why you're here?"

He didn't allow her to answer.

"Will there be tea?"

"The kettle is on," Austin said. "I told one of the aides."

"And you know how I take it?"

She smiled. "Everyone knows how to prepare your tea," she said, pointing to her purse.

"And it will be ready soon?"

"Yes, but you know, a watched pot..."

Demarais cut her off.

"...will boil no slower than an unwatched pot. Go see if it's ready."

Austin stood just as I began to hear a faint whistle from the other room. A few moments later, while we maintained an uncomfortable and anticipatory silence, Austin returned with a cup and saucer, then placed it next to Demarais.

"It's hot," she said.

"The steam was a clue," he said, then sniffed it approvingly. "Vodka doesn't have much odor, but there's something unmistakable about the vapors of alcohol. Salutary, I've been told."

"Early in the day," Austin said, "but not illegal, and if it's salutary..."

She took a flask from her purse and poured a liquid into the tea. Demarais looked pleased, breathed in the vapors, took a sip, nodded. "Keep the kettle hot," he said, "should I require a refill."

"Understood," Austin said. "Is there anything else I can get you?"

"No, but let's get on with this before I need a nap. Why is there a fifth chair? If it's for the coroner, tell me. If you know something...."

"Maybe it is for Sedna," I whispered.

"Oh yes," he said. "That would matter very much."

He looked at Austin. "They must pay you well," he said, looking surprised. "This is Grey Goose."

"Only the best," she said. "You aren't the only vodka drinker in this room."

"Good to have company," he said. "Now how can I help you?"

I didn't answer at first. What I'd really like to have known was why this guy—able to discern differences in tea-diluted vodka and throwing around words like *salutary*—had been placed, or allowed himself to be placed, in this dreary environment. But that would have been mere curiosity: I was there for a more significant reason.

CHAPTER 28

"A man named Jeremiah Queen told me to look you up," I said.

Demarais shook his head. "I don't know anyone by that name."

"He knows you."

"Of course," Demarais said. "My childhood exploits continue to follow me. Do you want me to cast a spell, Mr. McNally? I can maybe make it cold outside."

"We were hoping for a little more. Tell us about Sedna."

"You can look it up in any book."

"I want to know what you know."

"Sedna," Demarais said, then sipped some more. "Are you sure you want to mess with her?"

"I don't know. Do I?"

He turned the tea cup on the saucer. "Did you know," he began, "that in West Greenland they call Sedna the Mother of the Deep, but up near Coronation Gulf she's the Big Bad Woman? She's a threatening giant for some; for others a brutalized victim, a 'me too' member. Which one are you looking for?"

"Which do you think?"

"The stories about her are all the same and all different. There's the Sedna who married a dog, and the one who attacked her parents, and the orphan the locals tried to murder, and the beautiful maiden ravished by a petrel and mutilated by her father. Your choice."

"I don't like choices," I said. "I want the one who's guarding Tehek."

"Ah-ha. So now we get to it. Why does Tehek need guarding? And why is an Anglo asking me when you, Olin, have Inuit blood flowing through you?"

"I don't practice the old ways," he said. I don't think anyone there believed him, least of all Demarais.

"And yet here you are. Here you are."

Olin was silent, as was everyone else until Austin restarted the conversation.

"There have been...events," she said.

"Events," Demarais repeated. For some seconds he appeared to be staring, probing. Then I thought maybe he had dozed off, or worse that some sort of stroke had left him motionless and senseless. Finally he nodded.

"Sedna rules the sea," he said, "but she can create *events.*"

"When she is angry?" Olin said.

"When she is angry and even when she is not."

He attempted a somewhat subtle wink at Austin. "The tea is very good."

"I didn't want it to be too strong," she said. "This goddess, do things ever turn out well when she is involved?"

"I like the word goddess," Demarais said. "You make her sound like a beautiful young woman in a fairy tale."

Then he turned to me with a grimmer, darker expression.

"There are no fairy tales up here, no handsome princes. You should know that, McNally, your friend Wilkes learned it ten years ago. We don't produce happy endings. We have no goddesses."

"And we have no time either, Mr. Demarais. You have a world of stories and experiences, I get all that. But I want to know this: if someone set out to protect sacred ground, like Tehek, would that person be granted help? Divine or otherwise?"

"In 2018 you ask that?"

He drank some more, then scanned the room as if he were looking for someone.

"The orderly," he said, "the tall woman with the big breasts. She spies on me."

None of us knew exactly how to respond, though I did catch myself assessing the size of the female worker's breasts until I found his culprit. I felt like an eighth-grader.

"Would that person," I repeated, "even in 2018 get divine help?"

He looked confused: I was afraid of losing him.

"The person protecting the lake, Tehek," I added quickly.

"It's possible," he said, alert again. "It's more possible that we have overreached and landed beyond their assistance. Tell me about Derek Phillips. Is he a religious man?"

"No," I said. I wasn't sure: I just didn't want another excursion off the topic.

In the other room the kettle whistled softly, then faded but nobody moved while Austin condensed the events of the previous weeks. Demarais seemed to be taking in everything, occasionally nodding but otherwise betraying no emotion of any kind. At the end he held up his empty cup.

"Maybe one more?" he said to Austin, "now that it's later in the day?"

"Of course," Austin said.

Demarais watched her leave the room but didn't wait for her return.

"So you want my so-called powers, right? Not my historian's knowledge?"

"I think we want both," I said. "If you have a way of knowing something about Phillips, then yes, we want to know. But also if you can tell us if a spirit like Sedna would interfere in the lives of men...."

"Interfere?" he said, and laughed. "It is man who interferes. We do it over and over. Maybe Derek Phillips was interfering."

"And was murdered by a thousand-year-old woman," Austin said, returning with another tea and having heard some of the conversation. "I can't arrest some spirit for murder, so if that's the case, tell us and we can all go home."

"Going home is not a bad thing," he said, blowing some steam off the top of the newly-filled cup. "We're all home wherever we are."

"With all due respect," I said, "that sounds more like gibberish than wisdom."

Demarais shrugged. "Noted," he said. "And probably true. You seem impatient, Mr. McNally. Why?"

"My wife is ill," I said softly, "and I should be home with her. Instead I'm here trying to separate the wisdom from the bullshit. We're all home wherever we are? I'm not home. Phillips isn't home."

Demarais looked a bit chastened, though not enough for me.

"I was speaking metaphorically," he said.

"Of course you were."

I didn't want my sarcasm to alienate Demarais further, especially if he thought I was being condescending. I tried to tone it down.

"Your culture," I said, "full of angry gods and mythological vengeance, it's no different from any other culture filled with the same scary monsters. Satan. Beelzebub. Balaam. Throw in Mephistopheles and Godzilla if you'd like. But if you have nothing to share, I'm going home. Real home, not a metaphorical one."

I stood up.

"As a failure," he said.

"Who tried," I said, then let the frustration get the better of me. "At least I didn't sit there with the ability to help and scoff down a few free drinks before breakfast. In my home we have a name for people like that."

"Wait," Austin said. I think she thought I was going to hit the old guy, and in truth—for a moment—I understood why Martin Wilkes had already done the same thing years before. "I think what Mr. McNally means...."

"I know what he means," Demarais said, then looked at me. "I did not mean to anger you. These days...these days I trust the world only to betray me and I live in my mind and imaginings. With your friend Wilkes, my imaginings were so strong that when his wife came here, I knew her. I knew she would die here. Wilkes was angry with me, but I knew what I knew. And I knew the outcome. How could he not be angry?"

"And Derek Phillips," I said. "Tell me his outcome so that I can go home."

"He is in danger. But we are in danger too. All of us."

"You're doing it again...that's why people punch you."

"Is that what you want to do, Mr. McNally?"

"It sounds appealing," I said, "But then what? Is Sedna going to cut my fingers off? Pack them in ice?"

"Ice we have," Demarais said. I could just make out the trace of a smile before his face went blank again and he continued. "The gods are no longer powerful. Man can do what the gods once did and do it with the flick of a switch or the tap of a key. For Sedna to interfere there must be desperation."

"So these gods," I said, "they're really not that god-like?"

"Not in the minds of most people today—the gods cannot compete with technology."

I remembered Queen's comments about the gods that no one believed in anymore.

"Thousands of years of mythology gone to seed because of a smartphone," I said, sliding my palms together as if I were shaking off sand. "All those *god bless you's* and *god willings* and *god only knows*, all for naught."

"You make jokes, Mr. McNally," Demarais said. "I understand. But it is like a parent and a child. The parent provides the authority and the child accepts until the child realizes that the parent was once a child too. Then the aura of invincibility vanishes and the child no longer accepts. These days we can do what the believers in myth could never imagine. You can help, but it will not be easy. Still, if you try. Something good may come of it. For you."

"I have two simple goals, Mr. Demarais: getting paid and getting home in something other than a casket. I'll even forgo the first one."

"I know exactly what concerns you, Mr. McNally. As honest as you are, you lied about both. Only Linnie concerns you. I know why you need to get home. You asked what will happen with Derek Phillips. That answer will require one more day from you. In a life of so many days, that is not much to give."

"How did you know her name?"

"Maybe she will have more days than you think."

"I asked you a question. How did you know my wife's name?"

Demarais smiled. "You come to me expecting magic and then you question me when I pick the right card out of the deck? Listen to me. The gods, even if they are weak, will work *with* us, but not *for* us or independent of us. They no longer have any agenda except ours. They will not find Derek Phillips or lead you to him or carry him home in a golden chariot. But he has powers that can save you—maybe that is why he wishes not to be found."

"What if we do nothing?" I said. "What if Derek Phillips is allowed to disappear. Then what?"

"I think you know the answer to that," Demarais said.

"Actually, I don't. Tell me."

"It is difficult to survive in the Arctic without constant shelter and a food supply."

"Yes, I watch the Weather Channel. What happens to Derek Phillips?"

"He will be killed. I know that sounds cruel and...."

"Killed? You didn't say he would die, you said he would be killed. Who will kill him?"

"What kills mankind?"

"Stop," I said. "You're drifting again."

"Men with weapons," he said. "They kill mankind. I can't see their faces. But if you run the other way when the time comes, he may be saved after all."

"Run what other way?"

"As I said, when the time comes."

"More metaphor?"

"No. And I don't see the future," he said. "I see *a* future, but many are possible. One will come about because of your anger, Mr. McNally. Another because of fear. Concern. Uncertainty. They will all be different. But the first one—the one where you just go home—you will not like that one. You who hate failure—you will rationalize it and survive—but you will always hate it."

"So," I said—and I'm sure I looked pretty foul by then—"that means going back to Autumn."

"At least that," Demarais said. "At the very least, that. You know I cannot come with you, but if you are doing the right thing, maybe there will be help."

"Will Sedna plow the road for us?" I asked.

"She would never stoop. But maybe the Tuniit will pitch in."

"Do I get a wish?"

"Not if you waste it on something frivolous or stupid like plowing the road when you already have a snowmobile. Maybe the Tuniit will know what you need more than you will."

"And we'll run the other way."

He nodded, then waved the flask.

"Empty," he said. "And it's not even noon."

CHAPTER 29

If Derek Phillips possessed some mystique, then his outer appearance gave no indication. And seated at a desk in a functional but spartan construction shack, behind folders and papers that seemed to have been scattered by a sudden breeze, he looked more like a harried Manhattan accountant at tax time than an ecological terrorist.

But that, apparently, was what he had become.

"You're McNally," he said, laying his hands squarely on the papers and partially covering them. It was one of the more ineffectual security measures I'd seen. "You're from America."

"Yes."

"The PI."

"Not a secret."

"And you brought a cop and my old working colleague for good measure. How are you, Olin?"

I'm not sure how Olin was, but he'd been damn good at getting us there, picking up that side trail and all. He wasn't quite so good at providing Phillips with a civil response, though I guess a grunt is better than a punch in the face. Phillips turned back toward me.

"At least you didn't claim it was nice to meet me," he said. "I would think after all this you'd probably like to forget you ever heard my name."

"After all what? How do you know what I've been through?"

But of course he knew. Standing nearby was my ex-partner Manitok, who I'm sure had provided every detail of what had occurred the past few days.

"Glad you're safe," I said to her. "Sorry I missed your going-away party. Was there cake?"

"I couldn't very well tell you," she said. "I thought when you realized I'd gone, you could go home and forget all about me."

"Oh, I plan to. You, Phillips, even Mason at the hotel. I plan on forgetting I ever heard your names...tomorrow, or maybe even later this afternoon if the sun doesn't explode and we have to suffer our remaining hours in...in this place."

"These are rather bleak accommodations," he admitted. "Manitok says you're the best."

"She would know: we were partners. A couple of investigators searching for the truth. A regular Nick and Nora Charles, minus the dog."

Nobody knew what I was talking about, and I actually found that oddly pleasurable, considering the circumstances. Right about then Olin seized on the opportunity to excoriate his sister for being what I guessed was the Inuit term for an asshole, then asked her (in English) when she was going to quit this bullshit and come home.

She took unusually mild offense at the accusation, a fair indication that she was at least uncertain about what she'd gotten herself into. I thought that was an opportune moment to replace Olin's reference to bullshit with the more worrisome but equally appropriate "industrial sabotage."

Phillips was quick to respond. "That's not what this is about," he said, "it's...."

I guess it would have been polite on my part to allow him to finish the sentence, but I'd already been duped by Manitok's snowmobile gambit, jerked around at Autumn, then regaled by the goofball rantings of Demarais. For a knowledgeable guy I felt stupid and I didn't like the feeling. So no, he didn't get to finish the sentence; instead he heard me repeat the term and insist that whatever lofty and humanitarian goals he and his accomplices had in mind (I liked *accomplices*—it added an extra tinge of criminality), blowing up others' property was a crime and usually meant prison. I even volunteered to be a witness at his trial—though if he had known how much I desired never to come back, he'd probably have laughed.

My second little tirade made me feel better, but there we were anyway, no closer to convincing Phillips of anything. If he didn't feel threatened by incarceration for the next twenty years, I didn't think I could shame him either, but I tried that next.

"Manitok trusts you," I said, "and based on everything I know about her, one of two things is true: either her judgment has become clouded by another emotion—which she denies, or you're a lot better person than I'm giving you credit for. Tell me, Phillips, are you that paragon when it comes to trust and honesty? Because so far I have you listed as a thief and a liar."

"Equivocator maybe."

"No, liar. Then there's that whole married-to-someone-else thing we got going. So you see, Mr. Phillips, your trusting Manitok's judgment that I'm the best is meaningless. In point of fact, I'm pretty good, and because I operate on the right side of the law, I know that industrial sabotage is a really bad thing in the eyes of the industry being sabotaged."

Phillips smiled. "She also says you don't pull punches."

"You know what else she says? Whatever she wants. So why is she sitting here while we talk about her as if she weren't here? Is it because I no longer confuse lies and facts and you do?"

I looked directly at Manitok who seemed neither defiant nor contrite. But since you always need a follow-up question handy, I stumbled forward.

"So really, Manitok, why did I need to be here? You knew where the missing person is. Why hire a PI to find him?"

She didn't answer. Nobody answered. Nobody needed to. I didn't ask the question out of curiosity; I asked it because I was angry. I had been little more than her re-entry ticket into Autumn. She needed a diversion—someone to make it appear that the search for Derek Phillips was legitimate. Hiring an investigator—from America no less—would prove to the residents of Baker Lake, and more important to Autumn Mines, that finding Phillips was an earnest attempt to save someone they all liked.

When I told them that, the lack of denial in that little shack was deafening. Of course by that time, Austin had figured it out too, and Olin would have if he hadn't been even angrier than I was.

"I'll give you this, Phillips," I said. "You played it out to the end—another trip up here, this time with a cop and a witness. An unarmed cop, I might add. So if the Autumn militia drives by armed to the teeth—which appears to be their wont—who saves us from being killed?"

"You're not in danger here. We can defend ourselves."

"With what, your inherent goodness? Against an attack by a private army with high-powered rifles? Or against civil authorities who plan to arrest you for trespassing and sabotage, maybe eco-terrorism?"

At that, Phillips took notice, and even Manitok looked uncomfortable. Finally. Finally.

"Why would you...?" she began, but she didn't get to finish either.

"Why would I think that? Because I'm conscious and observant? I don't have to be a hotshot PI to see what's going on here. Where's Queen with the explosives?"

"He's not here."

"No, of course not, because Queen doesn't care what he says and who hears it. He's probably locked up somewhere, but he's done his job right? He got you the stuff you needed."

"He'll be taken care of. We're not going to just cut him loose," Phillips said.

"We? Who's we? You and Manitok?"

"There are others."

"Good. Good. Having friends in prison makes the days pass more pleasantly. I figure there'll be about 6,000 of those days. How about you MPP Austin? What's your guess."

"Sounds about right," she said, "though with the government tilting right, you never know what kind of judge will be making that decision."

"And through all this," I said, "you're going to protect Jeremiah Queen. Honor among...among what? What are you calling yourselves?"

"We're just...people...we're trying to prevent an ecological disaster."

"Describe it. You insist on getting your story out. Go ahead. Maybe when this is over one of us will be alive to tell it."

"You'll be alive, Mr. McNally," Phillips said.

"So then, tale of woe? Begin. It's about oil, right?"

"Of course it is. An oil extraction area this close to a major waterway is asking for trouble. One accident and Tehek will be ruined."

"A lake," Austin said. "One lake."

I was beginning to feel I had planted a flag in the moral high ground, but that answer, diminishing the importance of one lake, was wrong. I knew what Phillips would say (and Manitok and her brother would probably agree) so I backtracked.

"I understand," I said. "I really do. I believe the earth is warming. That the Arctic will suffer first. I believe we're responsible. And I believe that as long as it's profitable for a company like Autumn to make a profit, they're not going to care about some lake, or some river, or some ocean. I get all that. But what you're doing here is only symbolic. The real fight is being lost."

"Every first battle is symbolic—from your Lexington and Concord to Pearl Harbor to 9/11. They're declarations. This will be a declaration."

"People die in these declarations. People who didn't sign on for your cause."

"You're talking about yourself. I assured you...."

"...and aside from that, you have three kids at home. You haven't been much of a father to them but...."

"Watch yourself, McNally. You may be an old man, but I'm not above punching your face in."

"You're not really *above* anything, I imagine, but anytime you're willing to try, you know where to find me. But of course you do—you tricked me into coming here."

"All right stop!" It was Manitok, rousing herself out of the chair. "First off," she said, "we have weapons to defend ourselves."

She slid open a cabinet door. Behind it was a cache of guns, mostly rifles it looked like, but I'm not the best identifier of weaponry.

"Ah, a firefight," I said. "That should keep everybody warm and safe."

"The purpose of having weapons is to keep others from using theirs," she said.

"God, Manitok, what planet are you from? The purpose of having weapons is to kill things. You don't make a statement with a gun, unless it's 'look at me—I have a gun.' "

"Maybe in the United States. We are more disciplined than you are."

"You know, you might be right as a nation. But that's not going to matter when individuals are concerned. Like profit and loss. Whatever scheme you've got planned here is going to cost Autumn millions. Now maybe they can afford it, but affording it is never the issue. Only profits count."

"So your advice is what? Give up. Let this area be turned into a sludgy mess?"

"Exactly. Hop on our snowmobiles and head back to Baker Lake. You don't have to turn yourselves in. All you're doing is trespassing. No one's going to execute you for that. A good heartfelt *I'm sorry* ought to do it. And then expose this...this secret project. Let people know what's going on. Go through channels."

And I waited. Not for agreement or acceptance—that wasn't happening. I wanted to know where this went, beyond a storeroom full of rifles and some nebulous plan to impede an environmental disaster. I had already connected the dots—now I needed someone to color in the picture of this cockamamie plot.

"Or," I said, "do you just go ahead and blow up the place?"

"How do you know that?" Phillips asked, but he didn't seem upset that some major secret had been divulged. It sounded like a simple question, so I mentioned Jeremiah Queen. He was the procurer of the explosives, maybe of the weapons too. He may have had a lot of legitimate connections through whom he bought supplies for Autumn, but someone like Queen knew the other side of the law too and would not be reticent about straddling the line or drifting back and forth.

"But there's the problem, right?" I said to Phillips, "Queen provided the material but now he's not here to set it up."

"We don't need him anymore," Manitok said. "He fulfilled his responsibilities. And it was all legit. The explosives he sent here are exactly what was needed for early blasting. Autumn was fully aware."

"Were they?" I said. "Of amounts?"

"Not always."

"Not ever. And all the extra explosives. How did you get it here? Who fudged the paperwork, convinced the suppliers and the transporters that everything matched up?"

"It's all right here," Manitok said. She waved some papers—they looked like schemata and I was able to guess at the rest.

"That's us, right? I mean that's where we're standing. And scattered around us is all the explosives that Whitton couldn't keep track of. He told us he didn't know what was what but...what was it, Manitok?...they keep requesting and he keeps ordering? How did you get it from there to here?"

"We had help," Phillips said.

"Yes, the local indigenous people. The Tuniit. That brings everything to a proper conclusion. I'm the reliable witness, and I'll tell the story. And if I mention the Tuniit, people will say I've lost my mind, so I won't; and they'll pay attention only to what happened. Of course Ms. Austin here probably wants to arrest you, while Olin is formulating a way to break your neck—for any number of reasons, including sleeping with his sister. So of the three people you coerced into coming here, I'm the only one serving a purpose."

"I never slept with his sister," Phillips said, then turned to Olin, adding, "you know that. As for the rest, let me have you read something."

He reached into a carton of detritus on the floor and pulled out a folded sheath of papers.

"Is this your manifesto? Are you the new Unabomber?" I said.

"It didn't end well for him," Phillips answered. "I don't plan to hurt anybody."

"The road to hell," I said. "Let's see what you have."

CHAPTER 30

Experts always claim that, as we age, we need new experiences to maintain some degree of vitality. I probably satisfied that requirement by leaving a comfortable home in New York to end up in Nunavut which, until 1999, didn't even have a name. It was on the first day of that month that the Nunavut Land Claims Agreement was signed and Nunavut was born.

April 1.

Of course, the April fool, some might say, would arrive twenty years later in the guise of a sixty-year-old retired PI. I might agree

Irrespective of its birth, Nunavut is huge, constituting twenty percent of Canada itself: it extends from a few sea miles northwest of Quebec all the way to the Pole. Eight-hundred thousand square miles. Larger than Alaska and about as sparsely populated as Antarctica—about twenty people per square mile. If you want to put that in perspective, New York City where I prefer to find my miscreants contains about twenty-seven thousand people per square mile. And not to put too fine a point on it, but take away the ten largest towns in Nunavut and you have about 5,000 people left in the entire territory. We weren't currently in one of those towns—we weren't even close to one.

We had five people, one of them holding out a sheath of papers that would explain everything. Our own Rosetta Stone, Arctic version.

"Mr. McNally," Phillips said, spreading them out, "I understand you had a little earthquake at Autumn. Is that true?"

"Whitton said it was blasting, but I knew the difference."

"Do you know that this is an earthquake zone?"

"If I did, I've forgotten."

"We have little jolts all the time—kinda remind us where we are. If Autumn's plan was to drill for oil in an earthquake zone, I wouldn't necessarily oppose it. Drilling for oil wouldn't make it worse."

"What are you saying?"

"I'm saying the land could withstand drilling: it couldn't withstand natural gas extraction."

"You're changing the rules, Phillips."

"Some estimates claim there's twenty trillion cubic feet of the stuff down there."

"How many Olympic swimming pools is that?"

"Several—that would be my guess. Or think of a box five miles on each side filled with natural gas."

"We better get it out before it explodes."

"I'm glad you maintained your sense of humor, Mr. McNally. You'll have to forgive us if we take it more personally.

"It's the means of extraction," I said. "That's what worries you."

Fracking of course. Anyone following the news—and especially anyone living in Oklahoma—would have known that the daily, sometimes hourly earthquakes in that state were the direct result of cracking the earth's crust on a continuing basis. Some of the companies extracting the gas denied it, but recent rules restricting the pumping of water into the earth seemed to verify that it was true: fracking made for unstable ground, and though the earthquakes were not spontaneous seismological events involving a shifting plate, when the earth shakes, the people feeling it don't care why.

And worse, Oklahoma was not much of an earthquake zone. If, as Phillips said, the area around Tehek was prone to quakes, then injecting billions of gallons of water into the earth would only exacerbate the situation. And all that water had to come from somewhere, oh maybe a nearby lake whose surrounding area has some mystical significance? And when that dried up, maybe Baker Lake itself.

"So now what?" I asked him. "We're here. You're here. Whitton should be here shortly unless he's totally unconscious, which he isn't." I pointed to the papers. "And these papers? Do I have to read them all?"

"No," Phillips said. "Take them. Share them with friends. It's a summary of Autumn's Mid-Decades Plan. Mid-Decades," he repeated. "They plan to screw with us for a long time."

"I'm not sure what I'm doing here. If Whitton—anybody—knows what you're doing, they're not going to give us a free ride home, not with this material, not with you holding this over their heads. And if you have a story to tell, why not do it? Let the authorities handle it."

"These authorities," he said. "Don't you think they're involved? The way things work in America is the way they work everywhere. As for telling my story, that might have worked if all you people weren't looking for me."

We all looked at Manitok.

"It's not worth being a martyr for," she said, her tone more defensive than angry.

"I have no intention of being one," Phillips said. "I didn't plan to blow myself up."

"But one way or the other you'll be caught," she said, "and there'll be prison, and you still have a family."

"Nikki's a good woman and I haven't been much of a husband. Maybe a decent father, part time."

"Your daughter," I said, "Regina—she needs you."

He laughed. "She's six going on twenty-six. Her mother knows how to handle her. They'll leave Baker soon enough: insurance money, savings, Nikki comes from money. She'll remarry for sure, and she'll have a good life."

"And you," I said. "What will your life be?"

"If there's a trial, I'll have a forum to speak out against exploiters like Autumn."

I was skeptical.

"Ten years ago, even five," I said, "I'd have agreed. I'd have said that exposing the greed of a company like that—of exposing its lack of responsibility for the environment and its disdain for life in general—was a noble gesture. Not long ago that would have worked. But the world has changed. In America they want to open the Alaskan wilderness for oil exploration, they want to drill offshore, they want to burn coal and send men down to dig it up. I don't know, Phillips. You may find that your grand gesture can't compete with stockholders' profits."

"I know that," he said. "That's why this needs to be stopped now. We are headed in the wrong direction, but this applies the brakes, or maybe pumps them. Even if it's only a delay, it will give people a chance to reconsider. I'm not a zealot, Mr. McNally, but I'm not ignorant either. Autumn could run a fracking operation for the next fifty years and never have an incident, or they could create a magnitude-7 quake the first day, one that ruptures a pipeline and ruins Tehek and every small lake between here and Baker. And there are thousands of them."

"And eventually Baker Lake itself."

"So you see...?"

I looked at Austin. "You're the law," I said. "With what you know—and maybe knew already—couldn't you have...I don't know...forestalled this whole thing?"

"The law can't act on rumor," she said. "I don't have the manpower to conduct large-scale investigations."

"All due respect, Ms. Austin," I said, "this is the worst kept secret since the last solar eclipse: you'd be hard-pressed to miss it. And if it was just a rumor but you felt it had some credibility, why not alert the authorities in Toronto?"

"Iqaluit is our capital."

"I meant the national capital."

"That's Ottawa."

"Whatever," I said, my patience long since vanished. "You're not a Third World country. You have laws and people to enforce them."

"All due respect to you and *your* country, Mr. McNally, how many environmental reports cross your president's desk claiming that a new pipeline will have adverse effects on the environment? And then who decides whether the study is convincing? And then what fossil fuel lobbyist makes the ultimate decision? You think it's different up here? We inherited more than McDonald's from America. Speaking of which," she added, turning to Phillips, "in America the filthiest fossil fuel known to man is making a comeback...and you think this little display will matter?"

"But factor in the earthquakes."

She was adamant. "Factor in Oklahoma. You're not naïve. Why do I have to point this out to you? Fracking equals jobs equals money."

"Tell me something," I said to Phillips after she'd softened him up. "How long before we're discovered here?"

"With surveillance and patrols," Phillips said. "I'd say word would have gotten back to Whitton by now that there were trespassers at the site. In fifteen, twenty minutes, we should have company."

"Coming in the same way we did," I said, "which means if we leave, we meet them on the road. This was a great scheme you came up with. First we get the lowdown on your little eco-terrorism cadre, then I get to read why you're not really criminals but environmentalists, then on my way to tell your story I'm gunned down by goons on snowmobiles. *Goons on snowmobiles*— when they make the movie...."

"You'll be gone before that, Mr. McNally. Everyone will be gone except me."

"And by *gone*, you mean...."

"Safe."

"And this is where the fairies and spirits come in?"

"No, this is where the compass comes in. You leave to the east."

I looked at Austin whom I still trusted a little. She shook her head. "Nothing that way," she said. "Just a big loop that would make it easier for Whitton to nab us somewhere even more remote."

"East, toward the lake," Phillips insisted. "But you can't spend time deciding. Take those papers and go. You, Ms. Austin, you make sure these go through the proper channels, get to Iqaluit at least."

"I have connections in Ottawa," she said, "but again...."

"They may die there. I get it. Take them anyway."

The casual pace had turned frenetic.

"Okay wait," I said to Phillips. "This is all a wonderful plan and we're all gonna show those bad guys at Autumn how smart we are. But you, with a wife and three kids?"

"I already told you."

"I don't think you understand that whole parenting thing. Beyond that basic misconception, forever is a really long time when you have kids. And insurance companies don't stay in business by blindly drafting checks to policyholders. They investigate. Want to know how I know? I've done their dirty work. You really think that when this is all over, nobody here will ever have to testify under oath that your death was not a suicide? If they ask me,

I'm not going to lie for you. So what happens when the policy is revoked, or diminished? Your wife's money going to save everyone?"

"I've read the policy thoroughly."

"And your lawyer?"

"I don't have one."

"Ah, insurance fraud. Never mind *Goons on Snowmobiles*; here's your movie...except they've already made it a dozen times. So put on your parka, Mr. Phillips, we're all going back to Baker Lake to hire an attorney."

He said no, of course, but I had put the doubt into his head and I was watching it fester. And I was right, too. I'd been hired by insurance companies—by companies of all kinds—to investigate the veracity of some employee's claim. But there was another reason I came on a little strong: I'd come up here to find Derek Phillips—I suppose at that moment I could have left and claimed to have done my job. But implicit in my being hired was not only that I find him, but if he were alive, I was to return him home. I didn't want another failure: I didn't want to agonize over steps I could have taken or ways I'd fallen short. I'd done that in 2009 and it still annoyed me.

While Phillips was still contemplating, I piled on.

"Maybe you think that this will be a job-related incident and Autumn will be on the hook for your family. Again, too many witnesses."

I did have an ally of sorts in Marianne Austin. She was quick to verify what I'd said, emphasizing the perjury angle. She was not willing to relinquish her position with the government just to save an insurance policy. I was beginning to like her more, maybe not as much as Mason or in the same way, but she was quick.

Phillips went silent. An amateur would have taken that as a good sign, but I'm not an amateur: I had passed the point where I was getting through. It's hard to explain, but I'm sure trial lawyers know this—that there's a moment when you've just barely convinced a jury and you'd like everything to stop right there—but it never does, and you lose them, and it's over. I could see that same process occurring in Derek Phillips. I even knew why.

"A lot of planning, right?" I said. "And you can't let it go to waste?"

"It's important," he said. "It's a statement I have to make. We all do. If I leave now and this project proceeds, it'll be one more embarrassment for

Nunavut—we'll become another group willing to trade integrity for cash. Someone has to stay here and, you know..."

"Blow it all up."

He nodded.

I looked at Manitok: she seemed a little less resolute, but I think she was willing to stay, to carry out the assignment, to face arrest and imprisonment, if not death from whatever explosives had been planted.

"Olin," I said, "help me out here."

I think at the time—and this was probably ludicrous—I was counting on his physical strength to intimidate everyone and make them leave. But I also saw something else in him. Behind his gruffness and abrasiveness, there lay a spiritual depth—something I was hoping he might plumb at that moment. He was struggling with it all and his silence had not resulted from lack of interest. His sister was in danger and he wasn't sure he could convince her to save herself. Beyond that he wasn't sure he could save even his own self with her life in danger.

"Derek," he said, "you didn't do all this alone. You had help."

"Olin," I said to him. "This is not the time...."

"Let me finish. You are breaking the law, Derek. You will admit that, right?"

"If the law is...."

"Can you admit that?"

"Yes, I am breaking the law."

"Of the land."

"What other law is there?"

"Obviously your decision to go forward means that there is some other set of rules that you hold more binding. What are they?"

"You know what they are, Olin. They're the law of our people."

"Our? You're an American. Have you adopted the Inuit?"

"I believe in the spirit of...of your people."

"You can say *our*—I don't mind. But *our* people don't abandon their families. Never. If you leave Nikki and the kids to fend for themselves, *our* people will not be happy. Neither will their gods."

"Those gods are not famous for their happiness," Phillips said. Olin smiled. Even I, who had been there only a couple of days, got the joke.

"I'll give you that, but they will help. They've already helped. You haven't been able to haul explosives, to set up shop, to develop this scheme without help from the Tuniit. Am I right?"

"I don't know. Those times when my mind wanders—when time slows down...I don't know. I suppose they have helped."

"Then let them help now. They don't want you to die or rot away in prison. They don't want my sister to suffer. They don't want your children to have no father. I'm sure Ms. Austin here is not going to arrest you, and McNally just wants to go home."

"He's right," I said with an inappropriate but nervous grin, "Anywhere south is fine."

"We're settled then," Olin said.

Phillips frowned. "How?"

"The Tuniit will finish the job. Simple as that. What is it, a switch, a plunger, a code?"

"It's complicated."

"Derek. They're living inside your head. They'll figure it out. Now let's get out of here."

I thought maybe we had him convinced when his phone chirped. The call lasted only a few seconds, just long enough to undo every argument Olin had made.

"They're five minutes out," Phillips said.

I was astonished. "And they called to tell you?"

"Whitton. He's coming alone."

And there it was—the moment we had the jury won over—and then the moment vanished. Phillips took out his cell phone and made a few taps. Fifteen minutes," he said, "the clock is moving. This area will look much different after that, but we'll hear him out."

"We should," I said. As obvious as that sounds, I felt the need to say so, especially since I thought Phillips's new plan *du jour* may have involved shooting Whitton off his snowmobile.

CHAPTER 31

"We don't want a war," Whitton said. He had seen the scattering of weapons and wanted us to know. "I came alone."

He seemed neither surprised nor angry at what presented itself. His shrug was so noticeable, I almost felt he was in on it. He wasn't.

"We had a deal," he said, singling out Phillips. "I trusted you."

He didn't seem particularly saddened by Phillips's disloyalty; in fact, he looked like someone who had been told he had been sentenced to thirty years in prison, only to have the judge admit a mistake and extend it to thirty-one. He glanced about the room, saw me and nodded.

"A PI," he said. "I guess I shouldn't be surprised to see you here, but really, with all that's happening in your life, why this?"

"Kind of along for the ride," I said. I was about to add that I had no dog in the race, but even if it was true, I had become part of the story, or maybe more accurately, part of a group that was creating the story which, for the first time, I actually understood. So instead of separating myself from the others, I threw in with them. "Maybe the deal you had...maybe it was a bad deal."

"There's no such thing," Whitton said. "There's only the deal, and it affects people differently. This one would have injected a lot of money into this area. It would have created more jobs—some of them right in Baker."

"Right," Manitok said. "Those would be the ones throwing buoys on the lake to contain the oil spills."

Whitton shook his head.

"We're not looking for oil."

"No but every ship with every diesel engine that plows into Baker Lake will be spewing the stuff into the water."

Whitton shook his head. "God, I love the black-and-white world of the social activist. Oil bad. Water good. And when you burn oil to run a filtration plant to purify water for drinking, then your brain explodes from the complexity."

"Why not use solar or wind to run that filtration plant?" Manitok said.

"Or use whale oil for lamps? That's exactly what I mean," he said. "Your vision is a lake covered with a film of oil twelve months of the year, dead fish everywhere, the ones still alive scrawny and polluted, a smell of petroleum fouling the air. Is that about right, Manitok? Derek was never an environmentalist. Was his transformation your doing?"

"Nothing is ever that simple," she said.

"I agree. I really do. And yet, you've simplified this into good guys and bad guys. Your town does okay, but you have those shacks near the lake that fishermen use in the summer. You know there are people living there all year, burning scrap wood for heat, finding bits of food where they can. Maybe some of them would like jobs containing an oil spill, or operating machinery that prevented the spill in the first place."

"Who's going to prevent the earthquakes?" Manitok said

"That hasn't been proven."

"Maybe not in *Fracking Monthly* or whatever bullshit you read, but anybody within miles of a fracking operation knows the truth. Besides, if this is such a benefit to the community," she said, "why the secrecy? Why not call together the citizens of Baker and say look, we have a plan to extract natural gas near Tehek and build a pipeline to the town. Here are the pros and cons, the advantages and drawbacks, here's what you gain and what you lose."

Whitton laughed. "Look around you," he said. "Now you tell me why we were secretive, especially at the beginning. Eventually there would have been time for that," Whitton said. "Nothing moves forward without leases and licenses, government endorsement."

"Where is your lease for drilling here?"

"It will come. Authorizations come slow, but they come."

"And once the government gives the okay," Manitok said, "the will of the people becomes secondary."

"The will of the people," Whitton said, his sarcasm obvious. "Ask the workers at Autumn what their goals are, and they'll all tell you—make enough money to get out of here, to move somewhere else—anywhere else. You and your brother like it here, and that's fine. But you're in the minority. Ask the PI here what he thinks of Baker Lake after a few days. Ready to pick up and move your family here, McNally?"

"Where I want to live is not the question," I said. "It's where these people want to live and the conditions under which they'll live there. You have to give people the right to choose."

"They'll still live there," Whitton said, shaking his head. "This isn't even about Baker Lake, right? It's about Tehek, which is, if you'll pardon my lack of sentimentality, a giant block of ice that—according to some, not all—marks a sacred land area. That's what this is about. In your country, McNally, people vote against their own best interest all the time, then complain that the politicians don't help them. You have a minority government and the majority of people bend to its will."

"That can happen in a democracy."

"I respectfully submit that, in a democracy that does *not* happen. Look up the word."

The pitch of his voice was rising with his anger: he made an obvious effort to slow himself down.

"This project," he said quietly, "will proceed with or without your help. There are more personnel coming behind me, but I told them to wait until I could talk to you. Now I've done that—now you have to leave."

Phillips had been silent during most of the previous conversation, but now he spoke up.

"The project will not go on. You're drilling on public property on the expectation of leases and authorizations. Sorry, this project is done. You may start over again after today, but even then, it will never succeed."

"Derek," Whitton said, "I stopped using the word *never* a long time ago. You can impede progress, shut us down, but at what cost? And eventually when we're up and running, the stockholders won't absorb the extra expense: you will. And some guy in Calgary or Winnipeg filling up his gas tank will spend an extra dollar or two—multiplied by a few million...a day. When that guy is grousing about petroleum prices, you won't be his hero, you might not even be your own."

"I don't plan to be a hero."

"Good, then do what you have to do. Everything here—equipment, structures—it's all replaceable. Just don't kill anybody along the way, or Ms.

Austin here—who I believe is still paid to enforce the law—will hunt you down."

We all looked at her as if she held the key to everything. She didn't. If anyone did, it was Phillips, and he'd been sitting like some implacable Buddha during the entire exchange. Then he stood and faced Whitton.

"Where's Jeremiah Queen?"

Whitton was unfazed. "That isn't any of your business."

"Churchill? Or did you get him to Toronto already?"

"It doesn't matter. His tenure with us is over."

"He was good at what he did, wasn't he?"

"I'm not going to waste time talking about...."

"He told me that you were afraid to walk into the explosives storage area because you feared static electricity setting off charges. Is that true?"

Whitton stared at him but didn't answer. It was exactly what Queen had told me.

"I'll take that as a yes," Phillips said. "I can understand being skittish, but then you never delegated the inspection responsibility, just trusted Queen to keep everything up to date. He gave you a weekly summary that you never verified. You might want to delegate when you get back."

"What are you saying? Queen was skimming explosives? For what possible reason?" "You're standing on it," Phillips said. "Or near it."

"No," Whitton said. "Even if he had access, no possible way he could get it here, not without every guard and a hundred surveillance cameras monitoring everything."

"Wow," I said. It wasn't the most imaginative expletive I'd ever come up with, but I wasn't only surprised, I was impressed.

"So it's true."

"Ah," Phillips said. "A believer."

"In what?" Whitton's calm demeanor had returned.

"He had help," I said. "The supplies got from there to here by...oh...less than traditional methods."

Whitton exhaled. "Whew," he said, "I thought you really...so even a hard-nosed PI like you has bought into the local legends. That's kind of nice in a way, this spreading of cultures. Very...global. On the other hand, it's bad enough there are locals who believe it—we don't need visitors from foreign countries signing on to it."

"I wouldn't bet against it. Neither should you. Do you have a method for evacuating your workers?"

"We have only a skeleton crew."

"That phrase may be more meaningful than you think if you don't get them out of here."

"Oh, please, McNally,"

"He's right," Phillips said. "I'm not bluffing."

"No, I just think you're wrong. You may have stolen all kinds of paraphernalia from me, but you'll find that most of it is back at Autumn. Do you really think an organization this big would allow some penny-ante thief to sabotage us? Believe me, Phillips, I understand why you did it, and I'm not unsympathetic to whatever misguided cause you adhere to. But I'm not an idiot, and the other workers here are not idiots. Every controversial project expects this kind of thing, and we all provide for it. My crew is especially good. I could give you some names, but I won't. So anyway, push the button and send us all to our maker. Or just come quietly before you do any damage. Yes you'll face some conspiracy charges, maybe burglary, maybe trespassing if I feel particularly vindictive...which right now I don't."

Phillips stared at his phone as if it had suddenly become toxic.

I thought he was about ready to test Whitton.

"Don't," I said. "You have nothing to gain."

"On the contrary," Whitton said, "he has a lot. What's *conspiracy* now becomes *attempted murder* as soon as he pushes the button, even when it fails to work."

"It won't fail," I said.

"Based on what?"

"Jody."

"Who the hell is...you don't mean Jody Brackett? My receptionist? She's a ...she's a receptionist." He laughed. "Don't tell me she's a munitions expert. I guess I'm not paying her enough."

"She doesn't like you," I said. "Not many people do. Any loyalty you enjoy comes from paychecks you sign. And even then...."

"We're running a business here, not a popularity contest. You should know that. A self- employed PI," he scoffed. "How many people like you?"

"Very few, I'd say. But at least I figure that into my computations. You seem to think that a paycheck buys loyalty. It buys work, that's all. And most of your workforce, what are they? Locals with dreams of getting out. But you know what's funny, everybody wants to get out of Podunk, but god help you if you do anything to mess with that home town."

"You're new here McNally…"

"I stopped him.

"It's not *here*," I said. "It's anywhere. Phillips pushes the button and I'm betting on local pride to beat out whatever checks you've been signing. What do you think?"

Whitton was still dubious until Olin high-fived me. It was totally inappropriate and even silly, since I had to reach to find his hand. But I understood it, and the gesture from this otherwise stolid observer convinced Whitton more than anything anyone had said.

"How much time?" I asked Phillips. "Eight and change," he said. "Time to go."

CHAPTER 32

"Call this off," Whitton said, motioning toward Austin. "All the bluffing and bullshit. Do your job, officer."

"What would that be at this particular time, Mr. Whitton?" she said with obvious sarcasm. "Shall I confiscate Mr. Phillips's phone? But then if he's not bluffing, well...you tell me, Mr. Whitton. What's my next move?"

Whitton, disgusted, turned back to Phillips.

"Call this off. Punch in whatever code, number, just do it."

"Can't," Phillips said. "It's a twenty-number randomly generated combination that I should have memorized. I forgot."

Queen's little joke. If I had any doubts before that they had collaborated, the little doomsday line confirmed it.

"You can call in your stormtroopers," I said. "But there is another option."

"I'd like to hear it," Whitton said. He kept glancing at the door as if any moment a band of gun-wielding assassins would burst through. I wasn't convinced he was wrong.

"Simple. You go back and meet your reinforcements; we go the other way."

"East?"

"Yes."

"I wish you luck, McNally. East of here is nothing but frozen lakes and tundra. It'll be a smooth ride to oblivion. Nobody will ever find your bodies or your machines."

"He's right," Manitok said. "Those things I said about outposts—that's just rumor, maybe even legend. There is nothing east of here for five-hundred kilometers. Coral Harbor is the closest thing to another hamlet and we would get nowhere near there on a few gallons of fuel."

The evidence was daunting, but I remembered Demarais's words. Despite that affinity for vodka, there was something convincing about him. Besides, there seemed no other way for me to convince Phillips to get out of there, though convincing the others that Demarais was not some kook with a drinking habit was not going to be easy. Then my new friend Olin stepped up again. "I trust Demarais," he said. His size seemed to endow him with credibility I couldn't project.

"Brother," Manitok said, "that's a mistake."

"No, hear me out. Manitok, you explain to me—and you've seen Autumn and the security around it and you know the distance from there to here—tell me how Phillips moved explosives here."

"He didn't because they're not here," Whitton yelled. "This is all just...just a ruse. Blackmail."

"They're here," Olin said. "I never liked Phillips here, too weird for my liking. And other reasons. But he's not a liar, and he's not a fool. If he says this place is going up, it's going up. And if Demarais says go east, for whatever reason, I'm going east."

"Northward," Whitton said. "That's what they call it when the snow blindness and the cold and the infernal darkness collaborate to screw with your mind. Northward, all of you. Doesn't matter what compass direction you choose. Go. Maybe your Tuniit will guide you home safely. I hope so."

"Either you believe or you don't," Olin said.

Manitok looked dismayed.

"I believe you may be right, or you believe it, but going off in the wrong direction? Why?"

"You, sister, you with your faithfulness to Inuit traditions and always busting my chops for my Anglo name, why are you the doubter here?"

She was silent.

"I think I know," I said, though this was all new to me. "If there's a death here—if there's a martyr or two—people will have a name to attach to this protest. It's easier that way to rally support."

"We don't plan to die," Manitok said. "If we're arrested...."

"Your plans may differ from Autumn's," Whitton said. "I may have some authority at the mine, but Autumn is run by people who don't know who I am, who don't know who you are, and who don't care about either of us. A few deaths in the unforgiving Arctic? Who's going to notice? Blame it on the elements. Go. All of you. Go with my blessing. Put your faith in the supernatural and some old alcoholic. Be my guest. And you, McNally, any last words for your wife who's home waiting for you?"

"Tell her I'll be home day after tomorrow. Maybe you can get me to Churchill on that god-awful plane of yours. It would make things easier."

Whitton looked more sad than angry.

"This is your choice. It's not the one I'd have made. But I have to make a decision. He picked up his cell phone.

"You can come now," he said. "Weapons down."

"How far out are they?" Manitok said.

"Five minutes."

We started adding layers of clothing, all except Phillips.

"You're coming too," I said.

"No, I'm not. And the time you waste trying to convince me brings you closer to disaster. You did your job, Manitok—you got everybody here. Now get them out. Listen to the American. Go east and cross Tehek. You can pick up the trail again."

The American. Out of nowhere I had become a character in a le Carré novel, but without the subtlety and ambiguity, certainly without the determination. Or maybe I was the ugly American and my new designation was dismissive rather than complimentary. I did consider, as I always did, my previous failure, the deceit that got me here, and—this is the least surprising part—Linnie. She was dying—a little sentence I always had trouble saying or even considering—but she was. Months maybe? The first warm day of spring? Some afternoon during a summer shower? Her survival to the point where the leaves fell again seemed impossible. And here I was wasting hours on a hopeless cause. But in my mind, either fevered or frozen—I could no longer tell which—I tied her survival to Phillips's. If I arrived home and confessed failure again, it would make her final days worse. She wanted us to enjoy something together at the end, when everything else had been stripped away; and though it would be easy to say that the accomplishment would be mine alone, the recollecting and the celebration might very well become our last shared joy.

To get to that point, I had to trust Demarais. And I had to trust someone else too.

"Olin," I said. "We're taking him."

The big man looked at me, and for a second there was doubt about what I intended, but it was only a second if that.

"Conscious?" he said.

"Six of one," I said.

He walked toward Phillips, towered over him.

"You're coming with us," Olin said. "Get dressed."

"Not happening," Phillips said, and pulled a gun from his pocket.

Olin laughed. "You're going to shoot me in front of my sister?"

In one movement, not particularly swift or surprising, he took the gun from Phillips. If he had squeezed it into a huge ball-bearing and thrown it out the door, I wouldn't have been shocked. Not too shocked anyway.

"Conscious or unconscious," Olin asked, this time to Phillips. "I can knock you out right here, throw some clothes on you, and strap you to a snowmobile. Or I can break one of your legs and leave you in such pain that you'll be begging for a ride. Or you can shut off that timer and we can all leave and follow the American out of here. What's it going to be?"

"I won't shut off the timer," Phillips said.

"Okay, one more time, conscious or...."

"I'll go," he said, then turned to Whitton. "Keep your men away. I won't be responsible for their deaths when this place blows."

"That story is stale," Whitton said, his reply unconvincing. I tried once more to strike some sort of deal.

"Maybe if the town were brought in on the plans...."

"Don't bother," Whitton said. "Too late to negotiate."

"Well then," Austin said—she was calmer than the rest of us I think. "We'll go east. Maybe hit the next sunrise."

"Can I remind you," Whitton said, "that you represent authority? You're paid to enforce the law."

"Public safety," she said. "If we stay here, we blow up. If we head west, we meet your...um...associates." She looked at Phillips. "We're waiting for an answer."

He looked defeated. "I said I'd go."

"And since you're taking the safest path," she said for Whitton's benefit, "I guess I'm doing my job. Mr. Whitton, last chance to come with us."

He shook his head.

"Okay," Austin said, "and you, Mr. Phillips, since you're the reason we're all here, you didn't answer Olin's question. What's it going to be?"

We waited for the answer. It came slowly, almost as if he were being coerced into pronouncing not only every syllable, but every letter, and every bit of white space between the letters.

At last we were able to leave.

Phillips dialed a number and we heard alarm horns. "Other workers," he said. "I won't have their deaths on my conscience."

We agreed...and Olin did not have to carry anyone.

CHAPTER 33

It's half a year now since I left Nunavut for the last time, and just as I'd planned it took two days to get home.

I never saw Hal Whitton again. For all his bluff and bluster about the fraudulence of Phillips's explosives, he didn't stick around either, heading west to meet his army while we left in the opposite direction, heeding the advice of a liquor-addled sage and the town giant. Even though I'm alive to tell about it, I still wonder why we made that decision.

Faith, Linnie would say.

I suppose.

Whitton though—he's no longer at Autumn Mines, at least not in Nunavut, but he's still with the company, having been repurposed somewhere in western Canada at one of the new oil fields in Alberta. I doubt if he has the same responsibilities with which Autumn entrusted him, but then allowing hundreds of pounds of stolen explosives to be transported from one site to another for the purpose of sabotage probably isn't what's called *padding a résumé*.

He made one last plea that day, a plea directly to me. I think he gave me credit for more influence than I possessed, but I think that inherent in the credit was some deep-seated belief that I would understand the need to access that natural gas, to build the profits of Autumn, to make life "better" for Baker Lake, for Nunavut, for Canada, for the world. I was, after all, an American. If anyone understood the need for material goods, it was me.

I don't wear a "What Would Jesus Do" bracelet or drop by the chapel on occasion to pray for guidance. (Actually I've never dropped by the chapel to pray for anything. I doubt I could find the nearest chapel—in Nunavut or Westchester.) But often my decisions are informed by Linnie's beliefs, and with the truth rising clearly before me—she would die before I would—I'd begun to wonder what she'd want me to do with the world she left. She's not a zealot, but she'd been talking about solar panels and green energy and been looking at hybrids before she became ill. I didn't think tapping a five-mile square cube of natural gas would jibe with her developing environmental consciousness, though she'd probably agree it beat hell out of coal and oil.

But Whitton still singled me out for the last plea that day.

"You got caught up in all this," he said, apparently unconcerned with the fact that others could hear. "Nobody will blame you if you come back with me, testify against these people."

These people carried a tinge of condescension and I called him on it.

"Don't *these people* keep the mining company humming?"

He was ready to provide a dismissive assessment of the locals' importance, but probably noticed Olin lurking nearby.

"What I mean is, well, we're talking about business. Americans understand that."

"Some maybe, especially the Americans getting screwed by it. And what would I be testifying to?

"Industrial sabotage, endangerment, robbery, maybe even fraud and assault. If anyone gets killed up here, even murder." The list was loud enough for all to hear. "You're a PI. You know how the courts can frame a crime, can make a case stand up or not. They would go easy—trust your judgment."

Of course they would. I'm not some primitive native type who believes in weird myths. I'm not Inuit. I'm white and speak English.

If I had stopped him right there and called him a bigot, he'd have been shocked. But it was bigotry with an added touch of paternalism. Whitton and I were the great white leaders who understood, like the principals who run Autumn—or who run the larger conglomerate that encompasses Autumn and would have overseen that new natural gas bonanza. They didn't have time for even tangential knowledge of the Tuniit: their concerns nestled comfortably on the bottom line.

I could have pointed that out to him and sounded pompous and condescending, but I didn't. Neither did I want to make him the scapegoat. He was going to have enough difficulty explaining the theft and movement of materials from a secure and well-guarded site without being somehow complicit...or unconscious. Even if Whitton did admit to some mythological or spiritual explanation—some supernatural force, utilizing it to excuse what happened did not seem like the route Whitton would take. He wasn't the bad guy—there doesn't always have to be a villain—but he was on the wrong track, whether he'd laid that track or not. Yes, he was doing the job assigned to him; it was just the wrong job.

I told him I understood, even agreed that a natural gas pipeline could bring jobs and money; but trying not to preach (I don't know if it was successful) I said that sometimes the tradeoff isn't tenable and that this was one of them.

And so I never saw Hal Whitton again. It didn't matter.

As for our escape, explaining it makes me sound inebriated or insane. Your choice. Linnie believes me—after a year she's still with us, or with me, and though it may sound like burying the lead, that's another story. That day we escaped, Linnie was the primary thought on my mind, though I did give some consideration to what it would be like wasting away in a Canadian jail or listening to my extremities freeze, shatter, and fall off one by one.

When the five of us lit out of there that afternoon, we found terrain much less forgiving than the trail from Baker; but fortunately, every time I drove one of those machines, I felt a little more comfortable. By that trip I was almost confident. Once we got off into the weeds a bit, we took it easy. It was still flat and open most of the time, but there was a rougher quality to it, maybe like some ranch road in the west. I guess it was even mountainous if you think of the mountains as being very low. Hilly then, but like the trail from Baker, providing wide vistas. That ability to see a great distance was both a blessing and a curse, I suppose, because I kept turning around to see who might be gaining on us, this despite the fact that Derek Phillips never insinuated that we were running for our lives. He didn't have to: I knew we were.

And so... east. Without a trail our path was a little more disorganized, but basically Olin led and I held up the rear, looking for trouble like Phillips peeling away from the little caravan and fulfilling his martyrdom complex. After a number of miles we came to Lake Tehek, a frozen expanse that stretched out far to the right. There was no discussion when we saw it—no expressions of awe or reverence. It was a skating pond, albeit a large one. Olin turned in that direction and we followed.

It was logical: south would take us back to Baker Lake. But even with that, our pursuers—if they were pursuing—had faster machines and would overtake us regardless. We pushed on.

The rough terrain disappeared as soon as we touched the lake of course, its glass-smooth surface dotted only with occasional wisps of powdery snow. We rode into the sun—a romantic end to an old western maybe, but not for us: the low angle as it scraped the horizon was by turns annoying and blinding, though there was something vaguely comforting about the light and the promise that it emanated some heat...somewhere...a thousand or so miles to the south.

I don't think I ever relinquished the fear that we were being chased, but until we arrived at Tehek, we hadn't actually seen our imagined pursuers. But with those widening vistas (and the fact that I kept scanning the horizon behind us, I guess) I saw them. Or I should say I saw someone. I pressed on the horn button and everyone slowed down.

"Behind us," I said, "not far from the lake."

"Too close," Olin said. "They have greater speed. Let's go."

Greater speed—faster bullets too, I thought, but kept that particular observation to myself.

I guess I—we—never heard the explosion, nor did that explosion have any effect on the group pursuing us. I wondered if Phillips had failed—if all that planning had wound up in a pointless detonation and, instead of becoming a martyr, would settle for a convict's outfit. And with us running for our lives, and likely to be caught, his failure would have been complete. I don't understand martyrdom, didn't then, never will. It's one thing for a soldier to understand the risks and fight for the cause anyway, but it's another thing to die deliberately. The only person I'd give up my life for is Linnie— I'd gladly give her my lungs and make do without them. Of course it doesn't work that way, though when I volunteered to do it, she said it was worth a shot and handed me her best paring knife.

But dying for some piece of land or a fading way of life? I don't get that. At the time I didn't have to: there were more pressing concerns.

Olin was pushing his machine as hard as he could, and we were struggling to keep up. We all leaned forward like frozen Tour de France riders, as if making ourselves aerodynamic was going to win the day. I kept remembering Demarais's assurance that we would be safe, an assurance that seemed less credible every time I glanced over my shoulder. Note to self: advice from people whose breakfast centers on vodka must be vetted more carefully. In the future. If there were to be one.

I did wonder what these pursuers would do to us when (and it was *when*, not *if*) they caught us. Would they take us back to Autumn or right to Baker Lake? Or would they just blast a hole in the ice and drop us through? After all, we had taken some obscure path: who would deny the possibility that we took a wrong turn, got hopelessly lost, ran out of fuel, and died? Or who could say for certainty that we weren't killed in the same explosion that shattered the oil field?

Just about then, things became a little indistinct. I say that because it's true, but also because when I consider what seems to have happened, it doesn't hold up under rational scrutiny. And for someone whose life revolved around verifiable facts, situations like that are uncomfortable. We did, in fact, reach the other side of Tehek, or I should say *an* other side. Tehek doesn't so much end as it dissolves into a mass of smaller lakes and ponds and what appear to be rivulets set in ever-more forbidding landscapes. That annoying sun wasn't quite so annoying when it served as a compass. So we reached *a* shore and looked behind us. I think we all expected our pursuers to be halfway across and gaining, but they had stopped at a spit of land and seemed to be stationary. Then I saw what looked to be little wavelets on the lake and a blueness I had not detected before. Frozen lakes don't have wavelets, or ripples, or movement—or to be succinct—water in liquid form. I don't say that to promote my keen sense of the obvious—I say it to remind myself that what I was apparently seeing made no conceivable sense.

The waters of Tehek had ended the pursuit.

Warm springs, Linnie said when I got home. And that remains her story a year later.

Must have been, I usually answer.

Bullshit I invariably tell myself.

I did a little geological research on the area around Tehek and learned that there's no history of volcanic activity in that area, and you're more likely to find superheated water near volcanos. Still, its being an earthquake zone makes the possibility slightly less remote. In Yellowstone where the temperature can get to fifty-below in the winter, there are springs and pools that never freeze—even the river that runs though the geyser and pool area does just that—runs. So it's entirely possible for a lake to do the same—to be influenced by underground hot springs and face some substantial warming. Of course there's also the little factor of the lake thawing completely in the thirty-odd seconds between our crossing it and our pursuers' arrival at the shore. Even Linnie felt that was a little harder to explain.

If there was some miraculous aspect to our escape, I'll have to accept it. These Tuniit, if they do exist, keep to themselves and don't erect billboards to promote their skills as lake-melters for hire. Or the variously-depicted Sedna—friend to man or raging lunatic—isn't handing out brochures advertising her magical powers. It's left to us, the non-deities, to explain the inexplicable, or failing that, to report what we saw.

I guess I can imagine these gods helping people like Derek Phillips with whom they might be aligned spiritually—to save the integrity of the land and all that. But they don't have a history of pulling off miracles, especially really ostentatious ones like that—I mean "parting of the Red Sea" ostentatious. Melting a lake on which the ice must be a meter thick is like...no, it's not like anything. Shifting a few billion liters of water like that is just Biblical—I'll leave it at that. (A *meter* thick—billions of *liters*—'Ich bin ein Canadian' after all. Some days, anyway.)

Nunavut mythologies are pretty complex and encompass countless different characters with varying skills. If I'm going to accept the Tuniit, then I have to double down and accept all the others, some of whom are very powerful. And this Sedna—maybe she has friends whose powers exceed what we would expect. One of them melts lakes—another one...well, I'll get to that.

That day we stood on the far banks of Tehek and watched the vanquished. If it had been a cartoon they'd all be shaking their fists at us, but Olin brought us back to a semblance of reality.

"They can still go around," he said. "They may lose twenty minutes, maybe a half hour. We're going to need all of that to stay ahead of them. Come on."

We didn't argue with him. I took one more look at the lake. The wind had died and a thin layer of ice was already visible near the shore. Whatever spell had been cast or magic had been worked, it apparently had an expiration date, or minute. It would be a while before the ice thickened again to traverse in a snowmobile, but we didn't have much of *a while*.

With Olin in the lead and me turning around once in a while to see what was gaining on us, we made it back to Baker on the main trail and passed a few buildings just as Manitok pointed skyward and a helicopter with the Autumn "A" emblazoned on the side broke over the last rise. I think we all had the same thought—they won't shoot us here—but to be safe we waved at every human being we saw until we reached the co-op.

The helicopter hovered nearby for a moment, banked left and flew off.

CHAPTER 34

Once inside the co-op we pretty much forgot that the snowmobiles and the clothing had to be returned.

"I'll throw Ricard another twenty," Manitok said. "He'll survive the inconvenience."

But Olin volunteered instead: he didn't want to hang around for the post-mortem: I didn't blame him.

Manitok, though—I was trying to read her, to figure out if she was happy that Phillips had eschewed martyrdom, or disappointed that there had not been a grand spectacle to underscore the abuse planned for her community. Autumn had little interest in heritage or tradition—Inuit history would not be boosting profits for any conglomerates in the near future. Of course there might very well have been quite a spectacle when the explosives detonated, but at most Autumn would have lost a few months of work, only to be back at it—with heightened security—in short order. Someone more discerning— maybe more observant—than Hal Whitton would be at the helm, but those trillions of cubic feet of natural gas would not be ignored.

I never saw Marianne Austin's report, but she was anxious to get something on paper. She was justifiably nervous that the powers at Autumn were not through with us and that there might come some retaliation for her lack of action. I understood, though I don't know what more she could have done other than be a witness and provide an occasional intrusion of sanity.

I asked her what she was going to say.

She paused for a moment.

"I'll write what I saw: an attempt made to talk someone out of doing a job. Now I don't know why that was, but that's not my business. There was talk of sabotage and explosives and armed guards coming after us, but I never heard the explosion and those armed guards across Tehek, well they were too far away. I couldn't tell if they were armed."

"Tehek," I said. "What will you say about that?"

"Not part of the story. We crossed over it and came home."

"Whitton will tell a different story."

"If he tells one at all. He blew it, hiring Phillips here. There's protocol in companies like that, even a sense of responsibility. Whitton was going to make a name for himself by speeding up a process, cutting corners, working outside the lines. You know what, not to be crude, but fuck him. He wasn't thinking about anything except the profits. Let him explain the whole sorry mess to his bosses."

Marianne Austin was angry: it might have been the result of all these bigwigs conspiring to ruin her territory, but part of it, undoubtedly, was the blowback from a near-death experience. First comes the relief, then the rage. I was willing to let her rant, but she gathered herself.

"And you," she said to me, "when do you leave?"

"As soon as you find me a ride. You have connections?"

"Some. What do you need?"

"Shelley Norris, the pilot who brought us here, and who owes me a warm flight. Can you find her?"

"Try my best," she said before heading toward the door. I was curious about how she would be portraying the conflict. Would she favor the reputable company whose one renegade employee was a mere aberration, or the little hamlet on a lake, trying to eke out an existence? Optics favored the latter, but objectivity left it up in the air.

"Against my better judgment," I said to Manitok, "I'm leaving you and Phillips alone here. Try not to embarrass yourselves in case a customer walks in."

"I keep telling you," Manitok began, but I waved her off.

"Yeah, yeah, we know," I said. "I'd feel better if he were rushing home to see Nikki and let his kids know he's alive." I looked directly at Phillips. "Maybe you could squeeze that in before someone knocks on her door and says 'hey, I just saw your husband at the co-op.' "

He was struggling. I'm not sure if, when that day began, he expected to be alive at the end of it.

"I need a minute," he said.

There was something in his expression—disappointment? disillusionment?—that told me the last thing on his mind was reigniting some affair with Manitok.

"Just, you know, let her know you're safe," I said. "Tell her Austin is questioning you but you'll be home soon. Make up something so that she knows."

"You want me to lie."

"I want it to be your farewell to lying. I'm going to see Demarais again."

"Figured that," Manitok said, taking a pint of Stoli from the shelf, "at least make yourself welcome."

I gave her a twenty. "Give me the Grey Goose. This is Demarais we're talking about."

She put it in a bag.

"McNally," she said. "Do you think it worked? The explosives?"

"Jeremiah Queen," I said. "That's all you need to know. Anyone who looks as disheveled and ratty as he does couldn't possibly work for Autumn unless his talents exceed everyone else's. If he had anything to do with this, that area is unrecognizable. But Queen himself, he may need a good lawyer. You people better take care of him."

"We will," Phillips said. "When we were crossing the lake, I thought I felt a little jolt."

"Come on," I said. "On a snowmobile going that fast? Even on a smooth lake there are bumps and little rough areas. You don't know for sure."

"You're a visitor before. I'm not. I know the place. I understand the normal, everyday occurrences and those that feel different. This was different."

I conceded that he was probably right, hoped that he was, then took the bottle and left. I arrived at the assisted living center and realized that, for the first time, I hadn't noticed the cold. Even if I was the visitor—I felt a little less wary now. I no longer expected to be frozen mid-step on the main street.

Demarais was in the lounge, off by himself asleep with a book in his lap. While I debated whether to awaken him, one of the orderlies solved the problem.

"Augie! Visitor."

"Augie? You call him Augie?"

"He's a pain in the ass," the man said, checking off something on a clipboard. He was young—maybe Manitok's age—and had the harried look of someone not having a good day. "If I want to piss him off, I use Augie. It's one of my nicer names for him."

I would have felt like a traitor agreeing with him, but I knew what he meant. Demarais opened his eyes as I approached.

"Auguste," I said. "We made it."

"Of course you made it. If you hadn't you would not be here. When the jerk leaves the room, slip me the vodka."

"How do you know I have it?"

"I'm a psychic, remember? I'll take it now."

"Not a chance," I said. "I'm not going to be responsible for you drinking yourself to death."

"If I haven't done it so far, why today?"

"Because today is different from every other day. Do you know what happened on Tehek?"

"Was it on television?"

I took a chance and called the orderly over.

"Could you put the kettle on?" I said. I could not have been more obsequious.

"If it'll shut him up," he said, never finished the sentence, then walked away.

"Have you been a bad boy today?" I said. "Things getting out of control?"

"Every day is a bad day when you feel like I do."

"Give me a minute," I said, walked over to the receptionist—a much less harried and more pleasant young man—and asked if I could have a small glass of water for Mr. Demarais. He obliged, I dumped the water in to a potted plant, poured maybe an inch of vodka into the cup, and handed it to Demarais."

"Not much of a pour," he said, then winked and drank it. "Now, what do you want?"

"I want to know if you knew."

"Knew what?"

"About Tehek."

"I know the lake if that's what you mean."

I'd been standing but I pulled a chair close to him, then recounted the events I'd witnessed.

Although I knew he wanted to get at the alcohol, he listened attentively, even stoically. I could read nothing in his expression, even when I told him about crossing the lake.

"You're not surprised?" I said.

"I'm impressed, but no. I'm not surprised. The spiritual domain is much more powerful than we imagine. All over the world there are unexplained events happening. You just happened to be...."

"Stop," I said. "An unexplained event is seeing an old friend across the street who's been dead for twenty years. Melting a frozen lake into a few billion gallons of water is not an unexplained event. It's a scientific impossibility."

"The kettle is whistling," he said. I hadn't even heard it, though the orderly had and glared at me. I made the tea and made the usual Demarais-inspired adjustments.

He took a sip, showed some satisfaction with the result, and sat back.

"If you witnessed the impossible, what can I say to you?"

"You can tell me how."

"Of course I can't. You use the word unexplainable, then you want an explanation? Thank you for the vodka. Have a safe trip home."

"Will I?"

Demarais shook his head.

"I don't tell fortunes. I don't do card tricks. I don't bend utensils from across the room. I observe and I sense and I know my history. I trust you will have a safe trip home, but nothing more."

"And Autumn? The project?"

"Stopped."

"Forever?"

"A meaningless word. Even the sun will burn up in time."

"At least you won't notice it here."

He smiled. "I have enjoyed knowing you, Mr. McNally. Now go home."

That orderly was right: he was a pain in the ass.

"I worry about Manitok," I said. "I'm afraid that when the project starts up again, she'll get into trouble."

"And you'll be back?"

I laughed. "We're old, Gus, you and I. We're not dead and we're not ready to die, but we have to choose our living. No, I won't be back."

"And Manitok will be Manitok. Always. She and her brother will fight it out, but she will be safe."

"Of course you're not a fortune-teller."

"That I am not, but I can observe as well as ever. So you will leave. Then what?"

"Home."

"To what? Tell me about home. Tell me why you want to go there."

"That's a silly question."

"It is not. People always talk about home with a longing. Why?"

"It's a feeling. You can't define it."

"You can define anything if you try."

I told him about the community and my part-time job, but mostly I told him about Linnie, about her cancer, her prognosis, my fears.

"So, home for you," he said, "has become the unknown."

"With one constant."

"Your wife. I would like to meet her. Is she too sick to travel?"

I laughed. "No offense, Mr. Demarais, but if this is our last time to travel...."

"...It won't be here, I know. That's too bad. What if you had another year, and another? How many extra years would you need to come back here?"

I wanted to say fifty, but I didn't want to insult him either. Why I chose three I don't know, maybe because it seemed far-fetched without being absurd.

"Three," he repeated. "Maybe I'm the one who won't be able to wait."

"The cold preserves," I said. "And the vodka will keep your blood from freezing."

"Can you explain that to that miserable orderly?" he said, loudly enough for the miserable orderly to poke his head in, then disappear again.

"I guess you made your point."

Demarais shrugged. "You and Wilkes both. I admire you."

"Why?"

"You feel for something outside yourself. You, maybe always. Wilkes had to learn, but he did. He should marry again before his newfound knowledge goes to waste."

"He's hesitant."

"You tell him not to be."

"Shall I tell him that the advice came from you?"

"Yes, if you want him to hit you. Otherwise, just tell him that second chances should not go begging."

"Is that an Inuit saying."

"Yes, by way of the Chinese restaurant one street over. Now go. Catch your plane."

"I will. And listen," I said, handing him the pint which he quickly snuck into his robe pocket, "don't drink it all in one night, understand? I don't want to be responsible for your early demise."

"Too late for that," he said, "but yes, *Dr.* McNally. I'll be—what's that word another doctor used on me?—oh yes, abstemious. And you, get home and take care of your wife."

"Is she okay?"

He smiled. "I admire your pertinacity, McNally...."

"But you're not a fortune-teller."

"Right."

"Soothsayer."

"Mmmh, I like that better. But no."

"The lake," I said. I was determined to try once more. "Tell me."

"Tehek," he said, "has always been a place where spirits rule. Men come in the summer and fish there, but always there are stories of sudden storms, of waves on a calm day, of whirlpools, of shadows...."

"Shadows?"

"I don't mean from trees since there are none. Shadows in the water, or above it—shadows cast by something invisible."

"Have fishermen died there?"

"Drowned? No. But many have been frightened enough so that they'll never go back. Others return every August."

"The pure of heart?"

"What?"

"It's from the Bible—the pure of heart see God. The rest of us...."

"Catch fish," Demarais said. "I don't believe all that religious crap."

"Of course you do," I said, laughing at what even he knew was a joke. "You pick and choose. You believe in shadows. Isn't that just different religious crap?"

"I've seen them. I've seen Tehek. It's not a sacred place, but there's something there. And if I didn't know it before, what happened today proves it. Somebody or something does not want the lake fouled. For a time, at least, that side won, but in modern times, such victories are temporary. Still, you probably made some friends here," he said. "Maybe among the Tuurngait you are the pure of heart."

"Who are the Tuurngait?"

"Spirits. Powerful ones. They can possess people, inhabit them. They can do terrible things, but not always."

"Like today."

"Yes."

"What happened to the Tuniit? I thought I was working with them?"

"You are funny, McNally," he said. "Probably nothing happened to them. The Tuniit are tall; the Tuurngait are not."

"And so life's mystery is finally solved. Thank you, O wise one."

"Do you talk to everybody this way?"

"Yes."

"Good," he said, and his thin lips curled into a smile. "Now listen: the Tuniit once walked the earth, and maybe they still do. The Tuurngait never did so—never existed in the physical realm. Spirits always and forever. Their powers are limitless. The Tuniit have the strength to move mountains. The Tuurngait can create them."

"And I've been wasting my time with the Turniit."

"You all came back alive. Hardly a waste of time. Are we done?"

"No, because I don't want you chugging that pint."

"I won't. Who knows when another kind soul will replenish my supply. Is Marianne Austin still in Baker?"

"You are incorrigible."

"No argument there. Is she?"

"Yes, she is."

"Good, then as I said, go catch your plane."

"I will. And thank you for, you know, whatever the hell happened today."

I stood up, but Demarais grabbed my arm.

"If you really think I'm responsible," he said, "do me a favor—tell your friend Wilkes what I did, how I was the hero. When he falls to the floor laughing, don't help him up. Then he and I will be even."

CHAPTER 35

I settled up with Mason at the hotel and paid for one more night in advance: Austin had found me an ungodly early flight out and I didn't expect to be chatting near the main desk at four in the morning. Mason—versed in the art of hotel jargon—asked if I'd enjoyed my stay. The question reminded me of those old formulaic jokes—*aside from that Mrs. Lincoln, how was the play*; *aside from the iceberg, Mrs. Astor...* and the like. Yes, Mr. Lefebvre, aside from the gun-toting brigade and the chase through the tundra, a most pleasant stay.

I settled up with Manitok too—took exactly what we'd agreed on—then bought some overpriced trinkets to bring home in order to assuage my feelings of guilt for having given her a hard time, one I still believe she richly deserved. Olin had reverted to that stolid demeanor that I'd seen at the beginning. He was angrier though, not with me or even with Phillips; instead, modern Olin who loved to denigrate his sister's old ways was furious that his protected lands had been threatened and probably would be again. Activists are born under unpredictable circumstances: I think we'd witnessed the birth of one. Even so, if and when his radicalism interfered with earnings in the hamlet—negatively affected people's ways of life—I could envision a difficult path ahead.

In Churchill, where Shelley Norris and her colder-than-ever plane deposited me, I found some steadier cell service and called Linnie with an update. She didn't ask for details, probably because she didn't want me to explain again how things had not gone as planned. I wasn't sure if they really had; I mean Phillips was home but he'd never even been missing. It seemed that explanation would work better in person. I asked a ticket agent in the big blue box that constitutes the terminal if there wasn't a more direct method of getting to Toronto. He said yes, and pointed to a huge military transport that, he said, was headed to Michigan—Autumn's Greyhound on steroids. He joked that I would have to enlist quickly to be eligible and I'd probably have to stand during the flight. I told him that was the least tempting offer I'd had in a week of least tempting offers. I bought the ticket and prepared myself to fly west, then east, then home.

But every once in a while everyone draws a good card. Not even thirty minutes after I landed in Winnipeg, I got myself aboard a delayed United flight—fog at LaGuardia—and managed to avoid a night at the Grand Winnipeg Airport Hotel. Of course my car was nestled safely at JFK, so I added a cab ride from LGA to the already-very expensive day and pulled into my driveway shortly before midnight.

The house was dark except for the security light we have on the porch, the one on which I never adjusted the motion detection and which now blazes away whenever anybody sneezes within a five-mile radius. I had hoped to see a light on inside—that would have meant that Linnie was still up maybe watching Kimmel or one of the others—but that was pre-cancer Linnie, of course, subsisting on no sleep and none the worse for it. Not tonight.

I walked around to the back door to silence the alarm system, then quietly entered. We pretty much turn off the heat at night, but the house seemed warm—further proof that I'd been freezing for the past three days and had grown grudgingly accustomed to it. The kitchen hardly looked lived in—a glass in the sink and a clean pan on the stove. The refrigerator was full enough: whichever Amber had tended to the groceries had probably overbought, but that fact was reassuring. At least Linnie had not been neglected while I was gone. And if she required food because there was some semblance of appetite, that was good too.

Above me I heard the floor creak.

"It's me," I yelled. "I just got home."

"Okay," she said, her voice sounding no different than it had for thirty years. Strong, relaxed, half annoyed at being awakened, but relieved that I wasn't an intruder. When I got to the bedroom the light was on and she was sitting up.

"Did you find him?"

"I did," I told her, then sat down next to her and kissed her forehead. "What about you?"

"I wasn't looking for anybody," she said. "I was afraid to ask."

"I was afraid to tell. Not sure what constitutes a success these days."

"Getting home in one piece is a factor. You're okay?"

"Feel okay. You're up late. Is one of the meds keeping you up?"

"No, tell me more."

I did, trying to straddle the line between how dangerous it was and how in control I had always been. She would not have been happy if I'd taken risks, but she would have been just as disappointed if I'd been nonchalant. For the moment I left out the frozen lake that melted so that our pursuers couldn't pursue because, even now when I say it, I sound certifiable.

"At least the guy's okay," she said.

"We'll see how long that lasts. You didn't answer my question," I said. "How are you feeling."

"Well I didn't die," she said.

"That's always a good thing."

"Two nights ago..." she said, then stopped.

"Two nights ago...what?"

"I had this dream. I almost called you."

"You could have, although getting through...."

"You weren't in it, but it was about you."

Linnie and I tell each other everything, but not dreams. It's not embarrassment—it's just that she doesn't remember them, or claims not to—and I remember every illogical and surreal moment, all of which vanish within minutes of my waking. Still, I had nothing against hearing it, but in this particular situation there were more pressing concerns: had there been any physical setbacks, any negative reactions to medication, any loss of appetite, specific pains. There was a myriad of symptoms of which we were to remain cognizant, her dreams not being one of them. But when I told her as much, she said that it was all connected.

"What was?"

"The dream. You. An old guy."

"I'm an old guy," I said.

"Even more decrepit than you, if that's possible." She put her arms around my neck and we held each other for a few moments.

"Okay," I said, "since I'm too tired for sex, you can tell me about your dream."

"Too smelly, too. Were you fueling the planes you flew on?"

"Felt like it in one of the airports. The dream?"

She pulled away a little and leaned against the headboard.

"Remember when Wilkes was looking for his wife and you told me he punched some guy and sent him to the hospital?"

"Emergency room maybe, but yes. Auguste Demarais."

"I think he was in my dream."

"Was he drunk?"

"What?"

"I met him in Baker. He's in an assisted living center of some kind, moved down from Repulse Bay. Now he spends his days trying to get people to smuggle in vodka."

"Stoli?"

"He'll drink anything."

"No, I mean did you bring him Stoli? That was in my dream. I recognized the label because we have a bottle, don't we?"

"Yes. But he was drinking Grey Goose last I saw. Everyone kind of feeds his habit. I know it's irresponsible, but..."

"Yes? But what?"

"Nothing. It's irresponsible."

"That's what I thought. What's his name again?"

"Auguste Demarais."

She shook her head. The name meant nothing.

"Is he very tall?" she asked. "I mean unusually tall."

"He's unusually not tall. Kind of old and hunched over a bit. What happened in this dream?"

"A lot, I think. I know dreams last seconds, but this one seemed to go on for a long time in different settings. The one I can clearly remember is this big auditorium or something. This Demarais...."

"Gus."

"Easier," she said. "So this Gus was speaking with others who looked the same. Old guys, all of them. They were talking and we were listening."

"We? You and I? I thought I wasn't in it."

"You brought him the vodka, but it wasn't really you. Hard to explain, but the room was full. There was more but it didn't make a lot of sense. Except I wasn't sick."

"In the dream."

"Yes. I mean since the diagnosis everything is, well I guess clouded by the cancer. I don't see myself as just me anymore, I see myself as me with cancer. But in this dream. I was just...me...like everyone else. Even when I woke up that morning, I felt different."

"And now?"

"The same. Or maybe better. I mean you read all this stuff about positive thinking and not allowing yourself to be a victim and you figure it's all bullshit, but maybe it's not."

"My tolerance for bullshit has risen a bit these past few days. Tell me about the guys who were speaking. What did they look like?"

"I told you. Old."

"Not unusually tall or anything?"

She shook her head. "Why do you keep asking that? That's not important."

Maybe not to Linnie, but it was to me. I was trying to get her to admit to having dreamed about the Tuniit, but her description didn't fit. Instead she had dreamed a world filled with Demarais clones. I didn't think there was enough vodka in the world to keep that many frozen Svengalis going.

"Were you afraid of these old guys? I mean this dream—was it like a nightmare?"

"More the opposite, I'd say. This was two nights ago. Last night nothing. No dreams."

"That you remember. Do you still feel different? Better?"

"I feel...good. I guess the meds are working. Newland said there'd be good and bad days. Meds are so unpredictable."

She said that so haltingly that I knew she was sidestepping the issue.

"You didn't take them today, did you?"

"No."

"Yesterday?"

"Forgot."

"Jesus, Linnie, you need to, you know, do what they say to do."

"They? You mean the doctors?"

"Well I don't mean the old guys in your dream."

"But the old guys made me feel better. Even if it was psychological, what's wrong with that?"

"Nothing," I said, "if it doesn't make you worse in the long run. Maybe tomorrow you can start them again?"

"Maybe," she said. "What if I feel like the old me? I don't mean the old me from a week ago; I mean the real old me? Do I still need to take them?"

"We'll ask Newland," I said. A temporary evasion. The only sensible answer was yes.

"The guy, what was his name? Phillips. Was his wife happy to see him?"

"Their marriage is a little rocky," I said, "but they have a chance to save it."

"Will they work at it?"

"They have kids so maybe there's motivation."

Linnie wasn't convinced: I wasn't convincing. As I've said, I don't lie to her.

I dug out a pair of pajamas, took a quick shower to scrape off a day of air travel, and got into bed beside her. She was still awake.

"I want to see Newland tomorrow," she said. "Something is different."

"She won't be happy you're not taking the meds."

"Maybe," she said. "But I'm going to call."

I said she probably wouldn't get in unless it was an emergency, but Linnie said that was fine: a day here and a day there wouldn't matter. She actually did sound different, like someone who had seen certain death chasing her in the form of armed snowmobile drivers, then watched them stop—stymied— as a frozen lake melted in front of them. Yeah, that's how she sounded. That feeling I could recognize.

As exhausted as I was, I don't think I slept more than a few minutes that night, if that. In her nearness I felt warm and relaxed, but I couldn't cross the sleep threshold—the one that would have prevented my watching the digits on the clock slowly crawl toward dawn.

CHAPTER 36

Unobtrusively hidden in the World section of the *Times* yesterday was an article about Autumn Industries, the "Canadian behemoth" that had recently been exposed for a series of environmental offenses stretching back two decades. The story noted the irony in the fact that a crime *against* Autumn earlier in the year had exposed the criminal activity: an act of industrial sabotage in January. It had, as intended, crippled the development of natural gas exploration in Nunavut, but had also exposed to public view the fact that there was such a project in the works. The paper supplied a little map—it did not engender any great nostalgia in me, but I showed Linnie.

"This is where it happened," I said. "Way down here is Baker Lake—and there's Hudson's Bay. She put down her coffee and looked over.

Almost six months had passed: it was June. I'd spent the day before sliding air-conditioners into window openings and hoping, as I always did, that they didn't fall to the ground below. It was, however, an ibuprofen day-after as every "day-after" is when you get to be my age.

"Nunavut looks bleak," she said.

"It's not. It's just...pretty empty."

"Where's the little lake that melted."

I smiled. It sounded like the title of some kids' book—*Franny Mac and the Little Lake that Melted*. Of course Tehek was too small to show up there: it would be akin to Central Park Reservoir showing up on a globe, but Linnie seemed satisfied and went back to her paper.

A few moments later she said I should call the cop I'd met in Baker Lake.

"Austin?" I said. "Why?"

"To keep in touch. I don't want you to be alone after I die—she sounds like someone you'd like."

"I do like her. And I'm twice her age so after I die she can carve out a nice long life for herself on my money."

"She's 42," Linnie said. "Eighteen years. That's not much."

"I'll take it under advisement, as I always do."

It wasn't the first time Linnie had hinted that I should prepare for my life without her, but in the six months since I returned to the States, it had become more jest than concern.

Linnie is better. Newland would insist that's an understatement, but then Newland hadn't lived with the same trepidation as I had, or the same anxiety as Linnie the patient or the patient's husband, in this case. The death knell of the original diagnosis still echoed at times. So now I tell others, along with myself, that she's better: it's easy to see but not so easy to believe. What I find more difficult is what Dr. Newland insists is the truth—that the cancer is gone. Just...gone. A week after I returned and Linnie "complained" daily of feeling better, we finally decided to come clean with Newland. If nothing else, we said, it's spending a Saturday in the City. As usual Newland couldn't see us until 5:30—typical for someone of her renown—so we made our usual pilgrimage to the Met, arriving in the early afternoon, thus avoiding the morning chaos.

"Let's walk instead," Linnie said. It was a cloudy, mild (remember, I had just returned from Nunavut) January afternoon and the park was muddy and uninviting. I was still convinced as usual that too much exertion would undo any improvements, but we walked, held hands, shivered on a bench for a while, watched a football or two soar and then land and soar again. At one point I considered what Central Park would look like if Autumn Industries decided that twenty trillion cubic feet of natural gas lay under it and the time had come to access it, how the football tossers would feel about it, the nannies with strollers, the joggers and cyclists, Linnie and I.

"That would never happen," she said. "New Yorkers would lose their minds."

"It almost happened in Baker Lake."

"They're not New Yorkers. That's where you came in. You're probably part of their legend by now."

"I don't think anyone saw me as any kind of hero. It was Manitok's brother who turned that day around. And of course my next wife Marianne Austin was beneficial."

"If only I could die and still be around to watch her suffer. I still think you should call. She's gotta know things that never made the news."

"And probably can't talk about."

We sat for a while longer and talked about getting into the City a little more, maybe out on the Island once in a while when the weather broke. We sounded like two kids who had spent their childhood in their rooms, then one day looked out a window and said, "Hey, is that New York over there?" Our conversation was spiked with a hint of optimism—something we hadn't felt for a while. I think it unnerved us a little, and as the so-called mildness of January started to wear thin, it was back to the Met for an abridged visit.

Afterwards, on the cab ride to the medical building, we were unusually silent, and we remained that way until Newland saw Linnie.

"Your skin color," the doctor said before even exchanging pleasantries. "Have you been...I don't know somewhere?"

"We were in the Park this afternoon," I said.

Newland dismissed that out of hand and kept staring at her. "Tell me how you feel."

"Good, I guess," she said. "Better."

"Well what is it? Tell me the truth."

"Good."

"And today you were walking. Fatigue? Weariness?"

"No."

Newland appeared stunned—never a good look for a doctor.

"I'm ordering some tests right now," she said, pulling a sheet from a folder. "Quite a few. They'll be a pain in the ass but just for tomorrow when you come back. Morning, eight o'clock, can you do that?"

"Sure," we said. "On a Sunday?"

"The perks of eminence," she said. "It'll be an easy drive in. It's a quiet city then. I'm sure you know."

"What kind of tests?" Linnie asked.

"Diagnostic, mostly. Nothing invasive. Just, you know, don't eat first, the usual."

She paused for a moment, stopped writing, and held Linnie by the shoulders as she would a recalcitrant child.

"Something happened here," she said. "I feel dumb asking, but I have to—are you on some experimental protocol somewhere else? Were you in Mexico or something?"

Had the question come from anyone but Newland we'd have laughed, but she's so goddam serious we were afraid to.

"No foreign countries," I said, "but I was in Canada."

"That much I knew. Jesus, I'd like to run those tests now."

"Doctor," I said, because Linnie was probably hesitant, "is this a good thing?"

"Fuck yeah," she blurted out, apologized for her lack of professionalism, then repeated it. We mimicked her all the way home.

And most of the way back in the following morning. Later that week Newland FaceTimed us. One of the Ambers had given Linnie some technology lessons, and Linnie had taught me; in other words, neither of us had a clue. I kept falling out of the iPad's view and hung up at least twice, but eventually we got settled.

"I have a new abbreviation for a PI in NYC," she said. "N.E.D.—no evidence of disease."

"You were practicing that," I said.

"I was," she said. "I've never been much of a comedian. I was hoping I could pull it off." Linnie grabbed my hand as if we had just reached the top of the roller coaster and were ready to be scared witless. I was afraid to say anything.

"It happens," Newland said. "There are as many theories as there are cases, from miracles to spontaneous production of anti-cancer genes—a kind of self-generated regimen of immunotherapy."

"No acronym for that one?"

"Not yet. Whatever the case, you're it."

"I don't want to be some lab experiment now," Linnie said.

"We did the tests: we have whatever we need. Go live your lives."

"So," Linnie said, but like me, didn't know what to ask.

"It's a lot to digest," Newland said, "so let me just add a warning. No doctor will ever say that the cancer can't come back, or that it's not hiding. That's why I never use the c-word: telling someone she's *cured* leads to more trouble down the road. Let's just keep an eye on things for the next…let's say five years. And that doesn't mean you let five years go by before I see you again. It means every three months you better fucking be here."

"Professionalism, Doctor Newland," I said.

Upon which she gave me the finger.

"Also," she added, "it means you monitor yourself, pay attention to your body, all those things I can't do."

"Sounds like you're guaranteeing five years," Linnie said. Newland laughed, but it was the laughter of someone who had seen too many prognoses go sideways, or had made too many predictions that patients had construed as promises.

"As I said," Newland repeated, "N.E.D. Five years—we'll monitor everything and plan for the best. In the meantime, don't treat every ache and pain as a recurrence and don't ignore every concern because you're suddenly bulletproof. Find a spot somewhere in the middle, and let's just keep on top of things. After that you can enjoy the next thirty without my bugging you."

"Now it sounds like you're guaranteeing another thirty. What about my boyfriend here?" she asked. "How many years is he good for?"

"That depends," Newland said, "on how many years you can keep him out of trouble."

I promised Newland—and Linnie—I'd try harder to avoid snowmobiles and men with guns, and even Newland laughed, but reservedly. She possessed a wry sense of humor but always returned quickly to an uncompromising professionalism. She was all-business again by the time we signed off. Linnie and I were too, but only until we were alone.

"Five years," Linnie said to me, more than once that day. Her new mantra.

"Fuck yeah," I said more than once. Mine.

CHAPTER 37

I did try to reach Marianne Austin, left her a voice mail and didn't really expect to hear back. For months it appeared I was right, then near the end of June, one muggy night around 10:30, she called. The first thing she did was apologize.

"Time zone," she said. "I forgot."

"Only an hour. We're awake. Seems like the sun just set an hour ago— just like at your place, only the opposite."

"*Au contraire*," she said. "It's still light here, will be until midnight. You and your wife ought to come on up."

I issued a polite denial, then we exchanged the usual pleasantries that you would expect from two people who hardly knew each other. She was still working; I was working less. Baker Lake was beginning to thaw; there were some flowers poking through and buds on the stunted trees, but a missing persons case had everyone worried."

"If it's Derek Phillips," I said, "I can tell you where to look."

"It's a young woman," she said. "She just didn't turn up for work one day."

"At Autumn?"

"She's a teacher here in town. No indication of trouble. Nothing. Are you interested in a new assignment?"

I laughed. I think she knew what that meant.

"Get those Turniit to work," I said. "They're pretty good at doing things. Or bring Demarais some vodka and ask him to do a little séance."

"He won't be doing much of anything. He fell a month or so back— doctors think it may have been a stroke. He's lost some movement in one of his legs but his speech is coming back, slurred but better. You know, he's like the ancient here but he's not old, not really. I don't think he's even seventy."

"He's not exactly health-conscious."

"And we don't help by pumping vodka into him," she said.

"You're probably right. I'm guilty too. You know, if he goes and we're being chased by goons with guns, who's going to save us?"

"You don't believe that Demarais had anything to do with our—what are you calling it, our escape?"

"I refer to it as the timely incident."

"As opposed to what would have been our untimely deaths."

"Something like that. I don't deny Demarais' vision, but in my profession we still need facts and proof."

"We're in the same profession," she said. "Remember? And we both saw a meter of ice melt and refreeze in a very *unfactual* period of time. What do *you* tell people?"

"People like my wife? Everything. Everyone else? We escaped. Superior machines, better drivers."

"But you know it's not...."

"Superior machines, better drivers. Sorry about Gus," I said."

"We'll have to be real police, work this Laird case without divine intervention."

"Laird?"

"Deidre Laird. The missing woman. We're still in the early stages."

"Who's she sleeping with?"

Austin laughed. "I told Manitok I was going to call you, and maybe mention Deidre. She said you'd ask that."

"I didn't say I wasn't predictable, but I am pretty good."

We fumbled through some topics, straining to keep the conversation moving. It was tremendously uncomfortable and I knew why. Finally I just blurted it out.

"Linnie's doing fine. A kind of ongoing remission—I guess that's redundant."

I could hear the relief even before she spoke.

"I was so afraid to ask," she said. "It's more wonderful than redundant. How?"

"It can happen," I said. "Sometimes the body rises up and says enough! It goes on the attack and the bad stuff loses."

It's probably not that dramatic, but I liked the image."

"Wow! That is so...I was afraid to call and ask."

"You could have. We were so accustomed to ticking off days that I think I'd rehearsed what I was going to say a thousand times."

"Throw that speech away."

"Done. If you ever have an occasion to see Demarais, tell him about Linnie...oh hell, I'll bet he already knows. He is a nut case. But sort of a nexus, right?"

"Between?"

"I'm not sure," I said. "Past and present, reality and myth, faith and reason? I mean—I'm not saying I believe in all the Inuit myths and all those weird creatures of the cold—but without Demarais, you know...."

"Who's going to run the miracle machine?"

"Yes. Keep the caribou from getting shot, keep the wolves from eating the fishermen, that sort of thing."

"Somebody always comes along," she said. "Manitok relishes her heritage, and even Olin seems different. Maybe one of them will become the new Demarais."

"More a curse than a blessing," I said. "Let me just ask you, Ms. Austin...."

"Marianne."

"Marianne—I'm just curious—that day on Tehek, what's the story on that around town?"

"You mean is Olin doing a speaking tour?"

"Yeah, like that."

"He talks about it and people take sides. Harmless. In your country people watch the beaches get smaller every summer, but you still have a bunch of yahoos claiming global warming is a hoax. People 'round here will argue about this for a while, then it'll go away, then it will become a new myth."

"More a legend, I'd say. We owe Demarais."

"Sick as he is, he lives on in the ethos of the town."

"*Ethos*? I don't think I heard that word very often when I was there."

"Should have stayed longer—maybe next time."

"Not gonna happen," I said. "Give my best to Mason at the hotel."

"And Manitok? She thinks you're angry with her."

"She was just another client who lied to me. They all do it. I'm not angry."

"You didn't ask about Phillips. He's back home, got a job with the town."

"That's good, if for no other reason than it'll save little Regina from becoming a mass murderer."

"Still think he was sleeping with Manitok?"

"I don't care, really, but he was ready to abandon his wife and kids. That bothers me."

"We live. We fuck up. If we're lucky, we grow. Check back once in a while."

I told her I would, but we both knew that was what Linnie calls a phatic. Later I filled her in on the news from the Arctic. She was upset at Demarais's condition. "He saved a lot of lives, maybe yours, but he can't save his own."

"He isn't dead, just sick."

"So was I before he fixed it."

And that has become our story—one we share with no one—about a shaman who saved both our lives in the same day. I should add that we were drunk when we first contrived that little tale, but we had fun making it up and now we have fun recounting it—something we smile about while we worry that the cure is, as Newland warned, temporary, or illusory, or just fantasy.

But it was June, and a few warm days had convinced us we'd last out the summer. And I knew that September would bring that first autumn chill and then we'd know we'd make it through Thanksgiving, and maybe on to the first flakes, and on. And on.

One recent Sunday Martin Wilkes came by and we cooked out. We'd seen him briefly once around Easter when he was in the area, but this time he brought his on again-off again lady friend Elizabeth. She wore no grey that I could discern and I thought maybe they had both made some adjustments to their lives to make each other more suitable. Since I was not on the job that day—no, really, I wasn't—I was able to notice that the Elizabeth who sat on my patio was even more attractive and personable than the one I'd spied on many months before. I didn't bother pointing that out to Wilkes, at least not in those words.

The day was nothing special—burgers and beer—and the conversation was light and breezy for the most part, but when Linnie took Elizabeth inside to show her the house, Wilkes and I reverted to Nunavut, to Baker Lake, to what had initially drawn us together. His reaction may not have been typical, but had no trouble believing that something extraordinary had happened.

"I knew Demarais," he said. "Hell, I knew him so well I tried to kill him."

"You'd have to get in line for that, behind all the orderlies in that care facility."

And yet people put their lives in his hands," he said. "How does that happen?"

"I don't know," I said. "To be honest, for me part of it was selfish. I was convinced that Linnie was dying, that she had weeks to live, months at the outside. I had always admitted that I'd be lost without her. I wasn't sure I wanted to watch her die and then have to live with that too."

"So yours was a suicide mission gone wrong," Wilkes said. "I guess that isn't funny."

"It's fine. I'm more embarrassed than anything else, just to have thought that way, to have been selfish"

"Maybe a little cowardly too. Certainly irresponsible."

"Maybe," I said holding up a beer can, "that's enough confessing for one day."

"Did you tell Linnie?"

"I tell her everything."

"Oh yeah, I forgot. What did she say?"

"She said there was an upside: a simple, cheap funeral, and not even a grave to have visit afterwards."

He smiled. "Ask her if she wants to work on Wall Street. I can use people with that sense of practicality."

"We have some travel plans. You can check next year."

"Believe me, I wouldn't condemn her to a job like that. And to be honest, I don't blame you for believing Demarais. If Keira had had any desire to live, to fight through that, Demarais would have saved her. You felt guilty for no good reason. Maybe he did too. Maybe this was his chance to balance things out."

I know Wilkes wanted to believe that, and maybe at Tolliver & Byrne all the suits felt that balancing things was a desirable and attainable outcome, but he knew better than to apply that to real life. And he really had changed: he was good with Elizabeth, considerate but not fawning. He was a different man than the one who had been *inconvenienced* by his wife's disappearance nine years before. Linnie and I decided afterwards to maybe see them more regularly.

But later that night she woke me out of a sound sleep. Immediately I assumed the worst—that she'd felt something, some unexplained ailment or symptom that signaled a recurrence.

"It's not that," she said. "It's the Laird girl. Deidre. The one who's missing. Did you tell Wilkes about that?"

"I did. He remembered her. Bright, quick, a little quirky. She was a high school kid when Wilkes met her, but she had seen Keira and even spoken with her. Smart as she was, she had a loser of a boyfriend."

"That's not unusual. What happened to her?"

"Stayed at home, lived with an aunt or cousin or something, took a job as a teacher. One day she just didn't show up."

"And no one has an idea? Nothing?"

"No clue. It's not as isolated in the summer. She could be in Moosonee for all we know."

"Classes were still in session when she disappeared?"

"I think so."

She leaned up on one elbow and brought her face close.

"And she just left. What could have happened to her?"

"You know you already asked that."

"But your answer was weak. Where's your curiosity?"

"It's out near Manitoba somewhere, rattling around inside some single-engine puddle jumper."

I kissed her and said goodnight, again, then reached over and turned off her light.

"Hmmm, well I guess that's it," she said. She turned her light back on. When I looked over, she was still leaning on her elbow.

"Gonna read?"

"No. Just thinking," she said. "You go to sleep."

I sat up. "Okay, what?"

"I told you, just thinking. We're pretty lucky to get this extra time together, aren't we?"

"Yes we are."

"It would be a shame to waste it."

"We'll cook out again tomorrow. We'll drink more beer. I'll do chicken."

"You haven't thought about it?"

"Hot dogs are hot dogs. Chicken is...."

"Mac! You haven't thought about that girl? That's not like you."

"I'm not a do-gooder. People hire me and I do a job."

"I know. But what could have happened to her?"

"Again 'what could have happened to her?' She's young. Maybe she needed to get out of there. Maybe she met someone. There's any number of reasons why a twenty-five year old runs off."

"I hope she's all right," Linnie said. She couldn't have chosen a more effective phrase.

"Me too," I said, then finally fell asleep...only to awaken an hour later, racking my brain to remember the name of the little newspaper in Baker Lake. Just curious, that was all. Just wondering what could have happened to Deidre Laird.

CHAPTER 38

Regina Phillips was awake before anyone else.

Almost anyone else.

Derek Phillips could hear her wandering about, then heard the television click on: he had forgotten to remove the batteries from the remote. Nikki always double-checked, he seldom did.

It was Sunday, and though bad weather sometimes turned it into a workday for Phillips, spring had taken hold and road repairs progressed along non-emergency guidelines. The weekends were usually free. It was different from his days at Autumn. Then, Sunday's gloss was always dulled by the impending Monday plane ride to Autumn and the subsequent week of forced camaraderie and unity of purpose. That was all gone now, and though he missed the money, he realized also that escaping prosecution compensated for any reduction in their standard of living.

He missed Nikki, whose withdrawal from him had deepened over the months until eventually he moved on. He found a decent place not far from her—in a small town complete separation is almost impossible—with enough room for the kids to stay when his turn came to have them. It was a tight squeeze. He loved their visits, but spent most of his hours forcing himself not to ask if mommy had a boyfriend. At times he hoped she had found someone. Such an eventuality would have justified his constant and increasingly elaborate fantasies, none of which he had any inclination to fulfill. Even Manitok had pulled back somewhat, and some of the men with whom he worked said she had a girlfriend; but that too could have been a grudging resentment over her not responding to their crude come-ons. He remained fond of her, even protective, but there was little for either of them beyond a tentative friendship.

A glimpse of Nikki, though, would send him reeling, test his ability to recover. He always did—he knew the truth: they were two more victims of a relentless cold that had suffused every aspect of their lives.

He maintained a casual friendship with Marianne Austin, but she was absent from his fantasies. Instead he began to view her as what he could have been—someone whose talents had not been squandered scrounging for gold and participating in absurd schemes.

He had always considered himself a passably good father—now he was better than passably good. When he wasn't, he heard it from Regina. And when he avoided punishing her for bad behavior, she let him know that too.

"Reg," he said poking his head into the living room. "Too early for television. Go back to bed."

"No, wait, you have to see this. It's your friend. It's Manitok."

"Shh, don't wake up the others."

"Come on," she said, her voice no quieter for his having requested it.

He cinched his robe and entered the living room.

"I paused it," she said with the haughtiness that told him she had mastered the remote after all. "Look."

"Back it up," he said, "since you're so good with the remote."

She did, to the beginning of a news story out of Toronto, a missing girl in a Nunavut community. A wide sweeping panorama with a herd of caribou grazing, a cut to an aerial view of Baker Lake, then in to the center and the co-op—Manitok's co-op.

"There she is," Regina said. "Manitok."

"You're right," he said.

Her dark hair pulled back severely, she wore her usual outfit—the jeans, the black sweater, the requisite vest. She spoke to a reporter off-camera, spoke about the missing girl. Deidre Laird.

"Deedee used to come in to the co-op all the time," Manitok told the reporter. "Super smart, brilliant. Never any indication of trouble. Her students loved her. They're devastated."

Manitok was effusive in her praise, judiciously avoiding the fact that Deidre's own family were less than savory members of the community. Her father had served jail time for assaults, all of which evolved from barroom arguments. Her mother had been treated for drug abuse—meth at one time (the rumors said) and then opioids. Deidre had escaped somehow, but now she was gone.

"I heard about her. It's too bad," Phillips said.

"No, wait!" Regina said

The camera cut away from Manitok, back to the reporter, a young woman who had more than likely been assured that the plum assignments would come later. She summarized Manitok's comments before the story cut to a colleague at school—more praise and admiration and bewilderment over what could have happened.

"The authorities have been working overtime," the man said, his expression conveying the grim reality, "but…."

His voice trailed off as the reporter continued, filling the screen with a headshot.

"A few residents," she said, as the camera slowly pulled back, "have even pooled their resources and hired an outside investigator."

Phillips began to smile even before the nearby figure entered the picture. By the time the man's face appeared, Phillips was laughing so hard that tears were clouding his view.

He took the remote from his daughter: this time *he* hit the pause button.

"What?" Regina said. "What's funny?"

"The man on the screen," Phillips said, still convulsing but gradually regaining control. "I know him."

"Oh yeah," Regina said, "it's Mac and cheese. We all know him."

Lefora Mission

Our mission is to publish new literature, including fiction, poetry, memoir, and criticism, with a focus on contributions that best serve to enhance and represent the intellectual life of the New England region.

Lefora seeks to support a vibrant community of writers...

by stewarding writers through the editorial and marketing process,

by working with emerging talent as well as seasoned writers,

by sharing in the development of their careers,

by hosting an online journal,

by sponsoring writing contests,

by offering speaking opportunities,

and we will do each of these as we create the Lefora Publishing legacy.

Also by Chuck Radda

Dark Time

Absolute Truth

Flood Moon

www.ingramcontent.com/pod-product-compliance
Lightning Source LLC
Chambersburg PA
CBHW021420110726
47901CB00008B/2229